DEATHWATCH

CIA Director Richard Bushwick, with Grier sitting next to his desk, listened to the tapes, and the more he heard, the more of a threat Anderson became.

"He becomes the next President and there won't be any damn Company!" he said, angrily pressing the stop button. "I want him neutralized."

Grier rolled his eyes in dismay. "He can't be neutralized—at least not the way you mean it."

"Why the hell not?" Bushwick said. "We're the CIA, remember?" Then he paused. "You have a plan?"

Grier almost smiled. "Yes."

Bushwick scrutinized his Deputy Director for several moments, and decided to give him all the rope he needed. "You have a plan, use it. I don't want to have to think about John Anderson again. The next time I hear his name I want to be able to put on a *very* sad face!"

THE FATE OF AN EAGLE

BY IRVING A. GREENFIELD

ZEBRA BOOKS
KENSINGTON PUBLISHING CORP.

ZEBRA BOOKS

are published by

Kensington Publishing Corp.
475 Park Avenue South
New York, NY 10016

First printing: January, 1990

Printed in the United States of America

This book is dedicated to the staff and students of Susan Wagner High School, who have become such an important part of my life.

Irving A. Greenfield
Staten Island, N.Y.
July 1989

Chapter 1

"Good morning, Senor Santos," the concierge said, speaking Spanish from behind his high desk in the inner lobby of the Jan Luijken Hotel, which was located on the street with the same name in Amsterdam. He smiled at the tall, leathery-looking guest with horn-rim glasses that made him seem professorial, and continued in Spanish. "Another lovely spring day. If the weather continues like this for a few more days, all the tulips will bloom." The very first time the concierge saw Santos, a week before, he'd sized him up as being a man of means. A dilettante, in some out-of-the-way field. Something exotic. Something in keeping with his Honduran citizenship. A very wealthy man from Central America. Forty years of working in hotels had provided him with the necessary experience to make that kind of judgment. And from the way the man tipped, his judgment had proven right.

Santos returned the smile, marveling in the linguistic ability of the Dutchman. He had heard him, in a matter of ten minutes, speak to five different guests in as many languages, including a passable Russian.

"I would like to see the tulips bloom." Santos moved his head in a half turn toward the foyer decorated with white and blue tiles, which were splashed with brilliant sunshine. He had chosen the Luijken precisely because it was not a luxury hotel, and was away from the center of the city.

"On a day like this you will see just how beautiful the women are." Again the concierge smiled, almost conspiratorially.

Santos nodded. "I have already had that pleasure." The woman he had seen sitting alone on a bench in Vondel Park, close to one of the lakes, came to his mind. He had seen her reading a book in the same place on each of the past three afternoons. He wondered if . . .

"Will you require a cab, senor?"

His thoughts about the woman interrupted, Santos blinked.

"No, thank you. It's a day for walking."

"If there's anything I can do for you when you return, please don't hesitate to ask."

Again the look was conspiratorial.

The man was offering to get him a woman. "I won't," Santos responded.

"Enjoy yourself."

"Yes." Santos left the concierge's desk, crossed the small lobby into the tiled foyer, and out into the street, where he slipped a pair of clip-on, amber-lens sunglasses out of his jacket pocket, and attached them to his horn-rims.

The Jan Luijken was located on a residential street with red brick houses whose exteriors were exactly the same as the hotel's. Even their foyers, from what Santos could see, were decorated with the same tiles. There was a feeling of solidity and comfort emanating from those houses that was so characteristic of the Dutch.

Santos walked to the end of the street, where it met with Hobbema Street, and turning right, headed toward the Leideseplein, which would eventually bring him into the center of the city. There he'd be able to choose a place to breakfast.

By the time he crossed the bridge over the Prince Canal, he was aware of the many people on their way to work, and he felt some satisfaction in knowing that he was not one of them. Never was and never would be.

For the next two hours, Santos explored the various streets, sometimes referring to a guidebook to know more about what he was looking at. At ten, he joined a tourist group queuing up for a tour of A. Van Moppes & Zoon, Amsterdam's largest diamond-cutting factory. Throughout the tour, he amused himself by thinking of ways to steal the diamonds from the premises, and came to the conclusion that working from the outside would be impossible. If it could be done at all, it would require inside help, which, he had little doubt, could be bought. But the price would be very high.

Creating stratagems for stealing the diamonds occupied Santos even after he left the factory. But when he spotted a *broodjeswinkel,* a sandwich shop, he gave up his "game," and entering the place, chose a table near the window where he would have waiter service and be able to watch the people passing by.

He ate sparingly, leaving slightly less than half of his *broodje* uneaten. But he drank two cups of black coffee. After the second, he opened a tin of Dutch cigarillos, removed one, and enjoyed the next few minutes smoking it, while reflecting on what he would do for the rest of the afternoon.

Because he declared himself to be an antiquarian on his passport, Santos felt he should purchase several books and bring them back to his store in Tegucigalpa, the capital of Honduras. There was a man named van Kootje who specialized in erotica, which fit his fantasies perfectly. He had arranged an appointment for two o'clock with van Kootje, with whom he had previously exchanged several letters.

Having stubbed out what remained of the cigarillo, Santos paid his check and went out into the street again. It was now warm enough for him to wear his topcoat over his shoulders, in capelike fashion.

Van Kootje's establishment was located on the third floor of what had once been a warehouse, but in the recent past had been converted into an office building which also had several lawyers and import-export companies as tenants.

The office consisted of an outer room, where a gray-haired, middle-aged woman, who was both receptionist and secretary, sat behind a stylishly modern desk made of white plastic. As soon as Santos identified himself, she picked up the phone and announced him to van Kootje.

In moments, the door to the inner office opened, and van Kootje came toward Santos with his hand outstretched.

He greeted him in Spanish. "It is a pleasure to meet you, Senor Santos." He quickly ushered him into his office, pausing to close the door behind them before he said, "The chairs around the coffee table are much more comfortable than either of those at my desk." He took Santos's coat from him and placed it on the brass hook, next to his own, on an old-fashioned coatrack.

Santos made a quick survey of the office, taking in all of its decor, which included floor-to-ceiling shelves of books and a few prints of nude women, in various erotic positions, where empty wall space allowed. There was also a color photograph of a man and woman in the throes of a simultaneous orgasm—to judge from the look on their faces. Directly behind van Kootje's brightly polished teakwood desk was a semi-circular window, divided into quadrants by pieces of metal. Each sector was itself divided horizontally by another piece of metal shaped into a graceful arc. The entire window overlooked the street below and the canal.

Van Kootje approached Santos again. "The books I thought might interest you are on the coffee table."

They sat opposite each other, with the coffee table between them. Santos settled in a high-back chair, and van Kootje in a club chair.

"Would you care for coffee?" van Kootje asked. He had been surprised by Santos's appearance. Most of his customers were seldom as tan. Apparently, the man must spend a great deal of time out of doors.

Santos politely declined the offer, and continued to leaf through the first of the four books that were on the table, aware that the plumpish man with small round face and porcine eyes on the other side of the coffee table was studying him.

"Superb illustrations," Santos commented, glancing up.

"I assure you that those in the other books are as good, if not better."

Santos responded with a nod. The illustrations made him think about what the concierge had so subtly offered him earlier, and then he immediately found himself thinking about the young woman on the bench in Vondel Park. More than just thinking about her, he imagined her naked, and doing the things the women in the illustrations were doing. He closed the first book, then glanced at his watch. It was two o'clock. He had always seen her close to three-thirty. There was time enough to look at the remaining books without appearing to be rushed. To be sure he'd be there when she was, he would have van Kootje call a cab for him.

Santos spent another forty-five minutes looking at the other books, and without haggling paid the price van Kootje asked for them.

"Have them delivered to me at the Jan Luijken Hotel," Santos said.

"Certainly," van Kootje answered.

Amused by the look of surprise on the man's face, Santos said, "It's a hotel I highly recommend. Quiet

11

and dignified."

"Absolutely," van Kootje replied, looking down at the check for five thousand guilders that Santos had just written. He realized he could have asked for a thousand more, and gotten it without so much as a raised eyebrow.

"Now if you would be so good as to have your secretary call a cab for me, I would appreciate it."

"A cab. Yes." Van Kootje left the chair, went to the door, opened it, and asked his secretary to phone for a cab.

The two men shook hands inside the outer office, each commenting that it had been a pleasure to meet and do business with the other. Then Santos walked down the three flights of steps, and into the street, where a cab was waiting, just outside the doorway.

Traffic was heavy, and it took longer to get to Vondel Park than Santos expected. But despite his impatience, he used the time to think of various gambits he might employ to introduce himself to the young woman, knowing that regardless of which one he decided upon in advance, it would happen in a completely different manner.

When Santos finally began to walk in the park, he realized that the weather had begun to change. The sun had become pallid, and there was a chill in the air that hadn't been there earlier. People were already beginning to leave the park.

Quickening his pace, Santos hoped he was not too late. He also hoped the young woman had been as aware of him as he had been of her, and thus had not left, even if the day was turning raw. He almost smiled at his romanticism; it was so totally opposite from the way he viewed life, and the way he operated. But coming to Amsterdam was part of a month-long holiday, and on his vacation he could afford to be romantic.

12

After all, he wasn't married.

He came down the path to the lake, around the slight curve, and saw her!

Santos slowed.

She was engrossed in the book she was reading. The broad collar of her black seal-fur coat was turned up. Because her legs were crossed, the bottom of a brown tweed skirt was just visible, and through the partially open V neckline of the coat he saw she was wearing a white turtleneck jersey.

He moved toward the edge of the lake; then changing his mind, he went directly to the bench, and sat down alongside her. "Excuse me, miss." His use of the language was considerably less than facile.

She looked at him, and in Dutch told him to "fuck off."

Santos shook his head, and in Spanish said, "I am sorry, but I don't understand you."

Her eyes widened.

He saw that they were green. Her hair was light brown, almost dark blond. She had a pleasant-looking face.

She obviously didn't understand Spanish.

Santos switched to English. "I didn't understand what you said."

She hesitated before answering. This was what she had been waiting for. She smiled. "I said something nasty."

"It sounded nasty. I've seen you here before," Santos added.

She raised the book off her lap. "I come here when the weather is nice to read." He didn't look dangerous, yet she'd been told he was very dangerous.

He could see the title of the book, and the name of the author. She was reading a French edition.

"Ah, Simenon. He's one of my favorites. I especially

13

enjoy his psychological novels." He was a voracious reader.

She raised the book even higher. "*The Blue Room*. It's one of his psychological stories. Have you read it?"

He shook his head. "Not yet." Then he said, "My name is Miguel Santos." He extended his right hand.

"Hilda Borg." She shook his hand. "You speak English exceedingly well."

"I was just going to tell you the same thing," he said. They laughed.

Hilda's laugh was rich; it came from deep inside her. He liked it. "I had very good teachers," he told her.

She knew he was lying.

"Where did you learn your English?" Santos asked.

"I went to New York University." That part was true, but she neglected to tell him she'd been born and raised in Brooklyn.

"You're a native here then?"

She nodded. "I'm also here to do research for my doctoral thesis. But I've taken a few days off."

"I'm glad you did. Otherwise I'd have never met you."

"And you, what are you doing here?" Hilda asked, though she knew.

"On vacation from my bookstore. I live in Tegucigalpa."

She played stupid. "Teguci-what?"

He laughed. "The capital of Honduras."

"This is a good place for a vacation."

Santos agreed.

She began to move, preparatory to leaving.

"Hilda—I hope you don't mind me using your first name."

She shook her head.

"Would you join me for a drink? Coffee, perhaps?"

"Yes. I think I would like that."

They smiled at one another, and stood up together.

14

"Which will it be? A drink or coffee?" Santos asked as they began walking.

"I think coffee with a luscious piece of pastry."

"That sounds good to me."

He was already thinking about dinner, and beyond. He'd already seen her sitting on the bench, but as he walked alongside her, he was acutely aware of her physicality. She was somewhat shorter than himself, and he could see she had long, well-shaped legs. Because she did not close her coat, he also saw that, though she wasn't big-breasted, neither was she flat-chested. There was enough there to fill his hand.

"Aren't we going in the wrong direction?" he asked, becoming aware that they were actually moving deeper into the park. "The other way would get us out sooner."

"There is a place I know on Jac Obrecht."

Santos shrugged. "You're the resident here."

Smiling, she assured him, "We only have a short distance to go."

He took hold of her arm. "Mind?"

"No."

The walkway curved up, and away from the lake.

"Seems as if we're alone," he commented. The sky was gray now, and it had become cold enough for him to remove his coat from his shoulders and wear it.

Her eyes moved to a clump of cypress bushes ahead and off to the right.

"From April back to November in a matter of hours," he commented.

"That's Holland's weather. The same thing could happen in July."

"Does it ever go the other way, from November to July?"

"Never."

They passed the cypress bushes.

Hilda dropped her book.

15

"I'll get it," Santos said, stopping.

She moved to the left.

Even before he stooped down, Santos heard the muffled shot. He started to stand—the second shot tore into his chest. He was thrown on to his back. Drops of cold rain began to fall on his face. . . .

Chapter 2

It was three-thirty P.M. Friday afternoon. General Richard Bushwick, Director of the CIA, sat at his desk and stared at the far wall, at a large painting of his sloop, the *Sea Bird,* under full sail. He had hoped to spend the weekend cruising the Chesapeake on her — the first weekend of the season — even though temperatures in the low sixties had been forecast for the bay area.

He moved his pale gray eyes from the painting to the phone on his desk. Less than a half hour ago, he'd received a call from a Company man in Amsterdam, informing him that Cory Brant, a.k.a. Miguel Santos, had been shot to death in Vondel Park two days before.

Bushwick leaned his six-foot body back into the swivel chair.

Brant was the seventh agent killed in the past five months. Three had been taken out in as many different Central American countries. One had been killed when he'd lost control of his car. Forensics had later found he had been poisoned. Another operative had been shot to death on a street in Manhattan's Little Italy. Another's light plane had exploded on takeoff from a small airport in Fairfax County, Virginia.

Bushwick rubbed his clean-shaven chin, and muttered, "Not a fucking clue in any of them!"

He launched himself forward, picked up the phone, and punched out four numbers.

"Grier here," the voice on the other end announced after one ring.

"Have you finished that report you mentioned in your last memo to me?"

"Yes. But I haven't had time to put it in its final form."

"I'll take it the way you have it now," Bushwick told him. Before Grier could object, he said, "Brant went down in Amsterdam."

Silence, except for the sound of Grier's breathing.

"Like the others, no clues," Bushwick said.

"I'll give you what I've put together. But it's rough and contains my comments, many of which would not be included in—"

"Bring it. It's the only damn thing we have."

"Ten minutes?"

Bushwick didn't answer. He put the phone down and looked longingly at the painting of the *Sea Bird* again.

Grier entered Bushwick's office without being announced by the Director's secretary or knocking. He approached the desk. "The last two pages are handwritten."

"Legible enough to read, I hope."

Grier put his report down on the desk. "The usual chicken scrawl."

Grier didn't mince words with Bushwick. A short, tight-lipped man, he'd been with the Company too many years not to say what he meant and mean what he said. He was one of the few Deputy Directors with field service in Eastern Europe and later in South and Central America. The other top desks were political appointees.

Bushwick ran his fingers over the report, and looked up at Grier. "How much blue-skying?"

"You be the judge of that."

Bushwick's eyes narrowed. Grier wasn't his cup of

tea. He was used to men saluting him, even if it was only in the tone of their voice.

He hefted the report. "At least it won't take all weekend to read."

"It may well take a hell of a lot more than that to think about," Grier answered. "Don't be fooled by its lack of bulk." He knew Bushwick was a weekend sailor.

"You think—"

Grier pointed to a plastic red file folder in Bushwick's hands. "What I think is in there."

"I'll let you know what my reaction is on Monday," Bushwick said.

"If I'm right—"

"Monday."

Grier nodded, turned, and left the office.

The moment the door closed, Bushwick began to read.

EDITED FILE, DOSSIER JWA-2/22/29

TO: Major General Richard Bushwick, Director Central Intelligence Agency. (FOR YOUR EYES ONLY)

FROM: Peter Grier, Deputy Director, Central & South America

SUBJECT: John Wesley Anderson

REPORT FORMAT: Official interior and exterior sources, plus personal opinion.

THRUST OF REPORT: File was originally culled to isolate Highlight Material for initial evaluation re: possible Presidential appointment of Anderson as civilian overseer-ombudsman re: Agency.

President is known to favor creation of said office, and Anderson is much bruited about as the man for the job because of:

(1) extensive government experience, including years

of highly secret work for us,

(2) diplomatic experience in nations south of the border,

(3) public image.

To explain #3 — Anderson consistently ranks high in the polls of "Most Admired Americans."

Later in this report, I will demonstrate that Anderson's public image is not irrelevant to our current situation in the field.

The possibility of anyone looking over our shoulder is a disquieting one, especially if it turns out to be Anderson. But that would be a minor calamity in contrast to the other possibility regarding Anderson.

It's common knowledge that the President is seriously thinking of running again, and that the opposition party is casting about for someone who is not part of the Democratic machine.

A fresh face. Someone with proven charisma.

Anderson's name is mentioned more often than any other.

Because of this possibility, everything to do with Anderson has to do with us from now on. He can be — or already *is* — the cancer we've always feared.

PHYSICAL DESCRIPTION: Just turned sixty. Tall, lanky, gray-flecked sandy hair, blue eyes. Actually described by the press innumerable times as a "Gary Cooper look-alike."

HEALTH: Suffered a severe heart attack three years ago, approximately six months after having returned from a South American diplomatic post. Timing here is not insignificant. Only close family members and a few trusted associates apprised. Official cover story from the Anderson Foundation was that he was off on one of his many art-hunting expeditions. (See below.) He has fully recovered and the prognosis is for continued good health. Heart attack was regarded by our Psychiatric Analysis Section to be directly related to the situation re: "Venom" (see below), and the loss of his son (see below).

BASIC PERSONALITY PROFILE: Highly intelligent, complex man. Has been highly critical of U.S. Govt. while in various diplomatic positions (Chile, Mexico, Venezuela). In all instances circumstances proved Anderson correct re: local situations. He has to date kept away from partisan politics, despite his family's deep involvement in Republican Party matters.

NEXT OF KIN: Parents deceased. Two brothers, Wallace Anderson, sixty-four, is President of the First Intercontinental Bank, third largest in the world. George Anderson, sixty-six, is Chairman of the Board, Intercontinental Petroleum Corporation, the fourteenth largest in the world. (Dossiers for both men are on file, WA-3/9/25 & GA-1/7/25.)

IMMEDIATE FAMILY: Wife, Augusta, fifty-eight. The marriage was less a love match than a joining of economic interests. Son, John Wesley Anderson, Jr., born 1947, deceased in 1975 as a result of an accident during a mountain-climbing expedition in the Himalayas. Son's loss was a severe blow.

ADDITIONAL MATERIAL: Anderson has often been depicted as the American Eagle defending the poor and downtrodden of Latin America against an ogrelike Uncle Sam. There is no need for rehashing the various diplomatic and governmental posts he has held. All told he has spent three decades in the service of the country and this gives him an intimate knowledge of its inner workings. Anderson has shown us that the other side of the metaphor of the eagle is the serpent, and that *he* could provide the venom. He had the means and the talent to put together the best team of assassins (Code Name: Venom) the world had ever seen. He made Chile happen, and he made everything happen elsewhere that we wanted to happen. But this was before your time. Rumor was that he truly enjoyed the power that Venom gave him.

We know that Anderson had a love affair with Isabel Aroyo, a beautiful Mexico City woman, who is a political scientist, a leading feminist, and a revolutionist. We know from a source close to Anderson (Code Name: "Safe Deposit" — see your personal file on same) that he had considered divorcing Augusta and marrying Isabel, but nothing came of it.

After his heart attack, he spent most of his time running the family foundation, and now he spends more of his time at his East Sixty-seventh Street town house, where the cataloguing of his various art collections goes on. His father's collection will go to the Boston Museum of Fine Arts. But he has not yet announced where his collection of pre-Columbian art (reputed to be the best in the world) will go.

Now he is sexually involved with a twenty-seven-year-old woman, Marylee Jane Terrall, who works for him. We have several tapes of some of their intimate moments, if you care to listen to them.

This is just background. To give a rounded picture of the man. But after careful consideration, I have come up with the following:

1. I do not see him taking the job of ombudsman—it removes him from the limelight, which he enjoys.

2. He might declare himself a candidate for the Presidency—he is certainly unpredictable enough to do that, and he certainly has all the necessary credentials, including the necessary money to finance his own campaign. However, I do not see him doing either. Now we come to the tie between Anderson and the recent developments. This is strictly a hunch. I think Anderson, for whatever reasons—maybe in some spooky way it still has to do with the loss of his son—is behind the recent terminations of our friends. *I think Venom lives*. Bizarre as this sounds, consider the expertise involved in the hits. To make it even more *bizarre*, I believe Anderson is paying us back for what we "had" him do. If I am right, he's now on a moral crusade of his own—except he has been reborn as our enemy, not our friend. He should be considered very dangerous!

When Bushwick finished reading the report, he ran his hand through his close-cropped gray hair.

"Anderson . . . John Wesley Anderson . . ."

They had served in the same unit during the Korean War, and afterwards he had met him several times at various official functions. Their conversations had been polite, even inane, now that he looked back at them.

Bushwick turned back to the section of the report where Venom was mentioned.

While he had been Assistant Chief of Staff in the Canal Zone, he'd heard whispers about the existence of such a group, but he'd never believed them. As far as he had been concerned, such stories had been generated by the Communists. But even when he had heard them, Anderson had never been, even remotely, connected to Venom.

He reread Grier's reference to Venom.

"Son of a bitch!" he exploded, closing the report.

That was a damn dangerous leap Grier had made. Anderson just wasn't anyone.

Bushwick pulled a cigar out of a leather holder, cut the end with a small pocketknife, and lit up, sending a column of bluish white smoke toward the ceiling, instantly filling the room with pungent smell.

He looked down at the report. He thought he'd been grasping at a fucking straw when he'd asked Grier for it.

He left his chair and went to the window. The sky was mostly clear, with some light scud off to the right.

Anderson was one of those untouchables. He was one of the wealthiest men in the country, but, as Grier pointed out, one of the most admired. And those two factors didn't even begin to indicate the power the man had in and out of government.

Bushwick, with one hand braced against the glass pane, was aware that taking on Anderson could damn well turn the Agency into a house of cards. He blew smoke against the window, turned, and went back to his desk.

If fucking Grier was right, he'd have more than enough to think about over the weekend.

Chapter 3

Anderson, wearing a heavy woolen, red plaid shirt open at the neck, dark blue corduroy pants, and a pair of tan, handmade walking shoes, stood very close to the wooden dock's edge, and looked across a small lake, whose banks were still rimmed with ice. The lake, the ten-room hunting lodge behind Anderson, and a hundred and fifty acres of Adirondack wilderness belonged to him — more specifically to the Anderson family. But in the past, he had been the only one, after his father had died, to use the lodge. Neither of his brothers had a taste for rustic living, though conditions at the lodge were far from rustic.

On the other side of the lake, the slanting rays of the late afternoon sun turned the still, bare branches of the trees, some of which were covered from the previous night's snow, to gold, and an eight-point buck stood motionless in the golden light.

For several long, incredibly delicious minutes, Anderson drank in the scene, framing it in his mind.

Years before, when he attended Choate, before going on to Harvard, he had dreamed about becoming a painter. His art teacher, Mr. Perins, a grim, humorless man, had chosen two of his paintings to exhibit on Parents' Day, an honor that Perins, up to that time, had never accorded to anyone else.

Remembering that past glory brought a shadow of a smile to Anderson's lips.

Somewhere, in one of the many houses he owned,

those two paintings were locked in a storage room. They might even be in the hunting lodge behind him, though he doubted it. More than likely they'd be in the Manhattan town house, or even in Augusta's penthouse. He still kept many of his things there, despite the fact that he hadn't lived there for years.

The golden light was rapidly fading, and the buck was beginning to move back among the pines where now the grayness was deepening.

Anderson turned. The lights were already on in several of the lodges rooms.

The dock boards creaked under his feet as he made his way to the steps, up them, and into the lodge's main living room, where a roaring fire in the large fireplace spilled a comforting warmth into the room.

Three of his five weekend guests were enjoying a predinner cocktail, and acknowledged his entrance with a smile, or raised their glasses slightly in a toast.

"Thomas and Kevin?" Anderson questioned. Kevin Hogan was chairman of the state's Democratic Party, and Senator Thomas Post was the Majority Leader in Washington. This weekend gathering had been requested by Post, a longtime friend.

"Napping," Douglas Fitzroy, one of the drinkers, answered.

"Not together, I hope," Anderson responded with a straight face. Fitzroy was the Democratic party's media specialist, and because he was a newcomer to Anderson's circle of "friends," he'd had his people compile a dossier on the man. He was "clean."

The three men laughed.

"That certainly won't help you gentlemen put a man in the White House."

Another burst of laughter, and before it was over, a burly man with a red nose and a tracery of blue veins around his eyes entered the room.

"Your timing couldn't have been better, Thomas," Anderson said.

Post walked directly to the bar. "All this fresh air is enough to kill a man." He poured himself a double scotch. "To putting our man in the White House," he toasted, raising the glass toward Anderson.

"Here, here!" Fitzroy exclaimed. "I'll certainly drink to that."

The other two men, Charles Bing and Harry Pappas, lifted their glasses too. Bing, an almost cadaverous-looking man, was the party's chief strategist, and Pappas was the national president of the powerful Teamsters Union.

Anderson acknowledged the toasts with his famous smile, but at the same time, he put his hand up, palm out. "Too fast, gentlemen. Too fast. You see me as I really am. Just a country boy at heart."

Another burst of laughter followed.

"Am I missing something?" Hogan asked, entering the room.

"John was telling us that he's really a country boy," Bing said.

"To be sure, just as I am Peter Pan."

"And I thought that was supposed to be our secret," Anderson responded.

Hogan moved to the bar and poured himself a Jack Daniels. "Speaking for all of us, I'd like to thank you, John, for this invitation." He swallowed more than half the drink, while the others added their thanks to his.

Anderson nodded. "I always enjoy spending time with friends."

A white-jacketed servant stepped into the open doorway between the living room and the dining room to announce that dinner was being served.

Anderson led the small procession. He had the head of the table. Hogan was on his right, Post on his left.

The others were not seated in any particular order.

Despite the rustic setting, the table was set with Limoge china and exquisite Danish silver service. Dinner was an elaborate eight-course affair, with broiled, marinated venison steaks for the entree.

During dinner, the conversation was broad, encompassing everything from the latest on the Greenhouse Effect to the newest hit on Broadway, Jerome Robbins's *Broadway*. But it was after dinner, when the assemblage moved back to the living room and each of the guests was enjoying an after-dinner drink, that Post made the opening gambit.

"John, let's not beat around the bush. You know why we wanted this meeting and we know why you agreed to it."

Anderson allowed himself one cigar a day, and it was almost always after dinner. He smoked it, allowing Post's words to remain suspended. He was testing the waters, so to speak.

Post glanced at Hogan for support. He felt as if he were slowly sinking.

Anderson waited, blowing smoke toward the ceiling.

"The point is that we're prepared to make you the party's standard-bearer." Post moved his hand to encompass the other men. "We think you belong in the White House."

Anderson removed the cigar from his mouth. "There might be one or two others who disagree with you."

"Not enough, in our opinion, to make a difference."

"Gentlemen, my family's political associations are a matter of public record. Democrats to them are just one step away from — I was going to say Communists, but I'll make it even stronger — the devil's own."

There were smiles all around.

Hogan nodded. "But your politics aren't known."

"By choice, Kevin. By choice."

"Then perhaps, John, it's time to make them known by becoming our candidate for the Presidency," Pappas said. "Certainly you have the credentials."

"Pardon me if I'm frank."

"By all means be frank, John," Post said, pouring himself another drink.

"You people haven't been able to put a man in the White House for twelve years. What makes you think you can do it now?" He put the cigar back in his mouth, and rolled it to the right side.

"The conditions in the country," Pappas answered. "The people have had enough of trickle-down economics. They're ready for a change."

"He's absolutely right," Fitzroy said.

"Our surveys show—"

Anderson held up his hand. "I'm well aware of what the surveys show. But most people are earning more now, and certainly you would have to agree that glasnost is working. World tensions have been substantially reduced."

"Poverty has increased, and our social programs have been all but destroyed by the last few Administrations."

Anderson stood up and walked to the hearth, where for several moments he looked at the flames. He had thought seriously about running for the Presidency. That these men were here was proof enough of that. But he wasn't yet ready to commit to them. "Suppose the Republicans were to ask me to be their candidate," he asked, without turning to see the effect.

The question was answered with silence.

One of them cleared his throat; it might have been Post, because the next voice Anderson heard was his.

"That's a possibility, John. But speaking for myself, it has always been my opinion that your public statements, for the most part, on a variety of domestic and foreign issues, were closer to our philosophy than to

29

theirs."

Anderson made a slow turn. How little these men knew him astounded him! They seemed to be totally ignorant of whole decades of his life, when his public statements were one thing and his actions another.

His eyes, momentarily, went to the far wall where trophies of his various hunting expeditions were hung. A lion's head. The head of a water buffalo. A tiger's skin. Even the head of a moose. He had killed them all, and a great many other wild animals. He'd been younger then and eager to prove his mettle. But now he was a spokesman for many conservation groups.

"This is something that we do not expect you to decide now, or for that matter, over this weekend," Hogan said. "Our intention—the purpose of our being here—is to ask you to consider becoming our candidate."

Before Anderson could answer, Post said, "John, the country needs you, and to be frank, we need you."

"At least the second part of what you said, Thomas, is frank, and I appreciate it. As for the country needing me—well, that certainly is flattering, but nothing I would take seriously."

He was going to let them know, here and now, that beneath his easygoing manner, he was rock hard—Anderson hard—and that kind of hardness was never touched by flattery.

"Just to give you the opportunity to see our offer in its proper perspective," Post said, "you will not be burdened by political debts should you agree to join us."

Anderson nodded. "Interesting. If I stand here long enough, I am sure other changing, or rather enhancing, perspectives will be offered to me. But gentlemen, I've played some hardball in politics, and I know that there is a lot of horse trading before the reality of a situation falls in place. I will, as you have asked, consider your offer."

"That's all we ask now," Post said, knowing that if Anderson should agree to become the party's standard-bearer, he would do some sharp horse trading himself.

"Then be assured I will do it. But now, I'm tired, and any further discussion of the subject would tire me even more. I'll see all of you at breakfast tomorrow morning. Good night gentlemen."

Individually, his guests responded with their good nights.

Anderson stubbed out the remaining part of his cigar in an ashtray on the mantle above the fireplace, and leaving the room, climbed the steps to the upper floor, where his bedroom was located.

The discussion that had just taken place was the first of many that would occupy many hours over the next two days.

Chapter 4

Grier stood at the rain-spattered window, and looked out at a gray, soggy day. The rain had started before dawn on Monday, and now it was Wednesday afternoon.

It was Wednesday afternoon and Bushwick still hadn't gotten back to him on his Anderson report, though he and Bushwick had been in contact several times a day on various other matters. But he was not about to ask Bushwick about it. The ball was in his court. Now he had to play it or just let it go out of play — which was almost unthinkable, given the danger —

The intercom came on.

"Mister Grier, a package for you by special courier from New York," his secretary said.

He moved to the desk, and switched on his end of the intercom. "Thank you, Miss Cotter. Please bring it in."

The door opened, and his secretary entered before he had a chance to sit down.

From the size of the package, he knew they were tape cassettes. He sat down, anxious to unwrap the tapes, and at the same time aware of the young woman standing in front of him.

She was half his age, wearing a white blouse, with an open V neck that revealed the bare inside of each of her breasts, and a tight blue skirt. Her long black hair was braided, and her small sensuous mouth always seemed as if it was on the verge of smiling, or concealing a smile.

"Thank you, June," Grier said, his eyes resting longer than he meant them to on her breasts.

She nodded.

And to give the old goat something to really get him hot, she made her behind undulate provocatively as she walked to the door.

Grier's cheeks burned.

The door closed.

He bit his lower lip, and shook his head.

She damn well knew what he was thinking, what he wanted.

There were two cassettes, as he'd guessed. One was marked "A" and the other "B." He slipped the "A" tape into the portable machine and began to play it. Within moments, he realized that he was listening to a conversation between Anderson and the top people in the Democratic party.

Grier pressed the stop button, picked up the phone, and quickly punched out Bushwick's number.

He answered on the second ring.

"Grier, here. I received two tapes by courier from New York." He paused, savoring what he was going to say next before he said it. "Anderson and the big guns of the Democratic Party—"

"My office now!"

The line went dead.

Grier put the phone down and smiled.

They always put a fucking turkey in the top spot, don't they?

Bushwick, with Grier sitting next to his desk, listened to the tapes, and the more he heard, the more of a threat Anderson became.

The last of the conversations between Anderson and his guests ended halfway through the second side of the "B" tape.

Bushwick pressed the stop button.

"I'll hold on to these."

Grier nodded.

"This puts the proverbial fat in the fire, doesn't it," Bushwick said, after making several snorting sounds.

"Puts Anderson way on top of our list of priorities."

Bushwick fussed with a cigar and finally lit it. "I want him neutralized."

Grier almost rolled his eyes in dismay. But he stopped himself and waited for his boss to utter another stupidity.

"He becomes the next President and there won't be any damn Company." Pacing now, Bushwick puffed continuously on the cigar, shrouding himself in a bluish white haze. "The Democrats would like nothing better than to put the Company on their leash."

"He can't be 'neutralized'—at least, not the way you mean it," Grier told him, relishing the telling.

Bushwick came to an abrupt halt, and pointed the cigar at Grier.

"Tell me why the fuck not. What makes him so fucking different?"

"Venom."

Still pointing the cigar at him, Bushwick said, "I was waiting for you to mention that." He stuck the cigar back in his mouth. "Take Anderson out and you take out Venom. It's that easy." And he snapped his fingers to demonstrate just how easy it was.

"Take Anderson out, and Venom will—if I was right—get to me, to you, and anyone else it thinks is responsible. Even the President."

Bushwick dropped heavily into his chair. "You want me to believe that Anderson is still running Venom,

35

and he's running it as a payback operation?"

"I believe it. If I didn't, I wouldn't have suggested it in my report."

"Grier, *we're* the CIA, remember?"

"We don't even know the identity of any of Venom's people."

"You mean he ran them independently?"

"They were his people. He paid them himself. We only know that they ranged from Ph.D.'s to professional killers. They belonged to him."

"Holy shit, that amounts to a private army."

"Two, maybe three dozen at the most. But the very best, the very best."

Bushwick puffed several times on his cigar. "You have a plan."

Grier almost smiled. It wasn't a question; it was a statement. "Yes, I have one."

He had thought up a brilliant plan, and had it ready to put into operation.

"Then I can leave the matter completely in your hands?" Bushwick wasn't about to let his subordinate best him.

"Just exactly what do you mean by that?"

"You have a plan. Use it. I don't want to have to think about Anderson again. The next time I hear his name I want to be able to put on a sad face."

"Should I have to deal with Safe Deposit?"

If Bushwick was going to let him run the show, then he wanted all the players, and Safe Deposit was a key player.

Bushwick scrutinized Grier for several moments and decided to give him all the rope he wanted. If Grier's plan backfired, it would be all the easier to hang him.

"Okay, I'll give you Safe Deposit. But he's not to be used unless everything else fails."

"Agreed."

"Now tell me how you managed to have the conversations taped."

"It wasn't easy," Grier answered with a smile.

And Bushwick knew that was all that he was going to get from him.

Post was on the phone.

Anderson listened to the senator.

"I know you too long, John, to try and play games. You impressed the hell out of our friends."

"I impress the hell out of a lot of people. That's one of the Andersons' big assets."

Post laughed. "I know that. And that's precisely why we want you. We won't have to waste time and money building your image. You're already the 'American Eagle.' Practically every schoolboy knows that. We can concentrate on issues, for a change."

"Tempting . . . very tempting." Anderson eased back in his swivel chair and turned toward the rain-smeared window.

"John, you're too vigorous a man to retire from public life. You have the knowledge and the energy to make things, good things, happen in the country." He believed what he was saying.

"Give me another few days to think about it."

"We want to start early."

"A month," Anderson said.

"Good. Very good," Post answered with a smile in his voice. "And just to tip the scale, you're invited to my place—"

"There's really no need for that."

"It's non-political, John. The Missus is having a few friends over for cocktails on Saturday. Mainly arty types. You know she's into that sort of thing." The way he said it, he made it sound like some noisome creature he'd much prefer to avoid.

Anderson smiled. Post's taste in art went no further than crotch shots in magazines.

"Nothing large, John." He'd already told his wife, Iris, that Anderson would come. He certainly would be the stellar attraction for the other guests, no matter who would be there.

"What time?" asked Anderson.

Again with a smile in his voice. "Five-ish would be fine."

Anderson repeated the time.

"Good talking to you," Post said.

"Same."

Anderson didn't wait to hear the click on the other end before he put the phone down.

He really wasn't all that enthusiastic about attending the cocktail party. Iris Post was a tall, big-boned woman with a horsey face who spent a lifetime collecting terrible art and worse artists. But if he did decide to run for the Presidency, he and Post would be working very closely.

Anderson rested his elbows on the arms of the chair, pressing the balls of his fingers together. This time he turned fully toward the rain-spattered window. The two paintings he'd done at Choate came into his mind. Ever since he had remembered them, they'd moved in and out of his thoughts. He wondered why.

The drops on the window, when they became big enough, formed rivulets.

Perhaps one of the paintings had a rain-spattered window in it? He couldn't remember, no matter how hard he tried.

A soft knock on the door broke into his musings.

"Yes." He turned away from the window.

The door opened and Marylee entered, smiling.

"Mail's in."

She closed the door behind her and went toward the desk.

Anderson smiled up at her. She was the single most important human being in his life now.

"Anything interesting?"

"The usual requests for money, and a letter for you marked personal all the way from New Delhi, India."

She put the letters down, and settled on the edge of the desk, alongside him. She enjoyed the way he looked at her. The light that came into his eyes when he saw her gave her a warm feeling.

The unopened letter from India was on top of the stack.

Anderson looked at the name of the sender — Richard Gault — above the return address. The name meant nothing to him.

"Aren't you going to open it?"

"Eventually." He took hold of her hand, and kissed the back of it.

He never ceased to wonder that she preferred him to a younger lover.

Marylee bent down and kissed the top of his head.

"We're going to Senator Post's cocktail party — more precisely, his wife's party — on Saturday. Will you make the necessary arrangements?"

"First, you will have to tell me what arrangements you want made."

As Anderson thought for a moment, his eyes went back to the letter from New Delhi. The city was in northern India, a jumping-off place for those who visited Katmandu, in Nepal. His son had stopped there.

"John, are you all right?" She touched the side of his face.

Healthy though he was, she always feared he might

suffer another heart attack, especially after a morning session of lovemaking.

He regained his composure. "Arrangements for Saturday, yes."

"Well, what are they?"

"Suppose we fly down late Friday evening, and stay until Sunday evening."

Marylee nodded. "You want to use the Lear Jet or the helicopter?"

"The chopper will do fine. We'll use my suite at the Watergate."

"Consider it done." She stood up. "Are you sure you're all right?"

"Absolutely, in top form." He put his arms around her, drew her close, and while his hands cupped her buttocks, he buried his face in the deliciously scented hollow of her stomach.

She pressed him to her.

After a few moments, Anderson let go of her and moved back.

At his stage of life there were definite advantages to having a mistress who was almost always close at hand.

"Anything else?" she asked, pausing before she was halfway to the door and turning toward him.

"Not that I can think of now — except to alert Jeff and Pat that they'll be in Washington for the weekend." Jeff Hunter and Pat Ryan were his bodyguards. They'd been with the Company when he was, and gone with him when he'd left.

"Yes," she answered, and continued out of the room.

Alone again, Anderson picked up the letter from Richard Gault and hefted it, as if its weight would somehow tell him something about its contents.

He unsheathed a gold-handled stiletto and slid open the envelope. There was one sheet of plain white paper, folded in half. He spread the paper out on the desk, and read the very neat library-style printing.

Dear Mr. Anderson—
    For the past two years I have been traveling in northern Nepal to collect material for a book—I am a photographer—about the local people. Some six weeks ago, I happened to stop at a lamasery very close to the Tibetan border, where I had the pleasure of meeting your son, John.

Anderson shook his head. His heart raced. Tears came to his eyes. He'd spent several million dollars trying to recover his son's body. But no one could ever find it.

He used a tissue to wipe his eyes, and blow his nose before he continued to read.

He is well and sends his love to you.
    I will be returning to the States in about ten days. I expect to stay in New York for a while.
    I hope this letter brings you peace.

                                    Sincerely
                                    Richard Gault

Anderson jumped to his feet and started for the door. Then he stopped.

Aloud he said, "God, I want to see my son. Then maybe I'll have peace."

He returned to his chair, and looked at the date on the letter. It was postmarked eight days ago. Gault was somewhere in transit. He could even be in the States by now, maybe in New York.

He was on his feet again, this time pacing.

There wasn't any way he could find Gault. He'd have to wait until the man called him.

He went back to the desk, picked up the letter, and read it again.

There wasn't any indication that Gault wanted something from him. After John Junior had been reported lost, he had received hundreds of letters offering to find his son in exchange for money.

"Wait," he said aloud. "Wait." And with a complete feeling of impotence, he carefully folded the letter, put it back in the envelope, and placed the envelope in the top drawer of his desk. Then switching on the intercom, he said to Marylee, "If a Richard Gault should call, put his call through to me no matter who I'm with, or what I'm doing. And for the weekend, have all our phones covered by an answering service. Should Mr. Gault phone while we're away, I want his call transferred to wherever we are."

"That important?" Marylee asked.

"Yes," he answered, and switched off.

Chapter 5

Iris Post's idea of a "small gathering" was on the order of sixty people. As many politicos and high-level government officials as artists were present. There was even a sprinkling of journalists, whom Anderson immediately spotted.

But the weather cooperated, and the guests took advantage of the lovely spring evening by using the huge terrace more than the even larger dining room, where a lavish Chinese buffet had been set up.

Anderson, with Marylee at his side, moved easily among the guests. Most of those from the House and Senate he knew by name, and though the possibility of receiving a phone call from Richard Gault was never out of his thoughts, he had a smile and a firm handshake for everyone who greeted him.

He and Marylee found themselves the focal point of at least a dozen guests. Congressmen and their wives, a political columnist named Bill Haply, and General Bushwick, the head of the CIA.

The conversation had actually started with one of the Congressmen asking Anderson what he thought about the drought in the Midwest, especially in the wheat- and corn-growing states.

"I think what you're really asking," Anderson responded, "is whether or not I think the government should step in and help the farmers of the area. But that's only part of the question. The other part has to do with water conservation, or more precisely, water management. There the various Administrations, over the past twelve years, have done nothing. The result, when nature fails to provide the necessary water, is the disaster we now have."

At first Bushwick found himself more interested in looking at Marylee than in listening to Anderson. Divorced fifteen years before, when he was still a colonel, he'd had several affairs, but the women were always five, maybe six years younger than himself. But Marylee was almost twenty years younger than Anderson, and she was gorgeous. She had the body of a dancer, with shoulder-length brown hair, green eyes, and just a smattering of freckles below her eyes and across the bridge of her nose. Bushwick's own daughter was only a year older than Marylee, who suddenly locked eyes with him.

Marylee had sensed she was being stared at, and decided to silently challenge the person.

She glared at Bushwick, remembering his name and that he headed the CIA. She had been Anderson's lover long enough to be able to see in the eyes of a man when he wondered what she was like in bed.

Bushwick was doing it now.

She answered his question by not only staring back at him, but by linking her arm with Anderson's.

At that very moment, Bushwick imagined her naked, his face pressed against the brown hair on her love mound. At the very same instant he heard Anderson say, "We've supported all the wrong people in Third World countries."

Bushwick scowled.

The fantasy evaporated, as quick as the snap of a finger, and almost as jarring.

He blinked, and shifted his eyes to Anderson.

"Mr. Ambassador," another person in the group began, "how can we permit—"

"Please, just Mr. Anderson. Or if you know me, John will do. But not Mr. Ambassador. I'm just an ordinary citizen now."

Laughter followed.

"Excuse the interruption," Anderson said, smiling. "You started to ask a question."

"How would you prevent the Third World countries from going over to the Communists?" the same individual asked.

"By offering them a viable alternative, and by understanding that our way of doing things need not be theirs."

The longer Bushwick listened to Anderson, the more disturbed he became.

The man sounded very like a political candidate, even though he hadn't declared himself to be one. And there was absolutely no doubt in his mind that if Anderson became the President, he would, as Grier suggested, dismantle the Company—or at the very least greatly diminish its substantial power.

Anderson continued to hold forth on his ideas of what should be done to change, or at least improve, certain national and international conditions until Iris Post appeared. "Excuse me, people, but John has a phone call."

Anderson felt an immediate weakness in his knees.

Bushwick saw the color drain from his face.

"There's a phone in the den," Mrs. Post said. "You may take the call there."

Anderson nodded to the people around him, and whispered to Marylee, "I'll rejoin you as soon as I'm through." He freed his arm from hers, and followed Iris.

Aware of what had just taken place, Bushwick crossed the space between him and Marylee. "Must be a very important call."

She shrugged her right shoulder, annoyed with Anderson. "Must be."

"He seemed to be upset."

"I didn't notice." But she had. She had felt him suddenly lean against her.

Bushwick nodded. He wasn't going to challenge her. He wanted to cultivate her. "Would you join me—"

"No, thank you."

"You might have let me finish."

"It would not have mattered. Now, if you will excuse me . . ." And she walked away.

As he watched her, Bushwick suddenly wanted to hear the tapes that Grier mentioned in his memo.

Anderson picked up the phone and identified himself.

"Richard Gault here," the voice on the other end said.

For a moment, Anderson said nothing. He was sweating.

"Mr. Anderson, are you still here?"

"Yes. Yes. Where are you now?"

"O'Hare. I have an hour layover before continuing on to New York." Gault's voice sounded young, and enthusiastic.

"I can be in New York in a few hours."

"I'm going to be met by friends and go down to the Jersey shore with them. I won't actually be in New York, at the very earliest, until Tuesday."

"I want to meet you." Anderson couldn't keep the note of desperation out of his voice. "Is my son—"

"Fine. He's fine. I'll tell you all about him when I see you."

"When will that be?"

"Friday—"

"Yes, Friday. Where?" Anderson finally sat down on the chair behind the desk. "You name the place and I'll be there."

"Is Monte's in the Village still around?" Gault laughed. "All told, I've been away for two years."

Anderson knew the restaurant. A family-run place for almost thirty years on McDougal Street in Greenwich Village. "It's there."

"One o'clock for lunch," Gault offered.

"Yes."

"See you there."

There was a click on the other end before Anderson could ask if he had taken any pictures of John Junior.

He put the phone down, fished out a handkerchief, and wiped his brow. Totally drained, he leaned back in the chair and closed his eyes.

He'd told no one about Gault's letter, and didn't intend to until he met Gault, and found out more about his son.

But that he might have hope again that his son was alive suddenly brought a tightness to his throat which gave way to sobs.

"John?"

Marylee had taken it upon herself to seek him out, after a reasonable length of time had lapsed and he hadn't rejoined her. She had opened the door less than halfway.

"Is anything wrong?"

She was sure she'd heard him sobbing.

"No . . . no."

He wiped his eyes and blew his nose, and stood up. "I'm fine. Absolutely fine."

He crossed the room, opened the door fully, and took her by the arm. "You know, I'm actually hungry now. What about you?"

She smiled at him. "Famished."

As they moved into the dining room, they passed Bushwick.

"That man scowls a lot," Anderson commented.

"Yes, I've noticed that. I wonder why."

Anderson shrugged. "I'd prefer to think it was the result of constipation, rather than anything else."

They looked at one another, and simultaneously laughed.

"It's two o'clock in the morning," Grier said into the phone.

"I want to know what you're doing about Anderson." Bushwick cradled the phone between his left shoulder and ear while he poured himself another double scotch, the third since he'd begun to listen to the tapes.

"Where the hell are you?" asked Grier.

"Home."

Grier pulled himself up, and leaned against the bed's head board. He'd suspected that Bushwick had a drinking problem.

"I was with the son of a bitch this evening," Bushwick said.

"With Anderson?"

"Not the fucking Pope."

Grier cringed. He was a practicing Catholic.

"Him and that Marylee."

Grier didn't miss the growl—the male growl—in Bushwick's voice when he said the woman's name.

"I've been listening to the tapes."

Listening and probably jerking off, Grier thought.

"I want to know what you're doing about Anderson."

"Moving on it."

"I want the fucker out. He's even talking like a goddamn candidate."

Grier breathed deeply and slowly exhaled. "It has to

be done with finesse. Take him out and we're dead. Try to understand that. It can't be done your way."

Suddenly, Grier's wife Betty was awake. "Who are you talking to?"

He put his hand over the mouthpiece. "Go back to sleep. It's Bushwick."

"At this time of night?"

"Go back to sleep."

She turned over, and drew the cover over her head.

"You still there?" Bushwick questioned.

"I'm here."

"Give me a date," Bushwick said.

"I can't."

"You mean you won't." Bushwick didn't much like Grier, and sensed that the man felt the same way about him.

"I mean I can't," Grier answered stubbornly.

He had begun to initiate his plan when he'd first made the connection between Anderson and the murders of several agents, all of whom, at one time or another, had been assigned to Central or South American countries. This was one operation which would be carried out without any slip-ups. He was running it.

Bushwick mumbled something, but Grier couldn't make it out, and he wasn't about to ask him to repeat it. He wanted to go back to sleep, not that he'd be able to do it easily. He'd probably wind up having to take a sleeping pill, and that would make him feel groggy for the rest of the morning, while he was in church.

"She likes cock." Bushwick knocked back most of the scotch in the glass. "Did you hear what she said about oral sex?"

"Different strokes for different folks," Grier responded. Betty was strictly a missionary-style woman. Anything else she believed was perverted.

A sudden click on the other end seemed to indicate

49

that Bushwick had hung up, but then Grier heard him say, "Listen to this." And the tape came on.

"I love your mouth . . . you use it so exquisitely," Anderson breathed.

"As you do yours on me."

"I'm complete when I'm with you, and I don't really understand why."

"What, my lord and masturbator, don't you understand?" Marylee asked.

The two of them laughed.

"Before you answer, take hold of my cunt. Yes, like that! Hold it very tight."

"I don't understand what you see in an old fart like me."

"I enjoy myself with you. You're special, very special. And whether you believe it or not, and you should believe it, you please me physically, as much as any man ever has. I love the feel of your hands on me, and your mouth on my cunt—"

Bushwick clicked the tape off. "What the hell do you think about that?"

Grier wanted to tell him to take a cold shower.

"I've had more than my share of broads, but I can't remember one who talked to me the way that bitch talked to Anderson." Bushwick finished off the rest of the scotch. "What the hell is it with a guy like him?"

"Money."

Bushwick considered that, and before he could answer, Grier said, "The glamorous life."

"Have you seen her?"

"No."

"Let me assure you she wouldn't have any trouble experiencing the 'glamorous life,' as you put it, with— with any man of means."

"Anderson's our problem, not her."

"Shit," Bushwick responded, and clicked off.

Grier waited a few moments, just to make sure the line was dead; then he returned the phone to its cradle, and eased himself into a prone position, with his hands clasped over his chest.

Bushwick was bent out of shape because Anderson was fucking a beautiful twenty-three-year-old woman and he wasn't. What a turkey! The man didn't seem to understand the situation.

He unclasped his hands, and eased himself out of bed.

"Now where are you going?" Betty was out from under the blanket. She was a petite, bony woman, with a pinched face.

"To get a sleeping pill."

She switched on the night-table lamp.

"Get one for me too, and bring me a glass of water."

Grier padded into the bathroom, and before he opened the medicine cabinet, spent several moments looking at his reflection in the mirror.

When the time comes to take Anderson out, he'd make the decision, and only afterwards would he tell Bushwick, or for that matter anyone else.

"Peter?" Betty called.

"Coming," he answered, opening the medicine cabinet.

Anderson couldn't sleep. Earlier, when Marylee called him to bed, he had said, "I have some thinking to do."

It was his way of telling her he wasn't interested in making love to her. That was hours ago, but he was too excited by the prospect of meeting someone who had actually been with John Junior.

Several times, he resisted the impulse to call Augusta and tell her. Should the whole thing prove to be another

51

ruse, another scam to get money from him, he wanted to spare her the pain of another disappointment.

Now, standing behind the sliding glass door leading to the terrace, Anderson wanted very much to share his secret with someone. "Not yet," he said aloud.

"Not yet what?" Marylee asked.

He turned. She was less than a pace behind him, wearing nothing more than a blue pajama top of his.

"I woke up," Marylee explained.

"I'm going to bed now."

She took hold of his hand, and led him into the bedroom. She'd guessed that something had happened to upset him during the phone call he'd taken at the cocktail party.

"John, is there anything you want to tell me?" she asked as they got into bed.

He shook his head.

She turned her back toward him, and fished inside his pajama bottom for his penis. When it was free, she placed it against her bare bottom.

He reached around and, moving his hand under the pajama top, cupped one of her breasts.

"Good night, love," she said.

"Good night," Anderson answered, closing his eyes and giving himself up the warmth and fragrance of Marylee's body.

Chapter 6

"Stop here," Gault told the cabbie.

The slowing cab rolled alongside the curb, then came to an easy stop.

Gault paid the fare indicated on the meter, and gave the driver a fifteen-percent tip. The transaction took place without a verbal exchange, not even a nod from the cabbie.

Gault left the cab, and waited until the cab was several blocks away before he began to walk the two blocks north on Madison Avenue to Sixty-seventh Street, where Anderson's town house was located.

Because it was Sunday, and only seven o'clock in the morning, Madison Avenue was practically deserted, though Gault did see several joggers, either heading to or coming from Central Park, which was one block to the west, just across Fifth Avenue.

Whether it was Madison Avenue, or Second Avenue in the East Village, he appreciated the quietude of the morning.

There was something special in it, almost a palpable anticipation.

Gault smiled.

He was certainly anticipating his meeting with Anderson, and to intensify the feeling for both of them — he was absolutely sure that his letter and phone call had propelled Anderson's emotions to an even greater height than his own — he had delayed their meeting several days to allow the yeast of time to leaven, as it were, the man's memories of his son, whether sad or happy.

When he approached the corner of Sixty-seventh Street, Gault slowed, crossed the street, and looked west, toward Fifth Avenue. There were three parked cars. Two on the south side of the street and one very close to where he was. Even as he stood there, a jogger, wearing a red and blue running suit, headed in his direction on the opposite side. No one else was on the street.

Gault turned toward Fifth Avenue, and began walking. Making this "reconnaissance" was his own idea. He wanted to see where Anderson lived.

The town house was closer to Fifth Avenue than to Madison, and it was on the opposite side of the street. When he came abreast of it, Gault almost stopped, but quickly caught himself and continued to walk, though at a somewhat slower pace.

The house, like all of the others on the street, was a three-floor structure, made of red sandstone, with a steep flight of steps, capped with gray slate, leading to a stoop, and a lower level, between the basement and the first floor, that was three steps down, and could be accessed through a door at the side of the stoop. Each floor had wide, tall windows. But there was a marked difference between Anderson's town house and the others. His occupied the width of two lots, and probably, at some time in the past, had been two separate buildings. Now it was a single structure that by its massiveness and feeling of solidity proclaimed wealth, great wealth at that.

Gault reached Fifth Avenue, crossed to the opposite side, and was about to walk back to Madison when he suddenly noticed a gray Mustang parked on the west side of the street, with two men in the front seat.

He changed his mind, and walked south on Fifth Avenue. He hadn't seen the car before, but there was no doubt in his mind that the men in it had a clear view of the street and couldn't have missed him. Nor did he think that they were there by chance, not at — he glanced at his watch — seven-fifteen in the morning. Just as he had a purpose, so did they.

He went three blocks before cutting over to Madison, where he turned north, back toward Sixty-seventh.

Two explanations for the men in the car occurred to him: They were private security people, or they were involved in drug dealing, either waiting for a buyer or selling the shit themselves.

Gault saw a telephone on the corner, across the street, and that gave him an idea. He crossed Madison, went directly to the telephone, deposited a quarter, and dialed the police emergency number.

Five rings later a man answered.

He imitated a woman's voice perfectly.

"This is Ms. Paula Hemple. There's a suspicious car on Fifth Avenue and Sixty-seventh Street. One of the men has a gun."

"Are you sure?"

"I saw it. He was pointing it out of the window."

The cop asked where she lived, and her phone number.

Gault made up an address and a phone number.

"Is that here, in the city?"

"London, England. I'm here on holiday."

The man on the other end thanked her for making the call and said, "Someone will check it out." Then he clicked off.

Gault replaced the phone, crossed back to the other side of Madison, and quickening his pace, walked up to Sixty-ninth Street before he turned west, toward Fifth.

By the time he reached the corner, a blue and white was pulling in back of the Mustang. He crossed the street. He wanted to get a good look at the men.

The two cops were already on either side of the car.

55

The men were ordered out of the car. One was tossed against the hood, then against the back. Both were Hispanic-looking. The one bent over the hood was about five-ten with very kinky black hair, and not quite a white complexion. The man against the back of the car was tall, thin, with straight black hair and a black, walrus-type mustache.

They were clean, weaponless.

One of the cops searched the car, while the other one watched over the two men, with his right hand grasping the butt of his .38.

Gault had walked past the car, when one of the cops exclaimed, "Pay dirt, cuff them."

He glanced back over his shoulder.

One of the men smashed his fist into the face of the cop guarding them, and at the same time, the other grabbed hold of the second cop, just as he got back out of the car, felling him with a rabbit punch.

The two men ran toward Gault.

He pulled himself out of their way, against the stone wall that separated the park from the street.

The cop with blood pouring from his nose ran after the two men.

But they vaulted over the stone wall, and vanished into the park.

The second cop was on his feet, and back in the cruiser, no doubt calling for back up.

"They're in the fucking park," the cop with the bloody nose called out, now holding a blood-stained handkerchief up to his nose, as he returned.

He passed Gault without even looking at him, and joined his partner. Moments later, they left.

Gault moved away from the wall.

He was tempted to go back to the car and examine it. But there was a chance the two men would come back, and he didn't want to risk being anywhere in the vicinity.

Now deciding he had already risked more than he should, he recrossed Fifth Avenue, hailed the first empty cab that passed, and told the driver to take him to Sullivan Street.

By seven that night, the two men were in Brooklyn, walking on Eastern Parkway toward Classon Avenue.

Jesus Ortega, the shorter of the two, limped, having badly twisted his ankle while running away from the cops.

"I've got to stop for a minute," Ortega said in Spanish.

Without comment, Frank Velez, the taller of the two, stopped. Most of the day, it had been stop and go. He fished a pack of cigarettes out of his pocket, offered one to Ortega, who shook his head, then took one for himself. He lit up, and waited for his comrade to signal that he was ready to walk again.

"How far is it?" Ortega was referring to the funeral parlor on the corner of Classon Avenue and Sterling Street.

"Four, five blocks at the most." They were directly across the street from the Brooklyn Museum. "Once we reach Classon, the blocks are short." Velez too spoke in Spanish.

"Okay, I'm ready."

Velez cut the size of his stride to keep pace with Ortega's. He figured they'd make one more stop before they reached the funeral parlor, and they did, just a block away from it.

Two different wakes were going on at the same time, and despite Ortega's bad right foot, they were able to mingle with the mourners, then slip unobtrusively behind a heavy, black velvet wall draping, where a door led directly to the preparation room.

The naked body of a young black woman was on one

57

of the special tables, and a man wearing simple steel-frame eyeglasses, a heavy gray rubber apron, and rubber gloves was draining her blood.

"Crack," he said without looking up, and without emotion.

"We had a problem, Sanchez," Ortega said, speaking Spanish.

"Good-looking woman." Sanchez ran his hand over her breasts and her crotch. "Wasted. Wasted. It takes awhile to get all the blood out."

He removed his gloves and placed them on the bare stomach of the corpse. "She won't mind," he said, switching from Spanish to English. He lifted his glasses off the bridge of his nose and, massaging it, studied the two of them.

"We were almost busted," Velez said.

Sanchez, a professorial-looking individual, walked to a small table where there was a Mister Coffee and a sugar-coated doughnut. He poured coffee into three plastic cups. "How?"

"The cops just came down on us," Ortega answered.

Sanchez handed each of them a cup of black coffee, and broke the doughnut into approximately equal thirds and shared it with them. "Anything happen to make the cops—"

"The car maybe," Velez said. "Maybe it was reported stolen?"

Sanchez sat down on a high stool. "When did you take it?"

Velez looked at Ortega. "Three—three-thirty in the morning."

Sanchez shook his head.

"It wasn't the car," Ortega said, aware of the whirring sound that the pump was making.

"Okay, you tell me what you think it was." Sanchez sipped his coffee.

Velez took a slight step forward. "We've been discussing this all day—"

"Arguing about it, you mean," Ortega interrupted. "About ten, maybe fifteen minutes before the cops rousted us, we saw this guy walking up the street, the same street that we're watching. I said to Frank, he's looking at the same house we're looking at."

"Was he?"

Velez glanced at Ortega. "He was there when the cops came."

"We ran past him when we broke away from the cops," Ortega said.

"He was with the cops then?"

"No," Ortega answered.

Sanchez looked at Velez.

"No. I didn't even know he was there until I ran past him."

"I saw him walking, when the cop was frisking me. He was walking past the car," Ortega added, then bit into the piece of doughnut.

"Are you sure it was the same man?"

"Yes. I recognized the hat. It was tan, with a wide brim, which he wore turned down, and it had a low crown."

Sanchez glanced at Velez. "Same man?"

"I'm not sure."

Sanchez left the stool and, checking the equipment, closed one set of valves and opened another. "We're going to have to make another try." He went back to the table, and placed the empty cup on it. "This man you saw, was he a young man?"

"He walked like a young man," Velez said. "But he was wearing sunglasses, and the brim of his hat was pulled low over his face."

Sanchez's eyes shifted to Ortega, who shook his head.

"We might have competition," Velez commented.

Sanchez went back to the cadaver, and put on his gloves. "It doesn't matter whether we do, as long as Anderson is killed. But we will try to do it ourselves."

"Do you think the man—"

Sanchez's lips parted in a smile. "I think we go about our business, and not worry about what others might, or might not be trying to do. Now, we let things rest awhile."

Ortega pointed to his foot, and explained what had happened to it.

Sanchez clicked his tongue sympathetically. "If it's not any better after a few days, you'll have a doctor look at it. But stay off it, as much as you can, and soak it in hot water. When either of you go out, stay in the neighborhood."

"The cops have our guns," Velez said.

"By the time the two of you are ready for another try, I'll have new guns for you. Nine-millimeter automatics."

Velez and Ortega smiled.

Gault waited outside a phone booth on the northeast corner of Washington Square park. It was two minutes to noon, and because the day was warm and sunny, the park was already a stage for many different kinds of musical groups, from steel drums to brass. The ghetto blasters were turned up, adding the equivalent of a fourth dimension to the noise level.

The phone rang.

Gault immediately swung himself inside the booth and closed the door, dulling the sound of the outside noise.

"Gault here," he said.

"Richard, this is Mr. Anderson."

"Thank you for returning my call," Gault said. He'd called at eleven-thirty and left a message with the answering service for Anderson to all him back, even though the operator was willing to connect him to Anderson's phone in Washington.

"Is anything wrong, Richard?" Anderson's concern was evident in the tone of his voice. He'd had to clear his throat while he spoke.

"Some foolishness on my part," Gault answered. He let Anderson dangle a moment or two more. "I wasn't really thinking when I suggested that we have lunch at Monte's."

"Oh!" Anderson was instantly disappointed. "Perhaps another—"

"I want to meet with you, Mr. Anderson."

The sigh of relief was loud, and very clear.

"I just don't think that I will be able to tolerate Italian food, at least not for awhile."

Anderson laughed. "That's hardly a problem."

"I have eaten nothing but Indian food for—"

"Have you a place in mind?"

"I was hoping you might know of one. I certainly don't."

"Indian food—I'll call you and let you know where to meet me."

"Good, very good. But I'll be in and out a great deal. Suppose I phone you at, say, eleven on Friday morning. We'll still meet at one, and the two hours will certainly give us enough time to get to whatever restaurant you choose. I'm really very sorry about this change."

"Absolutely no problem. I'll wait for your call."

Gault had little doubt that Anderson would be waiting—waiting on the proverbial pins and needles.

"Thank you, Mr. Anderson, and good-bye."

Gault waited until Anderson said, "Good-bye," before he hung up and opened the door to the noise around him.

Chapter 7

Anderson spent a restless Monday morning, unable to concentrate on anything for more than a few minutes, without suddenly finding himself remembering whole sequences of John Junior's childhood, adolescence, and college years. It was almost as if there was a stage and a cast of family characters in his mind, which included himself, playing roles for his benefit.

He recalled one summer afternoon, on a Cape Cod beach in North Truro, when John Junior, who had a few weeks before passed his fifteenth birthday, had asked him several detailed questions about a woman's sexual organs. And he had answered by drawing them in the wet sand.

Before the summer had ended, John Junior had proudly announced that he had become a "man."

That particular memory brought a smile to Anderson's lips, albeit a sad one.

And with a shake of his head, he said in a quiet voice, "If only it was that easy to become a man, then men would be so much better than they are."

Hardly had he finished speaking when Marylee came through the half-opened door. "I knocked and when you didn't answer . . ."

He waved her in. "It's all right. I was thinking, a little too intensely perhaps."

She stood in front of the desk, her brow furrowed.

Anderson was not by nature melancholy. Thoughtful, yes. She had seen him that way, and when he was thinking intensely about something, he needed her — not sexually, although it sometimes would lead to sex, but her presence, as if her being close provided him with a special kind of insight.

But this was a different Anderson, one she was seeing for the first time.

"John —"

"Is anything wrong?" he asked, leaning forward with concern in his chair.

"That's what I was going to ask you. Ever since you took that phone call . . ."

"Close the door."

Marylee obeyed, and immediately returned to the front of the desk.

Anderson gestured her into the chair to his right. "There was another phone call yesterday."

"Threats?" she asked alarmed. Several had been made on his life in the time she'd been with him.

"No. Good things are in the wind, very good things."

She was sure that he was talking about his political future, and though she did not know the details, she was equally sure it had something to do with running for the Senate.

"You'll make a wonderful senator," she said.

Her comment amused him, and he decided to play along with her notion of what was really on his mind. "You really think so?"

"Oh, John, you'd be wonderful."

"Well, we'll see. We'll see."

"Have you told anyone about it yet?"

Anderson shook his head. "We'll keep it under wraps for the time being."

"I understand."

"Oh, by the way, would you make reservations in a decent Indian restaurant somewhere in the Village?" he asked.

She gave him a peculiar look.

"Politics," he answered.

Anderson stood up. "I think I'd like to go for a walk." He looked down at his desk. "Maybe I'll be able to get back to work when I come back."

"I'll tell Jeff and Pat," she responded.

Anderson uttered a deep sigh. "It would be a novel experience to walk outside without bodyguards."

"The price you have to pay for being John Wesley Anderson. Ah, that reminds me. There was a reason why I knocked on your door."

He lifted his eyebrows.

"The local precinct captain called, and told Ryan that 911 received a tip from a woman about two armed men in a car on Fifth Avenue, just down the street from here."

"Oh?"

"The cops who checked it out found the weapons, but the men got away. The car was stolen, apparently hot-wired, whatever that means."

Anderson smiled. Despite her worldliness in many ways, she also possessed an innocence that beguiled him.

"John, that's nothing to smile about."

"Probably drug dealers. I hardly think they even knew that I lived down the street. But I tell you this, unless the Federal Government shuts down the growers . . ." He stopped, and started to laugh. "I am really beginning to sound like a candidate, aren't I?"

Laughing too, Marylee vigorously nodded her head. "And I like it. It fits, John. It really fits."

Anderson took his jacket out of the closet, and as Marylee helped him put it on, he said, "I never did ask you whether or not you enjoyed yourself at the cocktail party."

"Not very much."

"I could see that General Bushwick enjoyed you, or was trying to."

They stopped at the door.

"The man gave me the creeps. I can tell you, he didn't like what you were saying."

"Probably not," Anderson said, opening the door. "He's way off to the right. He and I were in the same war—the Korean War—we were both second lieutenants then. He was straight out of West Point and eager to be a hero, and I was a ninety-day wonder. I guess I got the medal he wanted. For me it was just a case of being in the wrong place at the wrong time, and trying to survive it. But for him it was the right place at the right time, and nothing happened. That's the way those things go most of the time."

He opened the door. "Tell Pat and Jeff I'll be in the foyer."

"Have a nice walk, John," Marylee said. She knew that he'd been awarded the Silver Star for Bravery with several oak leaf clusters, but he had never mentioned it before.

He was truly a remarkable man.

Grier put the phone down.

He'd just spoken to Safe Deposit, and learned that two gunmen were spotted close to where Anderson lived. According to the description in the police report, both men were Hispanic-looking.

There would certainly be enough of those types with reason to kill Anderson, he thought.

The question he now had to answer was whether or not to let Bushwick know.

As far as Grier was concerned, the less Bushwick knew, the fewer problems he would have.

But Bushwick was still the damn Director.

"Those guys could just have been drug dealers," he told himself aloud. "There's nothing that ties them to Anderson. Absolutely nothing."

Grier chewed on the knuckles of his right hand for a few moments before deciding against telling Bushwick anything about Safe Deposit's call.

This was his operation, and he was going to call all of the shots.

Anderson, with Jeff on his right and Pat to his left, entered Central Park, at Seventy-second Street, and walked south, along a pathway that dipped into a small valley.

"You know, John," Jeff said, "I think you ought to put a few more men on until we're sure about the two that were here last night."

"I think so too," Pat added, without being asked.

Anderson was in no mood to discuss the possible danger he might be in. Though far from tranquil, he felt mildly expansive, as if the warmth of the day and the smell of spring in the air combined to be his special elixir.

"For ten days to two weeks," Pat continued. "That will tell us whether they'll be back, and if they come back, we'll have our people there."

"All right, do it. But get people you know and can trust. I don't want moonlighting cops or such."

"Strictly pros," Jeff assured him.

Anderson let the matter pass quickly out of his thoughts, and took notice of the early leafing of some of the trees and the thrust of new blades of grass through the brown carpet of last year's dead growth.

"I wouldn't be a bit surprised if we have a real spring this year," Anderson commented. "There hasn't been one for a good number of years."

"More than likely it will turn cold again, and then we'll leap right into summer," Jeff answered.

Anderson chuckled. "Always the optimist."

"That's because Jeff thinks a lot," Ryan said. "Me, I'm satisfied with a non-active brain. The wife, kids, a bottle of cold beer, and a good game on TV. That's it for me."

Jeff looked past Anderson. "Bullshit!"

"I'm even thinking of having a bumper sticker made that says. 'Idiots delight more when they do it.' " Ryan moved his right hand across his chest to indicate the length of the sticker.

Anderson glanced at Jeff. "He might have something there."

Jeff shook his head. "All wind, the proverbial fart in a windstorm. You know him as well as I do."

"It could be a new Ryan. After all, people do change."

He suddenly thought about himself.

He had changed from the time of Venom. But the change hadn't really started with him. He had actually enjoyed the immense power Venom had given him—and still did, if he should ever want to use it. The change had come through Isabel. She had made the difference in his life, she had been the catalyst that provided him with a new vision.

"Yeah, maybe. But not likely," Jeff said. "Pat will always be the painter, the man with an eye for beauty, even if he never picks up another brush or draws another line, while I will always be the misanthrope."

"There's no arguing with your self-evaluation," Pat responded.

"And none with my evaluation of you either," Jeff

said.

"Have you really stopped painting?" Anderson asked, looking at Pat.

The man had considerable talent, had even had his own showing in a small Upper West Side gallery the previous fall.

A look of guilty sadness came into Pat's face. He dropped his eyes. His painting had almost led to a divorce, and he might have gone that route if there hadn't been children.

"There's no need to answer," Anderson said, aware of the man's pain.

"It was getting in the way," Pat said. "And I wasn't going anywhere with it."

"Crazy, right?" Jeff questioned.

"For the thousandth time, what I do when I'm not working with you is none of your business," Pat said without conviction.

Anderson, though used to the exchanges between the two, which could become verbally fierce at times, realized that Pat's art was very important to Jeff, so important that he was trying to goad him into resuming painting regardless of the consequences.

In a low voice, Jeff commented, "He's throwing away the best part of himself, his unique vision."

Anderson agreed, though he didn't voice it. Pat looked sufficiently disturbed, and anything Anderson said would only fuel whatever anger had begun to build.

The three of them continued along the walkway until it was adjacent to a huge outcropping of gray rock that rose thirty to forty feet above the path and slanted back toward Fifth Avenue.

Anderson pointed to a bench, one end of which was occupied by a young woman with a toddler.

"I'd like to rest here for awhile."

Pat moved to a bench further down the path to where he could survey the rocks above, while Jeff sat down diagonally across from Anderson, a position that gave him a field of vision that covered the path in both directions and the semi-wooded area in front of him.

This was one of Anderson's favorite spots.

John Junior used to climb the rocks, and once, when he was no more than eight, possibly nine, he'd found himself on a narrow ledge, close to the top but not close enough for him to reach it, and too far from the base to make it down without risking a fall. He'd started to howl for his father to come and get him. And that was exactly what Anderson had done, dirtying a pair of white linen slacks to be the hero of the afternoon.

Anderson had no difficulty recalling the entire episode, even to remembering that afterwards he and John Junior had gone to the Children's Zoo, which was not far away, and eaten hot dogs with mustard, relish, and sauerkraut, followed by double ice cream cones.

Anderson smiled, and his eyes shifted to the baby.

"Boy or girl?" he asked.

"Boy," the mother said proudly, though she didn't look at Anderson.

"How old?"

"Two."

"Two," Anderson repeated. "I have a son too. He's thirty-four."

The woman didn't answer him, not that he blamed her, and as he expected, after a minute or two, she stood up, put her child in the stroller, and walked away.

Anderson looked up at the rocks again and thought about Augusta.

She certainly should know that their son was alive.

But her hold on reality, since the accident, had been tenuous at best. She'd become a recluse, a believer in the mumbo jumbo of astrology, psychics, and seances in a vain effort to somehow be reunited with John Junior.

Despite her constant failure, she always found an excuse to continue, though every failure chipped away another little piece of her being.

Anderson never maligned her efforts, or her hopes of making a connection with their son. He had made the same efforts, only his eschewed the occult and were more realistic — search efforts that cost several million dollars to finance. But none of them had returned with any hard evidence that John Junior had been killed. He had just vanished, taken by an avalanche.

For years, Anderson had had nightmares in which he saw John Junior entombed under tens of thousands of tons of snow, but somehow still alive, calling to him for help, reaching up to grasp his hands and be pulled up through the snow to life. It was a powerful dream that left him wet with sweat, and its memory that seemed to hang over him for days afterward.

But now, a stranger had given him new hope that his son was alive.

That was the way things often happened in life, his or anyone else's.

Not a religious man in the sense that he followed a particular creed, though he was a member of the Episcopalian Church, Anderson suddenly found himself filled with the sense that a more powerful force than any he had ever thought about was at work. That he was somehow being tested.

He looked up at the gray rocks, more cathedral-like in his eyes now, and silently said, "Give me back my son, and I will give you the rest of my life. Give me

71

back my son, and I will ask for nothing else, want nothing else."

Anderson bowed his head, and choked back the sobs.

Chapter 8

Bushwick sat across from the President in the Oval Office. Between them was a small black lacquered coffee table decorated with gold leaf, a gift from some Asian ruler.

"This is strictly informal," the President said.

Bushwick nodded. The President was a thin man, with a narrow face and wispy hair. Not physically imposing by any standard.

"You know, General, we're looking forward to the next election," the President said.

"That's certainly coming up."

It was the President's turn to nod, and he offered Bushwick a cigar from a teakwood humidor. "I'd have one myself, but the doctor advised me to cut down on all but a few pleasures of life."

"Are you sure it won't bother you if I smoke?" Bushwick asked, wondering if one of the few pleasures still enjoyed by the President was a good roll in the sack. The man in his younger days had had a reputation for being a "cocksman."

"Please, enjoy."

Bushwick lit up, waiting for the President to tell him why he was there.

"Our party strategists tell me that we won't come anywhere near controlling either the House or the Senate."

Bushwick blew smoke off to his left. "Has been that way for the last two Administrations."

His eyes went from the President to the far wall,

where there were several large color photographs of the President's champion quarter horses.

"We want to — we must retain the White House."

"No argument there."

"The party brains tell me that we won't if we run the same ticket as we ran before."

Bushwick instantly became more alert. He shifted the cigar to the other side of his mouth.

"We're going to change the Vice President. We think that someone who's older, with more experience — someone like yourself, General — would have more appeal than my former running mate."

Bushwick leaned forward.

This was coming totally out of left field.

"Is this an offer, Mr. President?"

"Let's say that you're very much a front-runner."

"And the field?" Bushwick asked, his tone becoming more military.

The President named a senator and a governor.

Lightweights in Bushwick's opinion, but he kept it to himself.

"But there is a problem," the President said.

Bushwick blew another cloud of smoke, off to the left this time, and waited to hear what the problem was, though he was sure he already knew.

"John Anderson, the American Eagle. My people are worried that he'll enter the race as the Democratic Party's candidate."

Those tapes of the meeting between Anderson and the Democratic honchos gave Bushwick a royal flush. But he wasn't prepared to play it yet.

"If he does run, we have a real fight on our hands, and one that we might lose." The President's brow furrowed as he spoke. "We want to prevent that possibility, and we think we can."

There was no longer any reason to allow the President

74

and his brain trust to remain in la-la land. "I have tapes of a meeting between Senator Post and some other members — important members — of the Democratic Party and Anderson."

The President started to stand, then changed his mind. "Then it has advanced to that stage."

"It was an offer," Bushwick said, very much aware that the President didn't ask why Anderson had been taped.

"And did Anderson respond?" the President asked.

"He held off giving a definite answer. Playing them a bit, I think."

The President did stand, locked his hands behind his back, and began pacing behind his chair. "May I have a copy of those tapes?"

"Yes."

The President stopped, and sat down again. "Anderson must not run."

"I absolutely agree," Bushwick said. He had no intentions of telling him that Anderson was as good as dead.

"To stop him in his tracks, I'm going to appoint him the civilian ombudsman for the Agency. That should . . ."

Bushwick wrenched the cigar out of his mouth as the President went on. That was the trade-off: In exchange for going along with this appointment, he'd be the Vice Presidential candidate.

"Anderson has been critical of the Agency," the President continued. "Now he'll have the chance to — "

"That would be like putting the fox in the henhouse," Bushwick said, interrupting. Having Anderson killed as quickly as possible became more imperative than it had been a few moments before.

"It would force him to — "

Bushwick was impatient. "What makes you so sure he'll choose becoming a clean-up man over a chance at becoming the President?" he asked. "He knows his own worth."

"Because if he doesn't, his American Eagle image will tarnish. He has presented himself to the public as the man who, if given the opportunity, would be able to keep the Agency out of difficulties that have plagued it in the past. Anderson will have to put up or shut up. The feeling is that he'll put up."

Bushwick thought about the President's explanation for several moments. He was sure that the man knew nothing about Anderson's tie to Venom, or about Venom itself.

"His ego won't let him back away," the President commented.

"Who's going to oversee him?" Bushwick asked.

The President grinned. "Oh I think we'll be able to find someone qualified to do that. That could very well be one of the new areas for the new VP to become involved in—not officially, of course."

"I can live with that."

"I was sure you would."

"When will you make the appointment?" Bushwick asked.

"Within the next two weeks, maybe a month."

The tip of Bushwick's cigar pulsated red for several moments before he said, "I'll send those tapes to you this afternoon, Mr. President. They make very interesting listening."

He almost offered him the tapes of Anderson and Marylee, but realizing he couldn't explain why the Agency had them, he changed his mind.

The President stood up, and Bushwick followed suit.

"We'll make a fine team," the President said, offering his hand.

Bushwick shook it. "I'm sure we will, Mr. President."

* * *

In the afternoon Marylee put the names of three Indian restaurants — the Nepal, the Raga, and the Katmandu — on Anderson's desk.

"I have no specific recommendation," she told him. "That kind of food is too spicy for my taste." Then with a small, playful smile, she added, "Besides, when it comes to spice, I prefer it in quite another form."

Anderson nodded appreciatively, and if she were on his side of the desk instead of in front of it, he would have acknowledged her comment by running his hand over her buttocks, which were so beautifully shaped, as beautiful in his opinion, as her breasts.

"I think you should make the choice," Marylee told him.

He agreed. "I'll have a look at them, and then choose. Have Pat and Jeff ready." He stood up.

"You're going now?"

"Now. I'll be back in time for cocktails." Evening cocktails had become almost a ritual. The kitchen would prepare a mixture of hot and cold hors d'oeuvres, Jeff or Pat would act as bartender — sometimes Anderson himself would fix the drinks — and the four of them would relax for an hour or so, usually until Pat announced it was time for him to go home.

Marylee wasn't sure whether or not Anderson wanted her along.

"Better wear your coat," he said, putting on his own jacket. "It gets chilly after the sun goes down."

"Yes," she answered, almost sighing with relief. Since the morning, when Anderson had intimated that a change was coming, she'd felt a growing uneasiness, as if his movement forward meant a retreat for her. It was something that she'd have to discuss with Doctor Hasse, her analyst.

Anderson raised his eyebrows. "Is anything wrong?"

She flashed him a smile. "Nothing. I'm on my way."

Before Anderson left his office, he opened the middle drawer of the desk, removed Gault's letter, and put it in his jacket pocket.

Usually, Jeff or Pat sat up front with the chauffeur, but this time, before the four of them got into the Lincoln, Anderson said, "I want the two of you in the rear with me and Marylee."

Marylee entered first, Anderson followed, and Pat and Jeff settled on the jump seats.

Anderson pressed the button that raised the glass divider between the front and rear of the car; then he said, "We're going downtown to look at three different Indian restaurants." He glanced at Marylee. "Does Roy know where to go?"

"He has the three addresses."

Anderson turned his attention back to Jeff and Pat. "On Friday, I'm going to meet a young man who has recently returned from India. That's the reason for checking out the Indian restaurants."

"All the way from India," Jeff commented.

"I want him checked out," Anderson told them. "I want him photographed, fingerprinted. I want to know every flight he took from the time he left India."

"No problem," Jeff answered. "We'll get as much info on him as we can."

"Do it as quickly as you can. I want to know everything there is to know about him."

"I'll put through some calls as soon as we get back to the house," Pat said.

Satisfied, Anderson nodded. "Work discreetly. I don't want the press to get hold of this one."

"What's the guy's name?" Jeff asked.

"Gault. Richard Gault," Anderson said.

The more Marylee heard, the more butterflies

swarmed in her stomach. She connected the letter to the name that Anderson had just mentioned, but she wouldn't dare ask for more information, though there was no doubt in her mind that Gault was in some way involved with John Junior, Anderson's dead son.

They moved slowly down Fifth Avenue, often waiting for three lights at a time before they could finally clear an intersection.

"Looks like everyone just happens to be here at the same time," Marylee commented. She did not like the constant stop-and-go routine, and was about to suggest they try going down the East River Drive when Anderson said, "I have plans for Gault, important plans."

The tone of Anderson's voice sent shivers down Marylee's spine. She'd never heard it before, not in the four years she had been with him, and certainly not since they had become lovers.

She looked at him.

Even the expression on his face belonged to a different Anderson, one she never knew existed.

Suddenly, Anderson shifted his position.

Their eyes met, and he instantly looked away, as if she had glimpsed the forbidden. And she knew she had.

As soon as they passed B. Altman's, on Fifth Avenue and Thirty-fourth Street, the traffic thinned out, and in a matter of minutes they were in the Village.

Of the three restaurants, Anderson chose the Katmandu, on Sullivan Street, as best suited for his purpose. Located in the basement of an old apartment house, it was the smallest of the three, only ten tables. There was one table against the window, where Jeff and Pat could sit and watch what was happening in the street as well as in the restaurant.

Pat came back to the car with a menu. "I hope you like this curry stuff."

"There are other dishes on it," Anderson said, looking

at it for several moments before handing it to Marylee.

Pat shook his head. "Not my kind of food."

Anderson switched on the intercom, and told the chauffeur to return home, then he said to Pat and Jeff, "Check out the place in the next couple of days. Get a rundown on who owns it and who patronizes it."

"It's just a small restaurant," Marylee protested. "I mean, why all the fuss?"

Anderson patted her hand, almost as if he were her father and not her lover. "Don't concern yourself with it."

"But I want to understand—"

"It's nothing to understand," Anderson told her. "Pat and Jeff will do it, and that's an end to it."

Again, there was a change in the tone of his voice, different from the previous one, but there nonetheless.

She had heard him use it before, demanding that something be his way and only his way. But he'd never used it with her, never.

"You know, I'm really looking forward to that drink this evening. Maybe I'll even have two." He laughed. "I feel good, very good." Then he did something he never did in public. He leaned over and, to Marylee's complete surprise, kissed her on the lips.

Chapter 9

The following day, just before lunch, Anderson received a phone call from Post.

"I just thought you'd be interested in this, John. The President intends to offer you the ombudsman of the CIA."

Anderson pulled the phone away from his ear, gave it a quizzical look, and guffawed. "How the hell did you find that out?"

"A leak. The President has a hard time keeping *anything* secret."

"I'm the last man the Agency would want riding herd on them."

"There's more," Post said. "It's rumored a deal was cut between the man in the White House and the present head of the Agency."

Anderson leaned back in his chair. "What does Bushwick get out of this?"

"Second spot."

Anderson leaned far enough forward to rest his elbows on the desk.

"How does that grab you?" Post questioned.

"That's quite a deal," Anderson responded. "Quite a damn deal. Does the President know where Bushwick's political head is at?"

"It could be up the proverbial shit's creek as far as he's concerned. The whole purpose is to cut you off at the pass. You can win, they know that."

"And they're banking on—"

"You got the picture. You've been critical of the Agency, and now they'll be giving you the opportunity to sanitize the operation."

"And you want me to enter the race before they ever reach the pass?"

"That's right," Post said.

Anderson took a deep breath and slowly exhaled.

"Come on, John. The country needs you."

"What happens to the deal between President and Bushwick if I go into your camp?"

"Let them worry about it."

"If it holds, Bushwick, as the expression goes, will be just a heartbeat away from the Presidency itself."

"Not if you run. If you run, you'll win."

There was an imperativeness in the senator's voice that forced Anderson to say, "All right, you have a tentative yes. But it's only tentative."

"Right now, I'll—we'll settle for that."

"I know you have to leak this to the press. But I don't want to be considered the candidate just yet. Get some other names into play, just in case I have a change of heart at the last minute."

"Yes, I understand."

Anderson wasn't at all sure that Post did understand, and maybe it wasn't important he did. Now, the important thing was to stop Bushwick from getting anywhere near the White House, except as a visitor, and an infrequent one at that.

"Have you any idea when the President intends to offer me the ombudsmanship?"

"By next week, certainly."

"All right, let your story out on the weekend. I'll be unavailable for comment."

"You got it, John."

"Good."

"You wouldn't have any idea when the tentative

could become a positive, would you?" Post asked, not really expecting an answer, but very much aware that Anderson was serious about running, or he would not have taken the first step.

"Don't push." Then in a softer voice, Anderson said, "Let it alone for now."

"Certainly."

"There are some personal matters that I have to take care of," Anderson said.

"I understand," Post responded, suddenly wondering if Anderson intended to change his relationship with the women in his life.

A divorce from Augusta to marry a younger woman would certainly lose him the election. A messy separation from Marylee might not lose him the election, but it certainly would tarnish his image. Even his present association with her would have to be explained in a very special way.

"Anything wrong?" Anderson asked, aware of the growing silence between them.

"Nothing. Nothing. All of us have personal responsibilities."

To Anderson's professional ear, Post was just mouthing words, but he was willing to let it go. Whatever had suddenly begun to bother Post was Post's problem, and not his.

"Anything else?"

"Not that I can think of now," Post answered.

"Good. I'm getting tired of holding the damn phone up to my ear."

"I'll be in touch," Post told him.

"I was sure of that," Anderson said, and without waiting to hear whether Post responded, or for the click on the other end, he put the phone down, leaned back, and pressing balls of his fingers together, thought about the conversation he'd just had.

There was no doubt in his mind that his chances to become the next President would be greatly increased if his son were at his side. It would be the melding of reality and fiction, something the American people could not resist. Because he'd never given up hope, he'd be the hero, a symbol of the special bonding between father and son.

Anderson stood up. "It could happen," he whispered. "It must happen!"

Bushwick summoned Grier to his office, but not in his usual imperious tone, which immediately aroused Grier's suspicions that something bad was about to happen, or had already happened. His feelings of uneasiness escalated even more when Bushwick gestured to the chair alongside the desk, instead of the one in front of it, and then offered him a cigar.

Grier was about to decline the offer, when Bushwick said, "Go ahead, take one. You'll enjoy it."

When the two of them were smoking, Bushwick said, "The other day I had a meeting with the President."

Grier accepted that without any comment, not even a silent nod. But that information did nothing to calm him.

"I've been offered the number-two spot on the ticket," Bushwick said with a smile.

Grier swallowed a mouthful of smoke, and instantly began to cough. "Went down the wrong pipe!" he sputtered.

Bushwick immediately poured water from a carafe on his desk into a glass, and handed it to Grier, who nodded his head appreciatively, drank, and after several tries sufficiently regained his voice to croak, "Thank you." And drank again before returning the glass to Bushwick.

Grier put the still-burning cigar down in an ashtray, and offered his congratulations.

"That's going to leave the top spot here open," Bushwick said.

"It's almost always filled by—"

Bushwick removed the cigar from his mouth and pointed it at Grier. "You'll be my recommendation."

"What?" Grier's heart started to race.

"You behind this desk."

Grier picked up the cigar again, not so much to smoke it, but just to have something to hold on to—or he'd have to grip the arms of the chair.

"I'll put it to you bluntly," Bushwick said, enjoying Grier's obvious confusion. "I don't particularly like you, and I know you don't particularly like me. But I admire your expertise, and I respect your experience."

"Blunt enough," Grier responded.

Bushwick nodded. "I'm a blunt man, when the situation calls for me to be."

Grier felt much surer of himself. "Now let's hear the other shoe drop."

"Nothing is free."

"I agree."

"Anderson will become the Company's ombudsman."

Grier started out of the chair. "You know my feelings about that."

"Sit down!" Bushwick ordered. "Goddamn it, man, sit down."

Grier dropped back on to the chair.

Bushwick's face was very red, and he was breathing very hard, almost snorting. "He must never become that," Bushwick said quietly.

"I told you it will take time to—"

"All right, all right. I just want to be assured that it

will happen."

"I said it will, and it will."

Grier understood the deal that was cut between Bushwick and the President. Now, he was the third party to the deal, and the President didn't even know it.

"The sooner, the better," said Bushwick.

"When is the offer going to be made?"

"Sometime during the next month."

Grier put the cigar back in the ashtray. He had to give Bushwick something now, or his own plan might be scraped. "Just to make it look good, I suggest we wait until he's actually here; then what happens can be attributed to others. There are others who would like to see him dead."

Bushwick nodded. "Good thinking, Peter," he said, using Grier's given name for the first time. "Damn good thinking."

Grier smiled.

If the turkey had a brain, he might be able to do some "good thinking" too. But the turkey didn't have a brain, at least not one useful to the Company.

"Well, hello, Rich!"

The voice came from behind Gault, who was nursing a glass of Beck's Dark at the bar in Chumley's. It was mid-afternoon. The lunchtime customers had gone, leaving the place to individuals like himself who had nowhere to go. Several were at tables, reading the *Times* or a book. A few were engaged in conversation. He and another man were at the bar, he almost at its center and the other man, on his right, at the end.

"Long time no see."

Gault saw the reflection of the face in the mirror behind the bar.

"Tad, good to see you again." Gault turned, and faced Tad Harris and the woman with him. They were an odd-looking couple, in a place where odd-looking couples or individuals were scarcely noticed, much less commented on. Tad was six and a half feet tall, very thin and almost bald, with deep-set eyes and a hawkish-looking face; while the woman next to him was probably an inch or two over five feet, and had dark brown hair that came down to her waist, a delicately chiseled face, and breasts just about the size and shape of small pears, with nipples clearly visible through the white T-shirt she wore.

"Rich, this is Maria Fusco. Maria, Richard Gault."

Gault smiled. He'd been thinking about his coming meeting with Anderson, making sure all the details were in place.

Tad said, "Heard you were doing a lot of traveling." He and Maria sat down at the bar, Tad next to Gault.

"India and Nepal."

Tad made a humming sound, and nodded his head appreciatively. "Man, I'd like a gig like that."

Gault shrugged. He didn't want company, and he didn't specifically want to meet an airhead like Tad.

"You know it's not like you were gone for a couple of weeks," Tad said. "You've been away for more than a year. I mean, the group really misses you."

"Tad always talks about you," Maria added.

The barkeep came up to them, and Tad said, pointing to Gault's beer, "Three of the same."

Gault held up his hand. "Thanks, Tad, but nothing for me. I just about have time to finish this one. Another time."

Tad said, "Then make it two."

"It must have been super to be out there," Maria commented. "I mean, Katmandu—like it must have been mind-blowing, right?"

"Right," Gault responded.

He guessed her to be twenty, perhaps a year or two older, but with a mind somewhere between thirteen and sixteen.

"Rich, Maria is from your neighborhood in Brooklyn. Maria lived on Bedford Avenue and H," Tad said. Then he added, "Rich lived on Glenwood Road. Your folks still live there, don't they, Rich?"

"Yeah," Gault answered.

He'd called them, but he hadn't been to see them yet. Maybe he'd go on the weekend; at least he'd thought about going then.

"I bet you graduated from Midwood High School too," Maria said, more animated than before—animated enough to make her breasts jiggle.

Gault shook his head. "Brooklyn Tech."

"Living there was really a drag."

"Yeah, a drag," Gault agreed, finishing his beer. "Listen—"

"You going to come down to the group?" Rich asked.

Gault shook his head. "Not likely, in the near future. I'm busy, but if I get some free time, I might drop in."

"We're in the same place. The church on Thirteenth Street."

Gault held out his hand. "It's been great seeing you, Tad. And meeting you, Maria."

Tad shook his hand. "Does Irene know you're back?"

"Haven't had the chance to phone her," Gault answered, letting go of Tad's hand.

"Give her a call. She'll be really glad to hear from you."

"Sure."

"Everyone thought the two of you—"

"See you guys around," Gault said, putting three

singles on the bar to cover the cost of the beer and the tip.

The stupid fuck was bringing up the past.

"Hey, this one is on me," Tad told him. "The next time it'll be dinner, and that, my friend, will be on you." He put his arm around Gault and squeezed his shoulder.

"You got it!" Gault broke free. Moments later he was out on the street, blinded by the bright sunlight; then, as he put on a pair of sunglasses, he started to walk uptown.

Chapter 10

By Thursday evening, Anderson was feeling almost ebullient. His "tentative yes" to Post had given him a sense of expansiveness, the feeling that perhaps he could, in the years left to him, make a difference on the world's stage. He'd done it before, clandestinely using Venom as his instrument. But now the possibility existed for him to rectify what Venom had done, and to go beyond—perhaps even take the first steps toward a unified world. Perhaps Gault's coming with word that John Junior was alive was an omen, a sign of the life to come, an epiphany that would enable him to regain his son and find his true worth.

Marylee entered the office.

Anderson had heard the soft knocking at the door, but preferred to continue to gaze out of the window and think a few moments longer about the future.

"John?"

Abruptly, he swung around, and faced her. "Let's do something outlandish!" He was on his feet, and grinning broadly before she could respond. "I mean, something we wouldn't ordinarily do."

Anderson rubbed his hands together, and came out from behind the desk. "Let's go out for cocktails, and then dinner."

Taken completely by surprise, Marylee almost gasped, then recovering herself, she said, "You have a dinner meeting with Mr. Edward Downing."

Anderson repeated the name. Downing was now a

respected art dealer, but in the past he too had been a Company man.

"For seven-thirty at Le Cirque." Marylee watched his brow furrow, then the ridges vanished.

"Come with me." He was smiling again.

Surprised again, she could only shake her head.

These past few days Anderson had been distant, even to the extent of not making love to her. That had happened in the past, but he had always satisfied her, even when, because of fatigue, he had been unable to have an orgasm.

"Does that mean *no?*" Anderson asked.

"It means that I can never even guess what you're likely to come up with next."

"We'll make a night of it."

"Yes, I'd like that."

"Very good. Now go, and change into something that will make you the envy of every woman there, and me the envy of every man."

Edward Downing occupied a corner table for four, where he and Anderson would be less likely to be noticed by the celebrities dining at Le Cirque. Anderson always sat at a table for four in a restaurant, even if he was dining alone.

Money had its privileges, especially in places like Le Cirque. A second table, a discreet distance from where he and Anderson would be, had also been reserved for Messrs. Hunter and Ryan. But they would have to make do with a table for two.

Downing sipped his Glenfiddich.

Anderson had phoned him two weeks ago, and had asked to have dinner with him. He'd said, almost offhandedly, he had something to discuss, but hadn't given the slightest hint about what it might be. That was Anderson. There just wasn't any way to guess what the man was going to do. He made his own rules, and expected other people to follow them.

Downing put the scotch down, and swallowed a water chaser. Tall, broad-shouldered, with freckles on his face and light brown hair, almost blond, he not only had the aura of a successful man, he was one.

At forty, he was a world-famous art dealer, and a recognized authority in pre-Columbian art. If he'd bothered to look at the clientele, he would have certainly seen several of his customers, but his only interest was why Anderson had asked to meet him for dinner.

Downing picked up the Glenfiddich again, and was about to finish it off when he saw the maitre d' coming toward the table with Anderson following slightly behind. To his astonishment, Marylee was on Anderson's arm.

He put the drink down, stood up, and in the few moments before Anderson arrived at the table took in every inch of Marylee, savoring everything he saw — and imagining everything he didn't.

She wore a green off-the-shoulder sheath, with a double strand of matched pearls that caught the light and reflected it with a low incandescence that fired each gem.

He knew she was aware of the impression she was making, and enjoying every moment of it.

Anderson was in front of him. He extended his hand.

"Good to see you, John."

They shook hands.

"You know Miss Terrall."

"Yes." He let go of Anderson's hand, and gently took hold of her hand. "A pleasure to see you, Miss—"

"Marylee, please."

Downing nodded, and as he brought the back of her hand to his lips, he saw Hunter and Ryan take their places at the table.

The maitre d' helped Marylee with the chair, and as soon as she was seated, Downing and Anderson sat down.

"Tonight, I am famished," Anderson announced.

"So am I," Downing said. "How's your appetite, Marylee?"

Before she could answer, Anderson said, "Ask *me*. She eats less than anyone I have ever known."

Downing cast an exaggerated look of appraisal at her. "I'd say it hasn't hurt her in any way that I could see."

Even as he spoke, he imagined those secret, naked places of her body that he now wanted to explore with his hands, his lips, and his tongue.

Marylee flushed.

"I'll let you choose the wine," Anderson said to Downing, seeing Marylee's cheeks redden.

"Fair enough. I'll even pay for it."

Anderson nodded approvingly, and after Downing's brief conversation with the sommelier, a bottle of Chateau Rausau Segla, a red Margaux, and a bottle of Meursault Domaine, a white Rouget, were agreed on.

"Well, Edward, what's the latest gossip from the art world?" Anderson asked. "I'm too busy with the Foundation to do much of anything else." He enjoyed playing the role of the innocent.

"Everything is going through the proverbial roof," Downing said. "But there are still good things to be had—"

"Don't sell me," Anderson cut in.

"Never entered my mind."

The sommelier returned with a bottle, and gave Downing the opportunity to inspect the label, sniff at the cork, and finally taste the wine.

"Absolutely excellent!"

"One of the best in the house," the sommelier answered, touching the gold-plated key on the end of the chain around his neck. Then he proceeded to pour.

There was more conversation, and this time Marylee joined in, asking how Downing and Anderson had met.

"We happened to be in the same place at the same time," Downing answered, "and shared the same interest in pre-Columbian art."

Anderson explained further. "Edward was in Tegucigalpa when I was the ambassador there."

What he didn't say was that Downing worked for the CIA, and his business provided an excellent cover for his information-gathering activities. Low-level to be sure, but absolutely necessary.

"And when I returned to the States, John introduced me to other collectors."

Marylee smiled affectionately at Anderson, and put her hand over his.

"You had the talent to succeed, or you wouldn't have succeeded," Anderson said. "If you lacked the talent, it wouldn't have mattered—"

"He's that way about everything he does for other people," Marylee said proudly, as if she were talking about her son, not her lover.

"That's his style," Downing said, suddenly remembering the rumors circulating while he had been with the Company. Rumors about Anderson, an Anderson who then ran his own killing machine, who made political policy by assassination. Those rumors were belied by the generosity of the man.

Anderson caught the waiter's eye, and when the man approached the table, he said, "I hope the two of you are ready to order, because I am. I don't have to look at the menu. But I will need someone to share it with me."

He smiled at Downing.

"Roast rack of lamb?"

"Yes."

Downing nodded. "Roast rack of lamb," he told the waiter; then to Anderson, he said, "May I choose my own—"

"Exercise your free will, Edward. Have you decided what you want, Marylee?"

"I'll start with the sea scallop fantasy in black tie, and then the grilled salmon. That will probably be too much," she said, closing the menu.

Downing ordered an appetizer of fettucini with wild mushrooms.

"An excellent choice," Anderson commented.

"I used my free will."

"Yes, that was evident," Anderson responded.

Marylee enjoyed listening to their verbal sparing.

Anderson seemed to have a special liking for Downing, and seemed to either be oblivious to—or not to mind—the way Downing devoured her with his eyes. She could almost feel the weight of them on her nipples.

Before the waiter returned with the two appetizers, Downing asked if Anderson had "any interesting plans for the future."

"I'll pass on the answer to that one until dessert."

Downing answered, "I hope it's worth waiting for. After all, I have my portion of your rack of lamb to digest while I'm waiting."

"It's worth it, I assure you."

Certain that Anderson intended to say something about his political plans, Marylee dropped her eyes lest Downing see a flicker of knowing in them.

The appetizers were delivered to the table, and as Anderson watched his two companions enjoy them, he too was enjoying himself.

Now and then he'd catch Downing's eyes trying to get

some clue about what he intended to tell him. The very fact that he'd asked him to dinner must have come as a surprise. Though they had frequent phone conversations, and lunched together several times a year, and though Downing had visited the Foundation, though not during the time Marylee had been with it, they had met for dinner on only two other occasions. The first had taken place when they had been in Tegucigalpa. Downing had come into possession of a rare Aztec piece, a ceremonial mask made of gemstones. Both of them knew it had been stolen, but neither had said as much to the other. Downing had asked for a quarter of a million dollars for it, but eventually had settled for two hundred thousand. The second time had been even more complicated. It had occurred in Mexico City, and because of it he had met Isabel Aroyo for the first time.

"You have that self-satisfied look, John," Marylee commented.

"Only because I'm watching the two of you eat."

"Good to the last noodle!" Downing proclaimed.

The empty plates were cleared away, and small scoops of lemon sherbet were served to clean the pallet.

The conversation moved from one topic to another, guided mostly by Anderson, who felt it was his duty as host to avoid long pauses that made everyone uncomfortable.

Finally the main course was served.

"Now that's almost too beautiful to eat!" Anderson said, looking at the rack of lamb.

"But we'll do our best," Downing commented.

The waiter divided the rack of lamb between Anderson and Downing.

"Your salmon looks wonderful," Anderson said, looking at Marylee's dish.

The three of them began to eat in earnest. What conversation there was revolved around food.

Marylee realized both men were gourmets, and had experienced tastes she had no idea existed.

Downing, to her surprise, was a fresh-game fancier, while Anderson, speaking about the past, before his heart attack, rather than the present, owned up to liking heavily spiced food.

"Food is often used as a metaphor for sex," Downing said, his eyes moving from Marylee's face to her breasts.

She flushed.

"Even some of the terms of intimacy used between a man and woman are the same used for expressing our delight with food."

Marylee's color deepened. She glanced toward Anderson for help, but he seemed to be totally unaware of her discomfort.

"For example, 'You look good enough to eat,' though that's more slangy than, say, 'I could devour you.' "

Marylee managed a smile. "Yes, yes. You're right, and you mustn't forget that wonderful scene in the film *Tom Jones.*"

"Too bad we can't act that way today in certain circumstances."

"Ah, but, Mr. Downing — sorry, Edward — your approach is no less unsubtle. It's only the surroundings that are different."

He grinned.

"I was waiting for Marylee to respond to your line," Anderson said.

Mimicking contriteness, Downing hung his head. "Caught in the act."

"Well, now that your libido is under control, let me ask what your plans are for the future," Anderson said.

"More of the same of what I have been doing. I travel enough not to have any need to do that. But in July and August, I'll probably spend a good deal of my time on a sailboat I recently bought."

"I didn't know you had any feelings for the sea," Anderson commented, laying his fork and knife on the plate. "My God, that was 'good enough to eat.' " He cast a wry grin at Marylee. "And I did, by God!"

Marylee laughed.

Downing was going to speak, but suddenly he too was laughing.

Then with a straight face, Anderson resumed the conversation. "Tell me about it." He, or rather the Anderson family, owned an ocean-going yacht, the *Sea Wind*.

"It's a forty-foot ketch. I've always wanted to own a boat."

"I didn't know you knew anything about sailing."

"I've been taking lessons out at City Island. That's where the *Wave Dancer* is moored. But I hope to sail her out to Ság Harbor soon, and make the Baron Cove Marina my home port."

"Wonderful!"

"I've been living aboard her for the last two weeks."

"Really?"

"It has all the amenities, and it gets me out of the city every night."

The dishes were cleared, and this time three servings of sherbet were brought to the table.

Finally, the waiter handed each of them the dessert menu.

Again, Anderson ordered without looking at the choices. "Chocolate mousse and coffee."

"I'll have the same," Marylee said, putting the menu aside.

"Chestnuts and ice cream and coffee," Downing told the waiter; then looking at Anderson, he asked, "Has it reached the telling hour yet, or do we still have to wait?"

Anderson ran a polished fingernail along the edge of

the white tablecloth. "I've thought about what I have decided to do for a long time, actually agonized over it."

Marylee's heart began to race. At first, she'd thought, he was going to tell Downing about his move into politics, but now—now it seemed that it would be even more personal. Perhaps it would have something to do with their relationship. He had taken her to Washington, and to dinner in a highly visible place, something he had never done before.

Anderson looked across the table at Downing, then at Marylee, before he raised his wine glass and asked them to join him in a toast. He said, "To the museum to which I will donate my entire pre-Columbian art collection."

Marylee's hand trembled, but she forced a smile, and managed to bring the glass to her lips, while Downing took a sip of the wine.

Anderson said, "I'm really glad that's done with."

"It's going to shock the hell out of the art world," Downing said.

The waiter brought their desserts.

"Of course, I haven't chosen the particular institution yet," Anderson said, beginning on the mousse.

"Oh, I thought you had made a choice."

Anderson shook his head, and smiled. "I'm ready to be wooed. Certain conditions must be met before I agree to placing the collection with a particular institution. And that's why I will need your services, Edward."

"To act as a go-between?"

"Something you do very well. Better than I could myself."

Downing sipped his coffee, then putting it down, said, "What sort of conditions would have to be met?"

"The recipient must agree to house the collection in its own facility, along with other acquisitions of Mezo-American Art."

Marylee, though interested in the conversation between Anderson and Downing, was having difficulty following it.

She had no idea that Anderson had even been thinking of donating the collection, and suddenly realized that she was more vulnerable than she'd thought — or more to the point, than she would have been willing to admit.

She took a quick look at Anderson. His face was filled with boyish animation, and a lock of pepper and salt hair rested halfway down his forehead.

Despite their intimacy — she knew every one of his sexual needs, and he knew hers as no man ever had before — she was now acutely aware of how much about him she did not know. And knowing that was extremely painful.

Suddenly Anderson was speaking to her. "You've scarcely had any of your mousse."

"I have already had too much."

Anderson wondered if she was feeling ill.

"I'll have the coffee."

He moved his eyes from her back to Downing. "I want you to arrange for the collection to be appraised."

"That's not a problem. I know several excellent people in the field."

"Good. I really feel good about this," Anderson said.

Downing nodded and asked Marylee, "How far along are you with the cataloguing?"

"Perhaps three quarters of the way through."

"There's no real rush," Anderson said. "If more help is needed to get the job done, then we'll get more help. Can you give me some idea about the number of people you might need to complete the work in — say, three months?"

"We don't need extra help. I have about a month's work left."

Anderson beamed. "Excellent!"

"When will you publicly announce—" Downing began.

"There will be no public announcement. Nothing, until everything is settled. You start the ball rolling, and let's see who picks it up and is willing to run with it."

"You know every curator in the country, and some probably not in the country, will be banging on your door."

Anderson laughed. "Let's enjoy it. It's not often a man gets to be wooed in his lifetime." He looked at Marylee, but spoke to Downing. "When was the last time you were wooed, Edward?"

"I must have been nine, or ten. What about you?"

"Probably around the same age." He was still looking at Marylee. There was something different about her that he couldn't quite put his finger on. But it was there.

"This has been quite a dinner," Downing commented.

"It's not over yet," Anderson said.

"That sounds almost ominous."

"Nothing of the kind. It's just that I have made another decision." His eyes moved back to Marylee.

Her heart raced; she could feel her breasts push against the tightness of the sheath, and for some strange reason her nipples hardened.

"I'm going to leave the Foundation," Anderson said.

"Christ, I can't handle that without something stronger than wine!" Downing responded.

Marylee remained silent. But her eyes raged at Anderson.

He'd shared nothing with her. She felt betrayed. She saw herself as his toy, something he enjoyed, not even a someone.

102

"When the time comes, I will make the announcement in the Foundation auditorium, but I want you to coordinate the releases to the media. No one must know about my plans for the collection just yet. I don't want the people who work for me to worry about what's going to happen to them. I'll take care of them."

Marylee glared at him. "I'm sure you will. You're always very considerate of the hired help."

Stung by her sarcasm, Anderson chose not to respond in front of Downing. "You two are the first to know. I haven't told Augusta, or my brother Wally about it."

Downing looked absolutely pleased. "Thank you, John, for the confidence."

"You have a lot to gain by our relationship," Anderson responded.

"Yes," Marylee said, "thank you." And then she asked, "Don't you think Wally will object?" She continued before he could answer. "He's such a fuddy-duddy when it comes to changes—unless, of course, he's making them—that this will send him up a wall."

"I don't doubt that it will. But I haven't exactly followed the family mold. There are things that I want to do in this life before I'm too old to do them. He might understand that."

"I certainly do," Downing commented.

Marylee was confused, and somewhat ashamed of herself. "Yes, of course. For your sake, John, I hope he does understand."

"Well, let's not try to figure out what my favorite brother will do or won't do. Now, I feel like I could drink something stronger than wine myself. What about you, Marylee?"

"Absolutely, but this time I'll have something to make me shockproof."

"Anything you want," Anderson said, putting his

hand over hers.

She withdrew her hand. "A very, very dry Bombay martini."

"Are you sure you can handle it?" Downing asked.

Marylee's eyes blazed. She looked straight at Anderson. "I'm not sure I can handle anything else."

Downing raised his eyebrows. There was no mistaking the woman's anger.

"I've changed my mind," Anderson said. "If the two of you want—"

"No, I'll pass," Downing said, relieved that Anderson had come to his rescue.

Marylee knew they were waiting for her to speak. She very much wanted a strong drink, but she also realized that to insist on it would be childish. "The majority always wins, doesn't it?"

Anderson summoned the waiter, asked for the check, added a very generous tip, and then signed it.

Sanchez was at the wheel of the gray Honda Accord. Velez was alongside him, and Ortega was in the back.

"Are you sure Anderson is in the restaurant?" Ortega asked, worried that his still-swollen foot would give him trouble if they were suddenly forced to abandon the car and run.

"He is there." Then to give credence to what he said, Sanchez added, "One of my people buses tables there. He recognized him and called me."

Ortega leaned back.

Sanchez turned onto Sixty-fifth Street, and rolled past Le Cirque. "We'll park up the street and wait."

"How many people are with him?" Velez asked.

"A man, and his whore."

"Kill them both?"

Sanchez shrugged, leaving the decision to be made at

the moment.

"It's a shame to kill a good whore," Velez commented, "especially if she's beautiful."

"Is she beautiful?" Ortega asked.

"Yes," Sanchez answered, slowing, and then coming to a stop next to a fire hydrant. Because the car was hot-wired, he kept the engine going.

Velez uttered a loud sigh, but did not say anything.

"How will we know when they leave?" Ortega asked.

"One of us will see them. I will stay here for awhile, then circle around the block."

"Suppose they go right into a waiting car," Velez said.

Sanchez took the time to light a cigarette before he answered, "Then we will try again, and if for some reason we don't kill him, we will keep trying until we do." He blew smoke out the window. "I owe him his death in payment for the deaths he gave to my father, my brother, my sister, and my wife."

For several moments no one in the car spoke, then Velez said, "I'd feel better if I was to fuck a beautiful whore rather than kill her."

Ortega rapped him on the back of the head with his knuckles. "You have your brains in the head of your prick!"

Velez was about to answer when Sanchez put the car into gear and started to roll again.

"We'll go around a couple of times."

Within a matter of minutes, Anderson, Downing, and Marylee were out of the restaurant and Marylee said, "If you gentlemen don't mind, I would much prefer to walk for awhile."

"I don't mind a walk," Anderson responded.

"I want to be alone!" Marylee exploded.

"The streets aren't safe."

"I'll see you in the morning, John."

"Marylee—"

"I'm old enough to take care of myself," she said hotly, and started toward Madison Avenue.

"Go after her, Downing. I didn't expect this kind of reaction from her."

"You really can't blame her. After all, she really is just a kid."

Anderson snorted. "She is not a kid."

"John, how old would your son have been?" Downing asked.

Surprised by the question, Anderson felt his mounting anger swiftly drain away. "Yes, of course you're right. Go after her, Edward." Then without another word, Anderson turned and walked in the opposite direction.

By the time he reached Fifth Avenue, he was toying with the idea of visiting Augusta. Perhaps even telling her about Gault. But the thought of having to deal with her occultism was enough to make him change his mind.

Jeff and Pat caught up to him.

"Walking home, boss?" Pat asked.

Anderson nodded.

He hoped Marylee would get over her mood and return to the town house. But it was just a hope. She was very angry with him. This was not the way he'd envisioned the evening ending.

Chapter 11

Downing caught up to Marylee.

"Please, I really do want to be alone," she said.

He didn't answer, but as he kept pace with her, he became more aware of the rose-scented perfume she was wearing than he had been in the restaurant, where it would have been obscured by the sharper and more prevalent scents of the food.

Recently divorced after fifteen years of marriage, Downing had suddenly rediscovered sexual passion, and found it even more exciting than he remembered. He'd also discovered—and this was a completely new discovery—that young women were not averse to having an affair with an older man, as long as he was tender and affectionate.

On the corner of Sixty-fifth and Park Avenue, Marylee started to cross.

An instant later, she was pulled back, and a cab came to a screeching halt where, moments before, she'd stepped.

"What the fuck is wrong with you, lady?" the cabbie screamed, and started to open the door.

Downing pushed Marylee to one side. "Get out of that cab and you're a dead man." His voice was flat, and cold.

The cabbie stared at him. "Shit, it ain't worth it!" he said. Slammed the door shut and defiantly burning rubber, he sped away.

Marylee turned furiously at him. "Just what is it you want?"

"You." He'd spoken before he could stop himself.

The light changed, but Marylee didn't move. "Just like that?"

Already in a high dive, he finished it. "Yes, just like that."

She took a deep breath. "Yes. On your boat."

When the light changed, he took hold of her arm. "My car is in a garage two blocks from here," he said as they crossed the street.

Marylee didn't answer. Whatever she would say, she would say later.

"Anderson," Sanchez said the third time he drove down the street. "Alone."

"Where's the whore?" Velez asked.

Sanchez slowed.

He could back up, and give Velez and Ortega a chance to get off two rounds before he'd have to floor the gas pedal and get the hell out of there.

"You ready?" he asked.

Both men answered, "Yes."

"Car just turned into the street," Ortega said, looking out the rearview window.

Sanchez eased to the right to let the car pass. As soon as it did, he moved back into the center and checked the rearview mirror. The street was empty behind him.

"Roll down your windows," he said.

Suddenly, he was sweating, and he could hear the thumping of his heart.

"We'll roll back slowly, then very fast. I'll cut to the right, stop, and you guys do the rest."

He stopped, and with his eyes on the rearview

108

mirror he put the car in reverse.

"Two guys just came out of the restaurant," Ortega said.

"I see them!"

Sanchez stopped, threw the shift into drive, and made the light on the corner before it turned red.

"Christ, they're his fucking watchdogs!"

"Maybe we could—" Velez began.

Sanchez shook his head.

Downing's boat rocked gently on the water.

Naked, Marylee felt the wonderful tranquility of mind and body—and yes, of soul—that came in the wake of an intense orgasm, like a cool sea wind after a long hot spell.

Downing was a skillful and considerate—it would have been inappropriate to use the word *lover* to describe him—partner. Yes, that was more appropriate.

The past few days had built up an enormous tension in her, and tonight at dinner—well, if John Wesley Anderson had his life apart from hers, then she certainly was entitled to hers apart from his.

"So quiet," Downing said in a low voice.

From the wordless cries of pleasure she had made, he knew he had satisfied her. But he also knew, from his years of marriage, and other intimate experiences with women, that what followed the orgasmic moment could have an enormous emotional range—anywhere from afterglow to sheer rage. And given the peculiar circumstances that had brought them together, he guessed that she was somewhere between pleasure and contriteness. Not an unusual reaction, by any means.

Marylee opened her eyes. The cabin was dark,

except for a small light over the bulkhead door. On either side, symmetrically spaced, two portholes provided momentary glimpses of the night sky and the lines that ran between the boat and the mooring piles.

"I'm listening to the sound of the water lapping against the boat," she said.

"Pleasant."

"Pleasant," she echoed. His hand was on her breast again, squeezing it gently.

"I'll drive you into the city in the morning," he said, wanting her to spend the night with him.

"It's probably morning now."

Downing glanced over to the side of the cabin, where a digital clock displayed the time in amber-colored numbers.

"Eleven-thirty."

Marylee didn't respond.

He was teasing the nipple of her right breast, and she was enjoying it.

Downing nuzzled her neck.

He hadn't had a woman as young as Marylee for several years. The last time had been in a very posh Bangkok brothel. The woman had probably been no more than eighteen. She'd been exclusively his for three days.

Positioning himself above Marylee, he kissed her lips.

She put her arms around his neck. "You're much nicer than I thought you were."

He laughed. "Do you usually go to bed with a man you don't particularly like?"

"I was very angry," she admitted.

"And hurt?"

"That too."

Downing moved slightly away from her, and as he

rested his head on the palm of one of his hands, he caressed her breast with the other. "This isn't really the time to talk about Anderson, but . . ."

"But what?"

"You're very young, Marylee, and John has reached that stage in his life where—well, most men have to make some sort of adjustment to what lies ahead and what lies behind them."

"I really did think I knew him. I—"

"Things are happening in his life—inside of him, in his head—that you couldn't possibly be aware of."

Suddenly, Marylee laughed.

"What's funny?" he asked, disconcerted by her laughter.

"Remember the story of John Alden and Priscilla?"

"You mean I should speak for myself rather than Anderson? All right, I will. But I'm not speaking for John Anderson, at least not as you interpret it." He paused, and moved his hand from her breast to a small patch of tangled hair on her pubic mound. "I would like us to have a relationship, but I know that this is probably the only time we'll ever be together like this."

She touched his face. "That's the way it will be," she said in a low voice.

Downing nodded. "I knew that the moment you agreed to come here with me. But that's no reason why I shouldn't help you understand Anderson."

"You like him a lot, don't you?"

"He made it possible for me to be where I am. But that doesn't mean I'm not aware of his shortcomings."

"Tell me what you think," Marylee said.

"For openers, he's not like other men. He doesn't think the same way."

She countered, "That's not it. He just makes his own rules, and most men don't have the wherewithal to do that. And even if they did, they really wouldn't know what to do."

"You're right. But do you know why he makes his own rules? Because he has his own vision of things. It's the vision, or rather the ability to have a vision, that makes it possible for him to."

"Do you have that vision?"

"Not the way he has. That doesn't mean that his vision is always right. It only means that it provides him with a goal. Any man with a goal, who believes in that goal, will make his own rules. But Anderson has the money, and the power that comes with having money, to make the rules more often than most men."

Marylee was very quiet. She realized that Downing had moved his hand from her love mound to her arm.

"He makes his own rules even in his relationships with women," she finally said in almost a whisper.

"Marylee, Marylee, Marylee," Downing sighed.

"Why the despair?"

"Because you're too intelligent to make the same mistake most women make when they sleep with a man over a period of time. They think they know the man. They don't; they only know one part of him. And a man like Anderson has more parts than either of us could ever imagine."

"I never thought of him as anything but complicated," she answered. "But we've been very close, and I believed he would be more trusting with me."

For a time, Downing didn't answer. He wasn't really sure just how much more he should say, and wondered if he had already said too much.

"I trust him," Marylee said in a small voice that suddenly erupted into the silence like a weak flash of light, and just as suddenly died.

"Anderson trusts no one," he told her, his voice

112

sharper than he'd meant it to be. Then he said, in a softer tone, "That's not completely true either."

"Tell me, who does he trust?"

"His brother Wally. Anderson trusts him."

She thought about that for several moments. "No one else?"

"You may not like what my answer will be."

She shrugged. "A woman?"

"At one time, Isabel Aroyo. Maybe he still trusts her."

"You're right, I don't like your answer. I have so much of him I want his complete trust too."

"Remember, he makes the rules. If you don't like them, you can always walk out."

Marylee suddenly became acutely aware of her position. "How much future do you think there'd be for John Wesley Anderson's former mistress?" The bitterness had almost choked the words off before she could finish speaking.

"Everyone can start a new life," he answered.

"It's something for me to think about, isn't it?"

"You're the only one who could answer that," Downing told her.

"Not much I can say to that. But you know more about him than I thought you did."

"I've known him for many years."

"And you've studied him?"

"That too."

Marylee listened to the water moving against the sides of the boat.

She wasn't sure she agreed with everything Downing had told her, but she felt better for having heard it.

"You never told me whether you'd stay the night," Downing said.

"Yes, I will."

113

He drew her close to him, and kissed her hard on the mouth until her lips parted and she gave him her tongue.

Anderson slept badly.

The third time he got up, he left his bed, put on a silk robe and a pair of slippers, and padded into the upstairs den, where he sat down in his favorite easy chair to stare at an empty fireplace.

That Marylee had reacted the way she'd had to what he'd said disturbed him, and he was even more disturbed by her absence, knowing she was spending the night with Downing.

Anxious about his meeting with Gault, he resented the intrusion of another emotional situation. Even as he had sent Downing after Marylee, he'd known what would happen. He had not been oblivious to the way Downing looked at her, though he had preferred to ignore it. Marylee was a beautiful woman, and he was used to the way some men looked at her.

Just as the grandfather clock on the other side of the darkened room struck four o'clock, the phone rang.

He let it ring three times before he went to the desk and picked it up, hoping it was Marylee.

"John, I had to call you," his wife said.

"Are you all right?" he asked. Her voice had the familiar high pitch it took on whenever she was upset or excited about something.

"Yes, yes. I am fine. I just had a remarkable experience."

Anderson tightened his lips.

"It started this afternoon," she said.

He was almost tempted to put the phone down on

the desk and not listen. But he couldn't do that to her.

"I went for my weekly reading with Doctor Roe, and she said that something was about to change in my life."

Anderson suddenly began to cough.

"John, did you hear me?"

He cleared his throat. "Yes, yes. Something is about to change in your life."

"She couldn't tell me exactly what," Augusta continued, "but she said it would affect the rest of my life."

Anderson cleared his throat again.

There had been at least two dozen different Doctor Roes in Augusta's life since John Junior had been reported missing, then presumed dead, and all of them had given her false hope. But now . . .

"John, then the most amazing thing happened while I was walking home," she said, her voice going even higher. "I didn't go straight home, John, the way I usually do. I walked over to that little park on Sutton Place that overlooks the river. The day was so beautiful, and there were lots of nannies and children out. I sat down on a bench. Really, I was just enjoying the warmth of the sun, when suddenly I realized there was a towheaded little boy looking up at me with big blue eyes. And then, John, he said, 'Mamma, Mamma.'" She stopped.

He knew she was too choked up to continue.

"That never happened before, John," Augusta said.

"No, I don't remember you ever telling me anything like that," he admitted.

"But that's not all. After I left the park, I felt more alive than I have in years. John, I started to remember things about us when we first married that made me smile — and blush a bit, I think."

115

"Augusta . . ." He was going to say something that would make her feel good about herself, but she said, "John, I had a dream about our son. It woke me up. That's why I called you. I had to. John, in the dream, I saw our son. I know he's alive. I know it!"

Anderson bit his knuckles. He wasn't going to tell her anything about Gault until he himself was sure.

"John?"

"Yes, I'm here, Augusta."

"John—"

"You've had several good omens," he told her.

"You never used a word like omen before," she said after a momentary silence. She knew how much he disliked, even hated, her interest in the occult.

"That's what they are, aren't they?"

He didn't want to become involved in a discussion with her about his use of a word. Besides, he wanted to give her something to which she could cling. After all, Gault had given him more than omens, and though he wasn't ready to share it with her, he no longer had the heart to deny her hope.

"John, you're not angry with me for calling you?" she asked in a tearful voice. "I wouldn't have if I hadn't had the dream."

"I understand. I'm glad you called."

"You are? You really are?"

"Yes. Now go back to sleep, Augusta."

"Thank you, John. And good night."

"Good night," Anderson said, and put the phone down in its cradle. For several moments, he made no effort to move.

"Omens," he said aloud. "Omens!"

Then he turned away from the desk, and left the room.

Maybe he'd be able to sleep, now that he was emotionally exhausted and physically drained.

116

Anderson was up at seven. He shaved, showered, dressed, and went downstairs to the office to wait for Marylee, who returned at eight-thirty.

He called to her from behind his desk as she passed the open door of the office.

She stopped, turned, and walked into the room.

"That was a long walk you took," he said, getting to his feet.

She resented his waiting for her, as if she was his property. She resented his tone. "I'm going to my room."

"You know, I made Downing. I can just as easily unmake him." He'd spoken casually, almost as if what he said had no import at all.

"How am I supposed to react to that?" she challenged.

He sat down on the edge of the desk. "You spent the night with him, didn't you?"

She ignored his question. "I'm going downstairs for breakfast. I desperately need some coffee and something to get my blood sugar up." She started to turn.

He was on his feet, furious with her, and more furious with himself for acting the way he was, but unable to stop himself. "Damn it, answer my question!"

"I did . . . I did . . . I slept with him," she yelled. "There, are you satisfied now? Now may I go, or do you want a detailed description of—"

He held up his hands, palms out. "I was genuinely concerned about you, Marylee."

"I know you were. But last night—well, there was just a lot for me to swallow, all in one gulp."

He looked at her questioningly. "Why?"

"I don't know where I will be a month from now

117

when the work is done. Don't you see that? It never entered my mind that you would donate the collection. John, I don't have any future here, not anymore."

Anderson made an attempt to embrace her, but she stepped back and said, "I really must have some coffee."

He dropped his hands. "I don't have any claim on you."

"Yes, I know that."

"I won't let anything happen to you, you should know that."

"I do," she answered with a nod. "But I don't want to be your, or anyone else's, mistress."

Her words took him by surprise. He was going to deny that he had ever thought of her as his mistress. But then he realized he had, or he wouldn't have waited for her, and they wouldn't be having the conversation they were having.

"John, I really didn't see, much less understand, where I was until last night."

Anderson retreated back to the desk, and half sat, half rested against it.

"I'm sorry if what I said hurt you."

"You don't have to apologize for being truthful. I should have been more aware of—what I mean, Marylee, is that you gave me something special."

"Any woman could have done the same, John."

He shook his head. "But it was you, and I'm grateful. More grateful than I can ever hope to tell you, and not because you were there in bed for me. It was always more than sex."

"But never love," she said in a low voice.

He hesitated. "I'd be lying if I said yes."

For several moments, neither one spoke.

Anderson found himself conjuring up the image of

118

the naked body next to his, the feel of her breasts in his hands, the pleasure he experienced just looking at her nude.

"I'll stay until all the work is done," Marylee said.

"Thank you. I appreciate that."

Marylee turned, started for the door, then stopped and faced him. "Last night I needed someone —"

"No need to explain."

She ignored him. "Someone else."

He nodded, and said, "I understand that. Believe me, I do."

Marylee gave him a small smile and left the room, closing the door after her.

Anderson stood up, walked around to the other side of the desk, and sat down. He was beginning to feel storm-tossed. Things were happening too fast. He felt as if he were losing control.

Chapter 12

At eleven Friday morning, Gault called Anderson from a street telephone on the corner of Jones and Lafayette Streets. A light rain was falling, bringing a grayness that washed over everything.

The phone on the other end rang once.

"The Anderson Foundation. Ms. Terrall speaking."

"Mr. Gault for Mr. Anderson."

"Yes. Certainly, Mr. Gault. I'll put your call through immediately," she responded.

He thanked her, aware of the flustered knowingness in her voice. Then Anderson came on, and said, "I'm all set for one o'clock."

"So am I."

"There's a place called the Katmandu on Sullivan Street," Anderson said. "I have reservations for two in my name."

Gault smiled. "I'll be there. See you." He hung up without giving Anderson the opportunity to extend the conversation.

Gault was already at the table when Anderson arrived, and as he stood up to shake his hand, he noticed the two men who took the table next to the window.

"My people," Anderson explained, conscious of where Gault was looking.

Gault nodded. "We might as well sit down, Mr.

Anderson."

Anderson smiled.

Gault was probably John Junior's age. A man of middling height, trim, with brown hair and matching beard. Green eyes. All in all a self-assured person. Much like John Junior. There was even a slight resemblance between the two.

"Do I pass inspection?" Gault asked.

"Sorry. I didn't realize it was that obvious."

Gault didn't answer.

Anderson shifted uneasily in his chair.

He needed this young man. The information Jeff and Ryan had collected on him checked out: He had been in Nepal and he was a professional photographer. His parents were still living in Brooklyn, in an apartment house on Glenwood Road. He had graduated from Brooklyn Technical High School, and attended Brooklyn College. Like Jeff, he had dropped out in his senior year.

"Are you familiar with Indian food?" Gault asked, picking up one of the small celluloid-covered menus.

Anderson took the other menu. "I've been to India several times."

Again Gault didn't answer. Instead, he summoned the waiter, a young dark-complexioned man with a narrow black mustache, and before the man could speak, he did—in Hindi, the basic language of northern India.

The waiter was momentarily surprised, but then he smiled and answered.

"I ordered a simple vegetable dish," Gault explained.

Anderson too was surprised at his ability to speak Hindi, and he acknowledged it by saying, "I defer to your choice. I'll have the same."

Gault spoke again to the waiter, pressed the palms of his hands together, and made a slight bow from the waist, even though he was sitting.

The waiter returned the courtesy, and left.

"Where did you learn to speak Hindi?" Anderson asked.

"Picked it up. I have a gift for that kind of thing."

"How many more do you speak?"

"The usual."

The waiter returned with a small woven basket filled with thin, flat pieces of hot bread, and a scoop of butter on a monkey dish.

Gault immediately helped himself to a piece of bread. "Wonderful, like pita bread but very much better." He buttered it, and before he began to eat it, he said, "French, German, Spanish, Italian . . . and Russian."

"And Hindi," added Anderson.

"And Hebrew."

"That's really remarkable," Anderson said.

Gault shrugged.

Though impatient to learn about his son, Anderson was acutely aware that Gault wasn't the kind of person to be pushed into anything.

"Do you have a publisher for your book?" Anderson asked.

Gault was devouring a second piece of bread. "My editor, Kevin . . ." He smiled. "I was going to say he was a horse's ass, but that would be too kind. He's a yuppy."

"Then he has to be close to your age," Anderson countered.

"Ten years older. But I've lived a dozen lives and he's barely making it through one."

Anderson nodded sympathetically.

"That's what I found so wonderfully exciting about John," Gault said.

Anderson's whole body jerked, as if he'd had a sudden contact with a high-voltage wire.

Gault pretended not to have noticed. "Try some of this bread," he said. "It's really quite good."

Anderson nodded, picked up a piece of bread, and with his hands trembling, buttered it.

"You were saying something about John Junior," Anderson commented. He couldn't keep the strain from his voice; it was as if his vocal cords were strained to their limit.

Gault smiled. "John lived many lives in this life and in other lives. He has a real sense of what it's all about, what our purpose is here." He looked straight at Anderson. "He has found his purpose, Mr. Anderson. He's at peace with himself, and with the universe."

"John . . ." Anderson had to stop, swallow hard, and drink some water before he could continue in his normal voice. "John always wanted to know more about himself and his place in the scheme of things."

"I think he has found the answers," Gault said.

The waiter came with two plates filled with vegetables.

Again Gault pressed the palms of his hands together and spoke in Hindi.

Flashing a broad smile, the waiter answered, then left them.

"I told him how beautiful these vegetables look," Gault explained. "He in turn answered that he personally goes to the market every morning to buy them."

Though Anderson nodded appreciatively, he couldn't care less if the vegetables had come from the frozen-food section of the local supermarket.

Then suddenly he and Gault spoke at the same instant.

"Please, Mr. Anderson, you first," Gault said.

Anderson attempted to defer to Gault, but he would not permit it. "Tell me about my son," Anderson finally

said, fixing his eyes on Gault. "I want to know everything."

"Everything," Gault repeated thoughtfully. He broke
another piece of bread, and held a piece in each hand.
"Neither you, his father, nor me, his friend, is capable
of knowing everything about John Anderson, Jr." He
put the piece of bread in his left hand down on the
plate. "He's well and fully recovered from the accident.
The monks found him three days after the avalanche,
and carried him in a litter to their monastery. He was
unconscious for several days, and during that time he
had—" He took a bite out of the bread, chewed, and
swallowed it before he said, "John had a vision, or so he
claims. Someone, or something—he isn't quite sure
what it was—told him to renounce his other life and
build a new one."

Anderson leaned forward and planted his elbows on
the table. "His mother would understand that better
than I do," he admitted. Then he asked, "Did he tell you
anything about the vision? Did he describe it?"

"It was amorphous, if you know what I mean. More
a voice than anything else."

"Then he's happy where he is?"

"Completely," Gault answered; then looking down at
his plate of vegetables, he said, "You really should try
these, Mr. Anderson. They are cooked to perfection
and lightly seasoned."

He was waiting for the big question, the million-
dollar one. He could see that Anderson was working up
to it, but still wasn't ready to throw it out on the table.

"John," said Gault, "tends their garden under the
tutelage of a very old monk whose seamed, weather-
beaten face looked as if some etcher had gone crazy on
it, and whose name comes closest to Bloody Warrior
when translated into English. But of course, an exact
translation isn't possible. John says that he has learned

a great deal from his ancient teacher, much more than he's ever learned in any of the schools he's attended, including Yale."

"I can understand that," Anderson answered. He was picking at the vegetables, and those he did put into his mouth, he hardly tasted.

"He asked me to tell you that he loves you and his mother very much," Gault said. "But I think I told you that over the phone, didn't I? If I didn't, I should have. That was one of the first things John made me promise."

Anderson's chest ached from a swelling of emotion. He put his fork down, and clearing his throat, asked, "Will you take me to my son?"

Gault put his fork down too, and placed the balls of his fingers together. The big question was out there in front of him.

"John knew that you would want to come to him."

"Will you—"

"It's not what John wants," Gault told him. "He doesn't want any part of his old life to intrude on his new one."

Anderson sighed deeply, leaned back, and looked squarely at Gault. "I have already spent several million dollars trying to find him, and now I am prepared to pay you a million dollars if you take me to him. Two million?"

Gault drew back, scraping the bottom of his chair's legs on the floor. He started to stand. "Money—ah, what's the use!"

Taken completely by surprise, Anderson started to stand too. But at the same time, he said, "Please sit down, Richard. I'm sorry if I insulted you. Please." He was pleading.

Gault nodded, and the two of them sat down at the same time.

126

"John said you would offer me money."

"He knows his father," Anderson said contritely.

"Better than his father knows him," Gault answered.

Anderson didn't respond, and for several moments neither one of them spoke; then in a very low voice, he said, "I love John Junior. I want to see him, nothing more." His voice began to break, and tears came to his eyes. He turned his head away, and wiped his eyes with a white handkerchief. "I apologize for—"

"No need to," Gault said. "I know this is an emotional time for you. But I came here as John's emissary. He trusted me to bring you news of him."

"I understand," Anderson told him.

Again Gault placed the balls of his fingers together.

"Is anything wrong?" Anderson asked, aware of the thoughtful expression on Gault's face.

"Perhaps it was a mistake for me to contact you," Gault said.

Anderson violently shook his head. "At least I know he's alive and well. You don't know what that means to me, and what it will mean to his mother. No, Richard, it was not a mistake. It was an act of charity to take the time and the effort out of your own busy life to do it."

"I promised John I would do it."

"You said something about having made other promises to him," Anderson said.

Gault nodded. He'd known that Anderson would pick up on that when he'd said it.

"Have any of them anything to do with me or his mother?" Anderson asked.

"I can't discuss them, Mr. Anderson."

"I'm sorry, it was a foolish question."

"John has also become an expert in herbal healing. It was medicine derived from herbs that the Bloody Warrior gave to John that brought him back from the grave, so to speak."

"From what you have told me, he really does seem to have made a new life for himself," Anderson said.

"Believe me, he has."

Gault signaled the waiter, and ordered tea when the man came to the table.

"Just how did you happen on this lamasery?" Anderson asked. He didn't remember Gault ever telling him how.

"Simply, I was lost. I was miles away from where I wanted to be. The monks were surprised that I spoke Hindi, and then one of them pointed to John, who was working out in the garden, and asked if I knew him. Later, I realized there is a slight resemblance between John and myself. And I guess the monk might have thought we came from the same village. After all, John came to them from the outside world too. They have no idea of anything larger than a village."

At the same time Anderson was listening to Gault, he was thinking of a way to change Gault's mind about taking him to John Junior. Given some time, he was sure he'd be able to do it. He'd not only need time, he'd also need a closeness. A bonding would have to take place between them before Gault would trust him.

Aware that Gault had finished speaking, Anderson said, "Your being lost caused John Junior to be found. A fair exchange, I would say."

The waiter came with their tea and Gault went through the same ritual with the palms of his hands pressed gently together. When the waiter was gone, he answered. "More than a fair exchange. I spent two months with John, and learned a great deal."

"I hope you brought back photographs."

"Only of the monastery. John, like the other monks, would not permit himself to be photographed."

Anderson looked incredulous. "But John took thousands of photographs."

"What's that old saw? When in Rome do as the Romans do? I think he really didn't want to go against their rules."

Anderson accepted that without comment.

"Well, I did what John wanted me to do," Gault said with a smile. "I really do appreciate having the opportunity to meet you." And he signaled the waiter for the check. "This is my treat, Mr. Anderson."

"Absolutely not!"

"I insist," Gault said.

"Waiter, I'll take the check," Anderson said, and he did. Then suddenly he had an idea that would keep Gault close to him. "Are you working on anything now?" he asked.

"After I leave you I have an interview."

"Work for me."

"What?"

"My assistant, Miss Terrall, said something about needing another person to help with the cataloguing," Gault told him, though he remembered her actually saying she could complete it without additional help. "I'll pay you a fair wage and you can have one of the rooms upstairs on the third floor in the town house."

"Cataloguing what?"

"A Mezo-American art collection."

"You're joking."

Anderson shook his head.

"Talk about good luck!" Gault exclaimed. "This has to be the best all-time example of good luck. Would you believe, I was planning to go down to Central and South America to do a book on the Mayan ruins? So much has been discovered about them recently."

"It's settled, then. You'll work for me. You can even use my darkroom in the basement. It's fully equipped."

"I don't know."

"Why the hesitation?"

"I keep kind of weird hours. I move around a lot."

"You'll have your own key," Anderson said. "Give it a try. If either one of us is displeased with the arrangement — well, we can deal with that if it comes up."

"How will you explain my presence? After all, I'm not a professional cataloguer. I'm not even —"

Anderson grinned. "I met you on an archaeological dig last summer in Colombia."

Gault cocked his head to one side. "A cover story?"

"Certainly a cover story, and it's a good one."

"Why are you doing this, Mr. Anderson?"

"I need another person."

Gault shook his head. "The real reason."

Anderson put his hands down on the table. "You're smart enough to figure it out for yourself, Richard."

"You think you're going to convince me to take you to John."

"I think I am going to convince you to take me to John. I don't know exactly how I'll do it, but I will."

Gault wasn't going to jump through the hoop for John Anderson. He reached across the table. "I'll think about it. That's the best I can do."

This young man was a lot more steadfast than he'd thought. "I guess then I'll have to settle for that," Anderson said, shaking his hand.

"I guess you will," Gault answered.

"When will you let me know?"

"Next week, Tuesday. Wednesday at the very latest."

They shook hands again, and Gault left the restaurant first.

Marylee was none too pleased when Anderson mentioned there was a possibility that Gault might join the staff. He said it over evening cocktails — a ritual that was held in the upstairs sitting room, on the second floor, whenever Anderson did not have a social engagement he was required to attend. Pat and Jeff were always there, and sometimes Wally, Anderson's brother.

"I'm sure I can finish the work myself," she said.

Anderson realized that she was still piqued from the events of the previous evening.

"By the time he knows what he's doing, the work will be finished," she said.

There was some truth in that, but he wasn't going to permit her to dictate who he should or should not employ. But more to the point, after having spent the entire afternoon thinking about it, he had come up with a plan of action that would convince Gault to take him to John Junior. And the keystone of the plan was to have Gault realize he was not the same man John Junior had known. That he too had come to a different "life," albeit in a very different way from his son's traumatic experience and the vision that had followed. But to do that, he needed Gault to be close at hand. If that were not possible, though, he would find other ways to accomplish what he wanted.

"Make the best use of him that you can," Anderson told her.

The tone of his voice told her that he did not want to discuss the matter anymore. But she was not going to drop it without a barb of her own.

"If he's content to be my gofer, then I'll be happy to have him."

Anderson nodded, but didn't respond to the challenge. Instead, he gave his attention to Pat and Jeff, and began talking about baseball season.

"I have my usual box at Yankee Stadium. Use it whenever you want to." He looked at Pat. "A couple of your guys must be big enough for the Little League by now."

"They are, and pretty good sluggers. The oldest is a southpaw, and throws a mean fastball."

"Of all the sports, I really like baseball the best," Anderson said. "It has a combination of so many skills, and all of them, at least to me, seem to have a grace that often becomes a poetry in motion."

His eyes went to Marylee. She was still fuming. "What do you think?" he asked.

"Hockey and football, in that order, are my favorites," she answered.

"Too violent for my taste," Anderson said; then with a rueful smile, he added, "They once were my favorites too, but I guess I'm getting too old to enjoy—"

The phone rang.

Anderson nodded to Marylee, who left her chair and went to the small table where the phone was located.

"It's Senator Post," she said.

Anderson put his martini down on a tooled, brown leather coaster, and went to the phone.

"John," Post began, as soon as he heard Anderson's voice on the line. "Everything is set. I'll be on *Meet the Press* Sunday morning. It will give us one hell of a clout."

"I thought you said you were going to leak the story," Anderson responded.

"Not to worry, John. It will sound like a leak, but it will create a flood of loyal supporters."

"Give me a minute or two to think," Anderson said.

"You want to call me back?"

"Just hang on," Anderson told him.

"Certainly, John," Post answered.

Anderson lowered the phone and put his hand over the mouthpiece.

Marylee was still close by. "Bad news?" she asked.

Anderson frowned, then realizing she had said something that he hadn't heard, he replied, "I'll tell you

132

about it later."

Running for the Presidency might go a long way toward convincing Gault.

He raised the phone to his mouth. "Go with it."

"I'll simply say at the right time that I have it from sources close to John Anderson that he does intend to become the Democratic Party's standard-bearer next November."

"Sounds right."

"I will try to deflect any close examination of that statement," Post said. But I can't guarantee that I will be successful."

"I understand that."

"Good. Tune in, and then tell me how you think it went."

"I'm sure it will go fine," Anderson said, and wished him good luck.

Post laughed. "Watch how good luck happens, after I make that statement. Good night, John."

"Good night," Anderson responded. He put the phone down, took Marylee by the hand, and led her back to where they were; then picking up his martini, he said, "Senator Post on the phone. He's going to leak my interest in becoming the standard-bearer for the Democratic Party. Sunday morning on *Meet the Press*. It's just to test the waters, so to speak. Nothing—"

"That's wonderful!" Marylee exclaimed, throwing her arms around his neck and kissing him on the lips.

Pat and Jeff shook his hand.

"You'll win, boss," Jeff said.

"You'll do it in a landslide. You're the American Eagle," Pat told him. "No one else comes anywhere near being that."

Chapter 13

"Do you want me to stay?" Marylee asked after Pat and Jeff left.

Anderson looked up at her. She was standing directly in front of him. Her full, young breasts were slightly above his eyes. The scent of her herbal perfume invaded his nostrils.

She smiled at him.

The invitation to enjoy her sexually was clearly there, but he shook his head.

"I wouldn't be very good company," he told her. "Besides, I have some paperwork that must be done."

Marylee hesitated. She was almost tempted to ask if he was punishing her for having spent the previous night with Downing.

"Go along," Anderson urged.

She retreated, and said, "I'll see you in the morning." Though she had her own apartment in a high rise on Fifty-fourth and Third, she almost always slept in the bedroom next to Anderson's. Most of her clothes were there.

He stood up. "Good night, Marylee," he said, and started out of the room.

"John?" she called.

He paused, smiled at her, and left the room, knowing he had just signaled the end of their affair.

Inexplicably, he felt very much relieved for having done it, though it wasn't something he'd planned, at least not consciously. It had happened without any dramatics on either of their parts. He wasn't sure whether it was the result of her spending the night with Downing, or his feeling that she was presuming more of a role in his life than he was willing to give her, or even the combination of both.

Anderson entered his office, switched on the light, and settled in one of the large, brown leather easy chairs facing the empty fireplace rather than sit behind the desk.

He was tempted to reach for a cigar. Though it was illegal to import Cuban cigars, he was always able, through his connections, to have several boxes on hand. But he put down the desire, and thought about his meeting with Richard Gault.

Gault was not nearly as self-effacing as he would have liked him to believe. On the contrary, he was a very self-possessed young man, who obviously wasn't the least bit intimidated by having lunch with him.

Anderson realized it was almost the other way around. He was intimidated by Gault, and Gault, he was certain, was sufficiently perceptive to sense that.

Anderson leaned forward, resting his elbows on his knees and lacing his fingers together, creating a platform on which he rested his head.

The question was whether Gault had exploited—

The phone rang.

Anderson turned to look at the flashing light, and hoped one of the servants would answer it.

It rang a second and a third time.

"Damn it, I have a house full of servants, and no one picks up the phone when it rings!"

By the fourth ring, Anderson had already launched himself out of the chair, and had the phone up to his face.

"John Anderson here," he said gruffly.

"This is Charles Bing. I was your lodge guest—"

"Yes, I remember," Anderson said. Bing was the

136

Party's chief strategist, and one of the most cadaverous-looking men he'd ever met.

"There's been—"

Anderson's heart skipped a beat, and began to race. Suddenly, he was sweating.

"Senator Post is dead," Bing said.

"What? I spoke to him not two hours ago. What happened?"

"A stroke."

Anderson sucked in his breath, and slowly let it out.

"I was with him, planning his appearance on *Meet the Press,* when suddenly his eyes opened very wide, his jaw went slack, and he fell over his desk. That was it. He was dead."

"Express my condolences to Iris—Mrs. Post," Anderson said.

"The interment will be at the National Cemetery."

"I'll attend," Anderson said.

"Now as for the leak—"

"Put a hold on that, Charley," Anderson said.

"You're still with us?" Bing asked.

"Yes. But I don't want to rush things now. Something has come up in my life that demands I remain free to travel."

"For how long?"

Bing was clearly irritated, but Anderson didn't care.

Post's death, sad as it was, presented him with the opportunity to free himself, at least for the immediate future, and concentrate on matters in his own life that were more important to him than the Presidency.

"The election is a long way off, Charley," Anderson said. "I'll be there to campaign when you need me. I don't want anything leaked now."

"That's your final word?" Bing asked.

"Yes, for now. After Post's funeral we'll talk. What I have to do will take more than a month, two at the most; then I promise you my full and undivided effort."

Bing was quiet for several moments. There wasn't any way he could oppose Anderson. Without him as its number-one man, the party might as well concede the election.

"All right. But we will have to talk," Bing said.

Anderson assured him that they would. "Get back to me in two, three weeks and we'll set something up."

"Good. See you Tuesday."

"Tuesday," Anderson said, repeating the day; then he replaced the phone in its cradle. "Post and I go back a long ways," he said aloud, still standing at the desk. "A long ways."

He started back to the chair, changed his mind, and instead went to the bar on the other side of the room, where he poured himself a shot glass full of scotch.

"To you, Tom," he toasted, then downed the scotch in one continuous swallow.

The sudden burst of warmth inside him felt good, and he returned to the chair.

"I need time to convince Gault," he said aloud, realizing that he had already decided to stop Post from leaking anything about his bid for the Presidency. He would have called him sometime that night, or the following morning at the very latest.

Anderson rubbed his chin.

Augusta would have considered Post's death an omen. Perhaps it was.

He lifted himself out of the chair. He felt old, and tired. The death of his friend, whose age was close to

138

his, suddenly put things into a more realistic perspective.

Gaining the Presidency was not anywhere near as important as regaining his son. And if there wasn't sufficient time to do both, he would give up any thought of making it to the White House. He'd devote the rest of his life, if need be, to being reunited with John Junior. That mattered most. Everything else paled by comparison.

The weekend passed slowly for Anderson, and though Marylee came in to do some work on Saturday morning, as she often did, he spent the morning at a benefit breakfast for the New York Foundling Hospital.

By late Sunday afternoon, the weather had turned nasty; a raw wind came off the ocean, bringing with it rain. Anderson spent most of the day inside, and began reading *Battle Stations,* the first book of a naval trilogy that followed the lives of four officers and their families from the beginning of the Second World War through Vietnam.

Monday began with cloudy skies, but by the middle of the day the sun was out, and spring had returned. And on Tuesday, he attended Post's funeral, which was conducted with a dignity befitting the man, and with the hypocrisy that was the hallmark of his profession.

The President, Post's political enemy, took the opportunity at the graveside to speak. "We were," he said, "in the same political arena, though on different sides. My purpose and his was always to build a better, stronger America."

Worried about whether Gault had called—or if he hadn't, would he—Anderson tuned out the rest of what the President said.

After the final words by the minister, the heavy bronze casket was slowly lowered into the grave while an army bugler blew taps. Then as the friends and family dispersed, Anderson, who had been standing next to a longtime friend, Admiral Roger W. Maylee, Chairman of the Joint Chiefs of Staff, was approached by a presidential aide.

"Mr. Anderson, the President would very much like to speak with you."

Admiral Maylee grinned, nodded, and said, "Why don't you drop by the OC this evening, John, and we'll have a few drinks together."

"I just might do that."

"Follow me," the President's aide said.

The Presidential black limousine was parked on the roadway, about forty yards away. A half dozen Secret Service and FBI agents were posted around it. The President was standing just in front of the opened door.

"Well, Mr. Anderson, this is a sad occasion for one of our infrequent meetings." The President offered his hand.

Anderson shook it. "Tom was a good friend of mine for many years, and a good public servant. He will be missed."

The President nodded, then said, "But life must go on. The business of running the country must go on. We who are here shoulder the awesome responsibility of making certain that it does go on."

The man was, as Lincoln might have put it, speechifying, and there wasn't anything Anderson could do to stop him. Anderson was a captive audience. The man was, after all, the President of the United States.

But Anderson did not miss the import of the

invitation for the informal conversation. He was just waiting for the President to confirm his suspicions.

Finally, the President stopped speechifying and said, "What would you say if I offered you a place within my Administration?"

"I'd have to say that I would be deeply honored," Anderson answered.

His suspicions had been absolutely correct. The President was testing the water, afraid there might be sharks in it, before he jumped in.

"What would you say if it was the ombudsman of the Company?"

I'd say you were playing a losing hand, Anderson thought. But to the President, he said, "That's something I would have to give a great deal of thought to, Mr. President."

"Would you be averse to the offer?"

"I certainly would consider it seriously."

The President smiled.

"But there are, I must tell you, many other things that I must consider before I'd be able to decide whether to accept or reject the offer."

The smile vanished.

"Personal matters may prevent me from accepting any sort of commitment that would require the major portion of my time. Watchdogging the CIA would not be a part-time effort."

"But if I made the offer, you would consider it?"

"Absolutely, Mr. President. I would weigh it against my other obligations."

The President smiled again, and offered his hand. "I'm glad we had the opportunity to have this chat."

Anderson shook the proffered hand. "My pleasure, Mr. President." He stepped away from the limousine.

Within moments the President was inside it, the door closed, and the vehicle moved slowly forward.

Anderson walked back to his own limousine, which had been rented for the day. Pat and Jeff were waiting for him. But before he reached it, Hogan and Fitzroy, the Democratic Party's media specialist, cut him off.

"What was that powwow all about?" Hogan asked.

Anderson told them.

"What do you intend to do?" Fitzroy asked.

"Avoid giving a definite answer for as long as I can. Then when I do, I will call a news conference, and explain that my reasons for turning down the President's generous offer is that I wish to serve the country on a much higher level, on a level where the decisions that are made not only affect the citizens of this country, but of the world . . . or some such words."

The two of them looked at him with undisguised admiration.

"Brilliant!" Fitzroy exclaimed.

"That will do it," Hogan said.

Anderson had thought of making the linkage between his refusal of the ombudsman job and his running for the Presidency on the spur of the moment.

"But don't pressure me," he told them. "I have to do all of this in my own time."

"It's your call, John," Hogan said, taking the liberty of calling Anderson by his given name."

"As long as everyone remembers that."

"No problem," Fitzroy said, holding the palms of his hands out.

"We'll talk soon," Anderson told them, shaking each of their hands.

"Look forward to it," Hogan said.

Anderson crouched down to get into the rear of the limousine, and a few moments later, Pat sat down alongside him and Jeff settled into the jump seat in front of Pat.

That afternoon, at four o'clock, Grier entered Bushwick's office. Bushwick was standing, not behind his desk, but at the window, staring out, with his brow furrowed, and one hand rubbing his chin — always a bad sign. Grier had learned Bushwick's body language, and what he was looking at told him that Bushwick was not only in a lather about something, but was also thinking, and that could be catastrophic.

Grier halted a pace or so in front of Bushwick's desk.

"I just had a call from the President," Bushwick said, without facing him. "To use the vernacular, we're in deep shit."

Grier immediately grasped the significance of the comment, but didn't move a muscle.

Bushwick slowly faced him. "Do you know how fucking deep? Well, let me tell you. He has spoken to Anderson and Anderson, he said, 'seemed responsive.' Responsive!" Bushwick practically shouted. "That's another fucking way of saying, 'I'll take it.'" He was breathing hard, and there was color in his face.

Grier quietly said, "Everything is in place. It will never happen, I assure you."

Bushwick ignored him, and gripped the back of his chair. "Just what have you got on Anderson that ties him to Venom?"

"Nothing concrete, just suspicions. The pattern of the various hits." Grier wondered if Bushwick ever retained anything he read.

Bushwick thrust the chair against the desk. "If we

143

could tie him to those hits, he'd be finished, totally neutralized."

Grier shook his head. "You'd have as much chance of doing that as a snowball has in hell. He's too smart to—"

"If he's so fucking smart, how are you going to get to him?" Bushwick challenged.

"By exploiting his weaknesses, that's how."

"As far as I can see, John Anderson's only weakness is that cunt he's been banging for the last couple of years."

Grier nodded.

"Don't tell me you're going to use her against him?"

He wasn't going to tell Bushwick anything, or more precisely, he'd tell him just enough to keep him the hell out of the way. "If it's possible, yes."

"We don't have time—"

"We don't have the luxury of making a mistake," Grier fired back. "We make a mistake and there won't be any more Company. Even the President wouldn't be able to save it from the wrath of Congress."

Bushwick considered that for several moments.

"We have time," Grier said. "Even if he accepts the appointment, he won't live long enough to do us any harm."

"You can guarantee that?"

"I can guarantee that."

Bushwick rolled the chair toward him, and rested his forearms on the top of its back. "How can you do that? Through Safe Deposit?"

"I already told you, everything needed to remove him is in place," Grier said stubbornly.

Bushwick squinted across the desk at him. He was aware that the man wasn't in the least bit awed or afraid of him. And that if Grier wouldn't voluntarily give him the information, he'd never get it out of him. "All right, like I said before, you have the ball and you damn well better play it."

"That's what I get paid to do."

Bushwick's curiosity was aroused; he couldn't let go. "Just tell me yes or no."

Grier knew he wouldn't come anywhere near his plan.

"Nothing more than that. You have a hit team dogging him. Those two guys were rousted on Fifth Avenue a few days ago."

To keep himself from smiling, Grier nodded vigorously, but didn't say either yes or no.

"All right, I have my answer. Tell your men to get it over with and then we can finally bury the bird." He laughed at his own joke.

Grier laughed too, not at Bushwick's joke but at *him*.

Anderson arrived back in New York at seven in the evening, and told his chauffeur to take him to the town house. But when the vehicle emerged from the Queens Midtown Tunnel in Manhattan, he changed his mind, and told the driver to take him instead to the New York Athletic Club. There he could work off the tension he felt by swimming the length of the Olympic-sized swimming pool a dozen times, spending some time in the sauna, and finally ending up with a Swedish massage.

Because of the hour, there were still a great number of Wall Street types around—some of whom he knew, and acknowledged with a nod. Others knew who he was, and couldn't help looking at him with admiration or just plain wonderment.

In his youth, Anderson had been a strong swimmer. He had even done some underwater archaeological work, off Cancun, before his heart attack. Even now, some of that previous strength was evident in the powerful strokes of his arms and the kicking movements of his legs. To push himself more, he did the entire last lap completely underwater. But when he finally surfaced, a momentary tightening on the left side of his chest forced him to pause, and hold onto the ladder, before he climbed out of the pool.

In those few seconds, Anderson experienced a renewed awareness of his proximity to death. A heartbeat, or more accurately, the lack of a heartbeat could dissolve that proximity, and his life would be over. He had adjusted to the possibility of suddenly dying as well as he could. But now that there was the chance that he might be reunited with John Junior, that "adjustment" was less certain.

"John, are you all right?" The voice came from above him.

He tilted his head up.

Downing was there, offering his hand for him to grasp.

"You're positively white as a sheet," Downing said.

Anderson took hold of his hand, and let himself be pulled up, while his feet stepped on each rung of the ladder.

Out of the pool, he said, "Pushed a bit too much. Besides, the day was more exhausting than I thought it was."

Downing nodded sympathetically and led him to a bench by the wall.

Anderson smiled wanly. "Every once in a while the old ticker reminds me who's boss."

"I think you should see a doctor," Downing said.

"It's over. As I said, it was just a momentary

reminder."

"Your color is coming back."

Anderson slapped Downing on his knee. "Thanks for helping me. Getting out of the pool was harder than I thought it would be. But I should be angry as hell with you."

Downing didn't answer. He felt no guilt about having fucked Marylee.

"But somehow, in the present circumstances anger would — if not be inappropriate — would smack of ingratitude, and I am grateful to you."

Downing accepted what Anderson said without comment, and immediately changed the subject. "I phoned your office today to tell you that I have retained an appraiser for your art collection. Mr. David Lee."

Anderson repeated the name, and said, "It sounds familiar."

"Should. He was one of the curators at the Archaeological Museum in Mexico City before he went out on his own."

Anderson said, "He's done some very fine work."

"He'll be ready to start about the time Marylee said she'd be finished with the cataloguing."

"I might have someone helping her," Anderson said.

"I thought she said she could do it alone."

"Having some help wouldn't hurt."

Downing looked at him quizzically.

But Anderson was already on his feet. "If you're free for dinner, why not join me?"

"Yes, I'd like that," Downing answered. "I'd like that very much."

Chapter 14

Anderson spent a restless night. It took hours for him to drift off into an uneasy sleep filled with strangely sequential dreams from which he'd awake. Then, when he'd sleep again, he'd begin dreaming the same dream, picking it up where it seemed he'd left it when he'd awakened.

The dreams were in color, and at the appropriate moments music added another dimension to them. Some segments came directly from his experiences in Korea, and were filled with sights of shattered bodies, blasted landscapes, and faces of men whose names he couldn't remember. Other portions were familial, and would have given him a feeling of well-being if it were not for the presence of his father, who without speaking constantly came between him and everything he loved.

Certain parts of his dreams were erotic, filled with the nude, perfumed bodies of the various women he'd made love to. But only one, Isabel Aroyo, remained standing proudly naked before him, as she had so many times when they had been lovers, after all of the others had vanished. Then there was the last, and by far the most disturbing dream.

A group of climbers is moving slowly up a snowfield.

149

High above them are the castlelike rock pinnacles of the mountain. The sun is very bright and all of the climbers are wearing snow goggles; then suddenly a wind comes, and the snow begins to swirl around them, obscuring them. But he knows they are there, he knows his son is with them. He shouts to them, calling his son's name over and over again. But neither his son nor any of the other climbers hears him. Then there is a rumbling that grows louder and louder, so loud that he is forced to cover his ears. It passes, moving down the snowfield. The wind drops off. It is dead calm, and when he looks to where John Junior is, he sees him, with arms lifted up, entombed under tens of thousands of tons of snow. . . .

"No . . . no, he's alive!" Anderson shouted, wrenching himself free from the vision of his buried son. He sat up and switched on the night-table lamp. His heart raced. He was perspiring. With trembling hands he managed to pour some water from a carafe into a glass, both of which were on the night table. Then, with the aid of the water, he swallowed a nitro pill, which he shook out of a plastic container that was also on the night table.

He lay down again, waiting for the nitro to take effect. His eyes went to the grandfather clock in the far corner of the room, where the light from the night-table lamp barely reached.

"Almost five," he said aloud.

Beginning to feel better, he took two deep breaths, and then sat up and planted his feet on the floor. Within moments, he'd put on his blue silk bathrobe, slippered his feet, and sat down in a rocking chair near one of the two windows that looked out on a small back garden.

"Well, the sweats are gone," he commented to

150

himself, and reaching over to the pull cords, opened the venetian blinds to the pre-dawn's grayness.

The memory of the nightmare was juxtaposed with the memory of Isabel, and for awhile he could dispel neither. It was as if each occupied one of the twin spheres of his brain. But as the grayness lightened, and some of the details of the garden and the rear of the house beyond it became clearer, the sense of the dreams dissolved, leaving him wondering at the beauty of the cherry blossoms, the multicolored pattern of the tulips, and the yellow blaze of the forsythia—a pallet of colors for any artist to appreciate.

Anderson smiled, and rocking gently back and forth, he decided to start painting again.

After all, Churchill did it when he was Prime Minister of England, and President Eisenhower was a primitive whose style was compared to Grandma Moses.

Anderson knew he was far better than either Churchill or Eisenhower.

Suddenly, thinking of Goya's "Des Nudia," he said, "I want to paint Isabel like that. But not reclining. Standing, in a three-quarter turn, with her long russet-colored hair undone and flowing down her back."

Anderson sighed, and lifted himself out of the rocking chair. "With her, I truly experienced a woman." And, as if she were there with him, he said, "I love you, Isabel. I love you." Then he went back to the bed, removed his slippers and robe, and lay down again, hoping to sleep a bit more.

151

Gault met him at the information desk in Grand Central Station. The family resemblance was so strong that he had no difficulty recognizing him.

"Let's walk," the man said.

Gault nodded.

They went out the Lexington Avenue exit. It was lunchtime and the street was very crowded.

"Walk east, down Forty-third," the man said. "Once we cross Third Avenue it won't be so crowded."

Gault answered, "I wouldn't bet on it."

But the crowd did thin out once they were past Third Avenue, allowing them to walk comfortably side by side.

"Tell me about yourself," the man said.

Gault smiled. "You already know everything there is to know."

"I didn't want this meeting. But our mutual friends insisted on it," the man told him.

"Oh, ye of little faith," Gault responded. He was getting strong negative vibes.

"Tell me about your work."

"I'll start in a few days. Cataloguing an art collection. I'll be living inside."

"That will make things very easy for you," the man said. He didn't care for Gault's brashness.

Gault shrugged: it probably would, but he wasn't going to admit it. Not to him.

"Have you accepted the position yet?"

"No. I intend to call later. Five, maybe six o'clock," Gault answered; then to be certain the man understood why he was waiting to call, he said, "A little sweating never hurt anyone, did it?"

The man turned his face toward him, then

quickly faced front. "You're that certain he won't change his mind?"

"Yes, that certain," Gault replied.

They reached First Avenue, and stopped for a red light.

"There's nothing else you want to tell me?" the man asked.

The light went to green, but neither of them moved.

"Nothing," Gault answered.

"Then I see no reason for us to continue to walk together," the man said.

Without speaking another word, Gault turned around and walked back in the direction from which they had come.

The meeting wasn't his idea in the first place.

As the day wore on, Anderson became more and more anxious. During the morning, he'd forced himself to work, jumping every time the phone rang.

His stomach was too knotted to eat lunch, and leaving the dining room, he returned to his office, where he attempted to work again, but couldn't. Finally, he gave up trying, and prowled the house, going from room to room, wondering why he was living in such a big house alone.

At four o'clock, Anderson confronted Jeff and Pat.

"We don't even know where to reach him," he said. "The man could be ill or worse, dead, and we wouldn't know it."

"We can run down to the Village and try to track

153

him down," Pat offered.

Anderson shook his head. "That could take days, maybe weeks."

He walked into Marylee's office.

She looked up at him, aware of his state.

"He'll call," she said, attempting to reassure him.

Anderson nodded. He was tempted to tell her about his meeting with Downing the previous night, but decided against it.

What had happened between her and Downing would probably never happen again, and even if it did, it was no concern of his. That aspect of his relationship with her was over.

He left her office, and returned to his own. He absented himself from the five o'clock cocktail session, claiming he had a headache.

At five to six the phone rang.

Anderson answered it himself.

"Gault here," the voice on the other end announced.

Anderson waited.

"If your offer is still open, I'll take it," Gault said. He heard the sigh of deep relief on the other end, and smiled.

"When can you start?" Anderson asked.

"I'll be there on Friday. I have to settle a few things."

"Friday will be fine."

"See you then, Mr. Anderson," Gault said.

Anderson heard the click on the other end, replaced the phone in its cradle, stood up, and squaring his shoulders, went to join his staff for cocktails.

Now, he had something to celebrate, something to toast.

After Anderson had greeted Gault on Friday, and introduced him to Marylee, whose coolness was immediate, and to Jeff and Pat, both of whom were reserved, he did not attempt to see Gault again until the following Tuesday morning, when he used the intercom to summon him to his office.

"The voice of God," Gault commented as soon as Anderson switched off.

Marylee, at the opposite desk, didn't look up, but she said, "He doesn't like to be kept waiting."

Gault made no effort to move.

Finally, Marylee exploded. "You're just doing that on purpose, aren't you?"

She'd disliked him even before she'd met him. She could have handled all the cataloguing on her own. But now that he was there, she disliked him even more. Not only didn't he know the rudiments of what he should have known—if he was, as he claimed to be, an archaeological student specializing in pre-Columbian civilization—but he was blatantly rude, staring directly at her breasts, and when she was standing, her crotch or ass, until a sudden burst of heat brought color to her face.

Gault answered with a lazy smile, but said nothing.

The moment Anderson had introduced her to him, Gault had known how she felt about him being there. But he didn't give a damn what she felt about him, or about anything else, as long as she kept out of his way.

"Damn you!" she exclaimed, leaping to her feet, leaving her desk, and walking out of the room.

155

"Easy," Gault said. Then he too left the room, crossed the hallway, and knocked softly at the door of Anderson's office.

"Come in," Anderson called out.

Gault entered the room, and closed the door behind him.

"Sorry I couldn't come immediately," Gault explained, "but I was explaining something to Ms. Terrall."

Anderson gestured to the chair at the left side of the desk. "Please sit down."

Gault wore western-style blue jeans, cowboy boots and a white polo shirt. He was more muscular than he'd appeared to be when they had met for lunch and he'd been wearing the loose fitting Indian-style shirt.

"Have you settled in?" Anderson asked.

"Yes."

"And how do you find the work?"

"Easier than a lot of other things I have done," Gault answered.

"I noticed you didn't join us for cocktails yesterday," Anderson said.

Gault shrugged. "I wasn't invited."

"Certainly, you're invited. You're a member of the staff."

"I'll be there from now on."

Anderson nodded. "It's just a way of relieving the tensions of the day, a way of unwinding."

Gault focused his full attention on Anderson, and changing the tone of his voice, carefully modulated it to give it a whisperlike softness. "There are better ways of doing that, Mr. Anderson. Ways that don't require the use of alcohol. Ways that bring sublime peace to the spirit."

Anderson was at a loss for an answer.

Gault smiled. "I'll be there, but naturally I won't imbibe."

"If you would like something special to drink, just tell me."

"Nothing special. Fruit juice of any kind will do. And . . ."

"And what? Tell me whatever it is that you want to tell me," Anderson said.

"I eat mostly vegetables, fruits, and nuts. I've completely lost my taste for animal protein of any kind. If this presents a problem—"

Anderson waved his right hand. "Not to concern yourself. I'll tell the cook myself."

"Thank you, Mr. Anderson."

"Then you haven't been eating in these last few nights?"

Gault shook his head. "It really wasn't a problem. I had people to meet on the outside."

"Speaking of people to meet," Anderson began, "my brother Wally will be here this afternoon and I'd like you to meet him."

"Have you told him that John Junior is alive?"

"I've told no one yet," Anderson said. "Wally is coming here to discuss business. Do you mind meeting him?"

"Not in the least," Gault answered.

"Good. When the time comes I want him to know the real reason for you being here, but for the time being we'll stay with the cover story."

"That's not a problem for me," Gault said.

"Inasmuch as we are talking about people, have you been able to come to terms with that Kevin—

your editor?"

"We have struck an arrangement between us. The rest remains to be seen."

"Arrangement meaning compromise?"

"The basis on which most of our endeavors come to their end." Gault smiled again. "It's imperfection in an imperfect world."

"I'll have to remember that the next time someone asks me to compromise," Anderson replied, smiling too.

There was a momentary lapse of conversation between them that gave Gault the opportunity to savor the luxuriousness of the room, from the shelves of books, all with leather bindings, to the darkly stained wainscot and the paintings. There were also handmade models of the *Constitution*, the *HMS Victory*, the old *Queen Mary* and *Normandie*, the battleship *Missouri*, and the aircraft carrier *Enterprise*. Each of the ships had its own shelf and lighting.

Then Anderson ended the brief interval of silence. "I'd much prefer being called John, or Wes, rather than Mr. Anderson."

Gault shook his head. "I don't think that would be appreciated by the rest of the staff. I'm very much the new kid on the block around here."

Anderson frowned. "Has anyone given you trouble?"

"Nothing that matters, nothing I can't handle." He was thinking specifically of Marylee when he spoke.

"All right, we'll let the informality go for the time being," Anderson said. "But I want you to feel welcome here."

"I do, and I want to thank you for having me

here. It will make my life much easier."

"That was the whole idea," Anderson said. "That and to change your mind about taking me to my son."

Gault nodded, but didn't answer.

There was nothing he could say.

Wally, a short, stocky man with a bald pate and wearing tortoise-shelled bifocals, paced the length of Anderson's office. Then suddenly stopping, he said, "You know, I hope, that you're shirking your responsibilities. You have always run the Foundation, even when you were with the government."

"I want time for myself," Anderson said. "The Foundation takes too much—"

Wally pointed a finger at his brother. "It's not as if you haven't indulged yourself whenever you were so inclined."

Anderson leaned back in his chair. He'd said nothing to his brother about John Junior, or about his coming bid for the Presidency on the Democratic ticket—that alone would probably make Wally run for the hills, or at the very least, accuse him of being a "traitor."

"I've thought it all out," said Anderson. "There are very good administrators—"

"They're not family!"

"You won't listen, will you?"

"Does Augusta know of this?" Wally asked.

"Not yet, but I intend to tell her soon."

Wally took several steps closer to the desk. "Just tell me what's so important that you have to give up the Foundation for it? It's not that Aroyo woman

159

again, is it?"

Anderson controlled a sudden flash of anger.

"Well, is it?"

"If you were anyone else, Wally, I would have asked you to leave," Anderson said in a flat but unmistakably angry voice.

Wally considered that for a moment. "All right, I'm sorry. I was out of line."

"Far out," Anderson said.

Wally was his favorite, and yet they were separated by a distance in their personalities that could be measured in light·years.

"Just give me one logical reason why you are stepping down from the chairmanship of the Foundation."

Anderson hesitated.

Wally misunderstood his brother's silence. "You can't, can you? Not a logical reason, anyway."

Anderson stood up, walked to the other side of the room, and facing Wally, said, "I'm also going to donate my collections to—"

"My God, John, have you gone completely over the edge?" Wally shouted, his face red with frustration. "You're talking about millions of dollars' worth of art."

Anderson remained calm. "Close to forty million, I should guess. I'm preparing it now for an appraiser."

Wally fished a handkerchief out of his inside breast pocket, and wiped the film of perspiration off his forehead. "Have you any more surprises to hand me this afternoon?"

"I'm sorry you don't understand. I really hoped you would."

"Lunacy can only be understood by other lunatics," Wally shot back. Then after a pause, he added, "I could perhaps understand what you intend to do if you were ill. But you're not, are you?"

Anderson shook his head. "No I'm not ill. But it is good of you to ask."

"There must be something—are you planning to go back into government?"

Inclining his head slightly to the right, Anderson smiled bemusedly.

Wally frowned. "You are, aren't you?"

"So the rumors are—"

"It's not the thing for you to do," Wally said earnestly.

"I'm not doing anything—at least, not now. Now I want to get out from under a load—yes, responsibilities—that I have been carrying for most of my life. I want the freedom to choose the way I spend the years left to me." He recrossed the room as he spoke, and stopped a short distance away from his brother. "Wally, I'm truly sorry that I have upset you. Truly sorry."

"I'll adjust, eventually."

Anderson squeezed his brother's shoulder. "You will, and it won't be as bad as you think it will."

"That remains to be seen," Wally answered glumly.

"Come on. The world won't stop turning because of what I do, or don't do. Come on, Wally!"

"All right, all right! Give me some time to get used to it."

"Has it ever occurred to you that we don't have all that much time left, and what we do have should be put to its best use? No, more than that.

161

It should be savored, enjoyed, as though it was a beautiful, enchanting woman, the kind of woman we must have dreamt of possessing when we were young and very, very foolish about life and living."

Wally gave him a quizzical look.

"Just sounding off," Anderson explained.

Wally nodded, then said, "I better be going, John. I have an appointment back at my office at five."

"Before you go, I'd like you to meet the newest member of my staff, Richard Gault. He's here to help Marylee with the cataloguing."

"If you don't mind, John, I'd rather not. Some other time, when I don't have more to think about when I leave than when I arrived."

Anderson shrugged. "Suit yourself. I'll walk you to the door."

"No need to. I know my way. I'll call in a few days."

"Send my best to Clare," Anderson said, returning to his desk and sitting down behind it.

"Yes. My best to Augusta," Wally responded, already closing the door behind him.

"I will do—" But the door snapped shut before Anderson could finish.

Wally started for the front door, passed the office where Marylee worked, and peered in. She wasn't at her desk, but the man at the desk opposite hers looked up.

Their eyes locked, and they exchanged nods.

"Mr. Anderson!"

Wally recognized Marylee's voice. He turned and

162

smiled at her. He marveled that such a young beautiful woman would find his brother so physically attractive that she'd become his mistress.

"It's a pleasure to see you again, Marylee," he said, smiling at her. She was holding a mug of steaming hot chocolate crowned with a thick swirl of whip cream.

She realized he was looking at the mug. "I needed a pick-me-up, and this is it."

He laughed. "And why not. To tell the truth, every once in a while, I give in too. My weakness is ice cream."

"Mine too, sometimes."

They laughed together.

Then Wally said, "Marylee, would you mind coming to the door with me?"

She raised her eyebrows.

There was never any doubt in her mind that Wally, despite his outward look of propriety, had imagined himself erotically involved with her. Perhaps John had told him that they were no longer sleeping together, and he was going to make his move.

"I'd appreciate it," he said.

Marylee glanced into the office.

Gault suddenly looked up, smirked, and just as quickly returned his gaze to the paper on the desk.

Furious, she pretended not to have seen him, and nodded to Wally.

"I'll go straight to the point," Wally said, even before they reached the door. "I'm worried about my brother."

She wasn't prepared for that.

"Has he been acting strange lately?"

They stopped at the door.

"What I mean," Wally said, attempting to clarify the question, "has he done, or said anything *outré*—something that would be completely out of character?"

Marylee shook her head. "I can't think of anything."

He wondered if she knew more than she was letting on. Conceivably, during pillow talk between her and John, he might have told her his plans to leave the Foundation and his plans about his art collections.

Then suddenly he had a vision of her naked in bed, with her long blond hair flowing over the pillow. But as quickly as it occurred, he expunged it from his mind.

"I'm sure John is fine," she said.

"You would know if he wasn't, wouldn't you?" he asked, alluding to their sexual intimacy.

She understood, and smiled coyly. "There's nothing wrong with John."

"I'm glad to hear that. Sometimes, when something happens to a man—well, you know what I mean." He suddenly felt embarrassed, and hunted for the right words.

She let him struggle.

"Other things begin to fall apart when a man no longer can be a man."

The words were spoken almost as if he were challenging her.

"That's not his problem, or mine," she answered, finally lifting the mug of hot chocolate to her lips. She'd no intentions of telling him that she and Anderson were no longer sleeping together.

Wally appraised her sexually. "I didn't think so." But he might have added, "not with you for a partner." "If you do happen to notice — a change, or anything unusual, will you notify me?"

"Certainly I will."

Wally put his hand on the knob, twisted it, and pulled the door open. "Thank you, Marylee."

She nodded.

Wally started out.

"There is one thing, now that I think of it," Marylee said.

Wally stopped and faced her. "And what's that?"

"He hired another cataloguer, Richard Gault."

"That, my dear, was absolutely necessary," Wally said. "Absolutely necessary," he repeated.

Marylee was too surprised to respond.

Chapter 15

Gault considered the weekend a drag. But on Saturday the weather was warm and sunny, allowing him to spend several hours in the park during the day working on his tan. And Saturday night, before he went down to the Village to meet two friends, he walked the few blocks east to the building where Marylee lived.

Contrary to what he'd been told, she wasn't sleeping with Anderson. She left every evening after cocktails and returned the following morning, stopping in the kitchen for breakfast about the time he was usually finishing his. But this could be a recent development, within the last week or so, and his information dated back at least a month.

Gault even checked to see if her last name, Terrall, was on the directory. It was, and her apartment number, 6J, was next to it. For a moment, he half considered inviting her to join him, but decided against it.

He had her off balance, and he intended to keep her that way.

At three o'clock in the morning, Gault was walking west on St. Mark's Place in the East Village. Less than fifteen minutes before he'd left a party that would probably continue through most of Sunday.

He and a china-doll-like woman, with long raven

hair and cat's eyes, had had a fucking good time on one of the twin beds in the bedroom, where two other couples were also doing a lot of heavy action.

He hadn't been in a situation like that since . . . He sensed someone behind him, but continued to walk, neither quickening his pace nor slowing to give them any indication he knew they were there.

He had seen two guys sitting in the doorway of a house with one of those high stoops, a few houses in from the corner.

Probably, they had dogged him for most of the block.

He was almost at Third Avenue.

"Hey, dude?"

The accent was New York.

"Maybe the dude can't hear so good," a second male said.

There wasn't any other way.

Gault stopped, and faced the two men, both white.

One wore a red headband, a denim shirt, and dirty white jeans. The other's head was shaved. He wore an olive green T-shirt under a fatigue jacket, and black slacks without a belt. Both were bearded.

"No problem, mister, just give us your wallet and your watch and we'll be on our way," the one with the red headband said.

"No problem," Gault repeated, then he added, "for me. But you fucks have a real problem. You're going to have to take them."

He kicked the skinhead in the groin, then threw a quick chop at the other one's nose. The bone crunched under the blow, and blood suddenly gushed from it.

"Holy shit!" the man screamed, dropping to his knees.

Gault slammed his foot into the skinhead's stomach.

Groaning, the man twisted away in agony.

He went for the one with the red band around his head.

"Told you you'd have a fucking problem," Gault said, grabbing him by his hair, pulling his head back.

The man flailed his arms.

Gault wrenched his head farther back.

"You're breaking my neck!" the man screamed. "You're —"

Gault backhanded him across the mouth. "You play fucking rough. Now I play rough."

Suddenly a shrieking siren came up the street.

Gault let go of the man.

The blue and white, with its red lights flashing, jumped the sidewalk and came to a squealing halt.

Two uniforms came out of the car, with guns drawn.

Gault pointed to the two men on the sidewalk. "My work," he said. "Both of them need a doctor."

"They try to take you?" the stockier uniform asked. His partner wore glasses. Both were in their thirties.

"Failed," Gault said, realizing he was breathing hard.

"Punks," the cop with glasses said. "I busted them a couple of weeks ago for snatching a purse."

"You want to press charges?" the stocky cop asked, looking at Gault.

"Get them to the hospital, and tell the doctor they ran into a truck."

"It's just routine, but do you have any ID?"

Gault took out his wallet, fished out an ID card, and passed it to one of the uniforms. "I don't want to become involved. I'm here on business."

The cop passed the card to his partner, who handed it back to Gault. "We'll take care of these two pieces of garbage," he said.

"Thanks," Gault said, putting the ID card into the wallet and then replacing the wallet in his back trouser pocket.

"You shits are lucky he left you alive," one of the cops commented.

"See you guys," Gault said, and walked away.

The last thing he needed would be to become involved with the police and appear in court. That would blow everything.

When Gault returned to the town house, he found the door to Anderson's office open. Anderson, wearing a blue silk dressing gown and white scarf, was at his desk.

Gault tried to pass the open door without Anderson noticing, but Anderson called out, "Couldn't sleep."

Gault stopped and faced the open door. He wasn't in the mood for socializing.

The punks he'd decked had ruined the good feeling he'd had. Now all he wanted to do was go to sleep. Sometime late in the afternoon he was going to visit his parents.

Anderson motioned him in. "I hope you had an enjoyable evening—or should I say night."

Gault approached the desk. Even in the glow of the desk lamp, Anderson looked pale.

"I was with some Indian friends," Gault said. "I find I'm more comfortable with them than with— well, some of the people I used to run with, as the expression goes."

170

"Sit down and chat," Anderson said. "That's if you don't mind chatting at a quarter to four in the morning."

Gault dropped into the chair next to the desk.

"I wanted my brother Wally to meet you," Anderson said. "He was here Friday afternoon."

"I saw him when he left," Gault commented.

"He was running late, otherwise I would have introduced the two of you." He smiled. "I guess he was a bit rocked by our conversation. Wally, like most people, resists change."

Gault nodded. "Understanding change, or the cycles of change, is fundamental to becoming one with the universe. The universe is constantly changing."

Anderson studied him, not sure whether to take him seriously.

"The great wheel of life never changes, though our fortunes on it are ever changing."

"I am not a mystic," Anderson admitted. "I'm a realist, a person who has learned that life is a series of compromises."

"I can't argue against your experience," Gault said. "But I also have had certain experiences—one, of course, was having the good fortune to meet your son."

"Tell me about him. Really, all I know is that he is alive."

Gault shifted in the chair. This wasn't the kind of conversation he wanted to have, if he had to have a conversation. He was tired, and afraid of making a mistake.

"He could have been anything he set his mind to," Anderson said. "Anything."

"He is what he wants to be, John." Gault purposefully used Anderson's given name to give himself an

171

equality that their differences in age would not permit. "He is a pure, burning spirit who is loved and respected by those whom he teaches and who teach him."

Anderson was too choked up to answer.

"He has found the peace and tranquility that elude most of us," Gault said, unaware that he was rubbing the fingers of his right hand until Anderson reached over and took hold of it.

"Your hand is swollen. Looks like you might have banged it against something."

Gault eased his hand free. "I don't remember doing anything like that."

"Those fingers are going to be stiff in the morning."

"I'll soak it in hot water before I go to sleep." He stood up.

Anderson did the same. "I might as well go too. Maybe I can sleep for a couple of hours. Sometimes, I find I get the best sleep, a really deep sleep, just before dawn, and for a couple hours afterwards."

Gault agreed with him, then said, "But it's hard to get out of bed."

They were out in the hallway, and Anderson closed and locked the door to his office. "By the way, if you need a car for any reason, go over to the rental agency on Second Avenue. It's up the street, a few blocks from here. Take whatever kind of car you want, and charge it to my account."

"That's very kind of you, John," Gault said as they climbed the steps together. "I just might do that tomorrow. I'm going into Brooklyn to see my parents and have dinner with them."

Anderson smiled broadly. "Good. Excellent! Get a big car, a Caddy or a Continental, and take them for a ride in it."

Gault laughed.

They reached the second floor, where Anderson's room was located, and stopped.

"Do it, Richard," Anderson placed his hand on Gault's shoulder. "They'd enjoy it. Hell, I know I would, if John Junior would make the same offer to me. I really would."

"Yes, I'll do it," Gault answered earnestly, though a moment before, when Anderson had first mentioned it, he'd instantly rejected the idea. But there was something about the way Anderson spoke that made him change his mind.

"Good night," Anderson said.

Gault answered in kind, and continued up the steps.

For him the image of Anderson as the American Eagle was becoming transformed into Anderson the grieving father—a kind of male Pietà.

Anderson awoke just before noon, and ate break-fast alone at the kitchen table, with the cook serving him. Then he went out for an hour walk in the park accompanied by his weekend bodyguards. He much preferred the park on weekdays, when it was left to people like himself and young children accompanied by their mothers or nannies. Now, it was crowding up with tens of thousands of people all hungry to possess a piece of green grass the size of a blanket, and enjoy the cool shade offered by a tree's umbrella of leaves, or feel the heat of the sun on their bare skin. More than the shouting children, or even those families who violated the law and barbecued their meats using strong spices that overwhelmed the scent of the grass, he resented being assailed by the blasting, nerve-jarring music from the "boom boxes." Everything else he saw or smelled was part of the city's remarkable kaleidoscope, and he viewed it with the eyes of a painter, wondering if there would be enough time left in his life to sketch and paint it.

He returned to the town house just as Gault was closing the front door behind him.

"How's the hand?" Anderson asked.

The two of them were standing on the top step. One of the bodyguards was on the street level, while the other unlocked the front door and was waiting for Anderson to enter the house.

Gault flexed his fingers. "A bit stiff, but nothing serious."

"On your way to Brooklyn?" Anderson asked, almost hoping he would be invited to join him.

Gault could almost read the man's thoughts.

"Yes," he answered, and was tempted to invite him along. But an instant image of John Anderson with his mother and father was so far out, he had to force himself not to smile. Despite his loneliness, John Anderson was still John Anderson.

Gault started down the steps.

"Enjoy the day," Anderson called.

Gault waved, but neither answered nor looked back, knowing that if he had done one or the other, he would have taken the bull by its horns and invited him.

Anderson went inside, and directly to his study, intending to read the *New York Times*. He sat down with the news section, and scanned the front page.

None of the stories interested him.

He went through a few more pages, and finally put the newspaper down.

"Sunday, Bloody Sunday," he said aloud, remembering the title of a British film that had played in the late sixties—or was it in the early seventies?

Hell, it didn't matter when it had played. It had said everything there was to say about Sunday.

The only time he'd ever enjoyed Sundays was when he'd spent them with Isabel.

They'd stay in bed, sometimes making love, and sometimes just dozing in each others arms. Then they'd have a leisurely brunch, and spend the rest of the day—

"Christ, there's no reason for us not to see each other!"

He picked up the phone, started to dial Isabel's number, and then put the phone down. He hadn't spoken to her in over a year.

Anderson shook his head.

She would be the most logical person for him to tell about John Junior, even before he told Augusta.

He started to dial again.

Three rings later, Isabel was on the phone, speaking to him as if they spoke to each other every day, while his heart was racing.

"I'd very much like to see you," he finally told her.

"And I would like to see you, John," she answered. "Why don't you come over about six. I'll cook dinner for you."

"I'll be there."

"John?"

"Yes."

"I'm glad you called," Isabel said.

"So am I," Anderson answered, and waited to hear the click on the other end before he put the phone down.

Now that he had something to look forward to, Anderson was able to sit down and read the *Times*.

Gault chose an emerald green Lincoln to drive, and parked it across the street from the six-story building on Glenwood Road where his parents lived.

Welcomed with a kiss and hug by his mother, a birdlike woman with graying brown hair, he was greeted by his father with a handshake.

"I saw you park that boat from the window," his father commented, using the slang word for car from the nineteen-twenties. But his father was a throwback, a big burly Irishman who viewed everything from the viewpoint of the Depression. "You own it?"

Richard laughed. He'd expected the question. "Rented, Pa."

The three of them moved out of the foyer into the living room, and sat down. Richard on a high-back chair, with a yellow lace doily on the back and lace antimacassars on the arms; his father on the brown upholstered easy chair; and his mother in the middle of the couch under a very large painting on black velvet of a beach and a burning red sunset.

"Ethel is coming too," his mother said.

Ethel was his sister, older than him by five years, and married to Arthur, a thirty-five-year-old Peter Pan.

"What's her husband doing now?" Gault asked.

"Teaching physical education in a high school," his mother answered.

"And Ethel?"

"Still with the same sportswear company. But she makes very good money, very good."

Gault nodded.

Then his mother said, "There were two men here asking questions about you."

176

"When?"

"When would you say they were here?" she asked, looking at her husband.

"About ten days ago."

"They said they were government men," she told him.

Gault figured Anderson would have had him checked out, and he described Pat and Jeff.

"You know them?" his father asked.

"Yes. It's nothing to worry about."

"I told him you were away in India for almost a year. Just like you told me to," his mother said.

"You weren't there for more than a couple of months. Why the cock-and-bull story about being over there for a year?" his father asked.

Gault smiled. "It's part of a game."

"Your mom told me you're working for this guy John Anderson," his father said.

"I'm helping to catalog his art collection."

"What do you know about art?"

"Nothing, Pa, but that's part of the game too."

"This guy Anderson, is he one of the players in this game of yours?"

"He's the main player," Gault answered.

His father seemed satisfied, and said, "When Ethel and Byron are here, don't get involved in any kind of a conversation that will lead to an argument."

"Not to worry, Pa," Gault told him. "I'll let them say whatever dumb thing they want to without calling either of them a horse's ass."

This time his father just glared at him.

Though he could smell it—and for as long as he could remember Sunday dinner had always been the same: chicken fricassee, followed by chicken soup, and finally roast chicken—Gault asked, "What's for

177

dinner, Mom?"

"What we always have for Sunday dinner," his father said, adding as he always had in the past, "and be damn glad you have that to eat. There are millions who have nothing."

Gault stood up and looked down at the Lincoln.

He'd rather be in it, tooling along some open stretch of highway, than be where he was. But life's a bitch, especially when you first learn that you don't get to choose the family into which you are born. Even after you've learned it, and lived with it all of your life, it's still a bitch.

He turned into the room. "After dinner, we'll all go for a ride."

"Where?" his father asked.

"You name it, and we'll go."

"Take your mother. I'll stay home and watch the game."

Gault could feel the anger begin to build in him. "Just think about it, Pa. That's all for now, just think about it."

"I'll think about it."

Gault was about to tell him to forget it when the downstairs bell rang.

That had to be his sister and her husband.

"I'll open the door," he said, crossing the room.

At that moment he would have crawled across the room. He would have done anything to avoid having to speak to his father.

The two of them stood on the terrace. A cool breeze blew off the Hudson River, and thirty floors down and a short distance away was Lincoln Center.

Just looking at Isabel gave Anderson enormous

178

pleasure.

She was leaning against the side of the building, and the breeze caught her red hair, making it stream out behind her like some unfurled, silken ensign. She was a woman of middling height, with a dancer's legs, now covered by a pair of gray slacks, and a dancer's body, except for her breasts, which were half the size of grapefruits and fitted so perfectly into his hand. Her face was speckled with freckles, more on the bridge of her nose and under her eyes, which were sparkling blue in the kind of sunlight that drenched the terrace.

He reached over and took hold of her hand. "Did I ever tell you how beautiful you are?"

She smiled. "Many times, Wes."

She was the only person who ever called him Wes. The memory made him smile.

It was the third time they made love. She was sucking his cock, and he was tonguing her cunt, when suddenly she stopped, raised her head, and said, "I'm going to call you Wes. Andrew is too formal, and Andy too ordinary."

He'd had no objection then, and none now.

"What are you laughing at?" she asked.

He told her.

A slight color came into her face, and flowed down her neck.

"Those were heady times," she said softly.

He kissed the back of her hand.

With her free hand, she gently touched his face, and suggested they go inside.

Anderson opened the sliding glass door, followed her into the living room, and easing the door closed behind him, said, "I'm resigning from the Foundation."

179

Isabel stopped, and faced him. "Is that what you wanted to talk about?"

Anderson sat down on the couch. "No—well, not exactly."

She too sat down on the couch, leaving a cushion width between them.

"I've already started making the preparations to donate my art collections."

Isabel laced her long fingers, and asked, "Have you told Augusta?"

He shook his head. "Wally knows."

"How did he take it?"

She knew Wally—she actually knew the whole family—but she knew Wally the best, and for reasons unknown to Anderson, she'd never trusted him.

"As you can imagine," he answered.

"I can imagine."

"But if your decisions are firm, why discuss them with me?" she asked.

Anderson rubbed his hand across his jaw, stood up, and went to the sliding glass door, where he stood looking at, though not really seeing, the high rises on the New Jersey side of the Hudson. Miles behind them was the dark smudge of the Watchung Mountains, where John Junior had first begun to climb.

She came alongside him, took his hand, and gently pressed herself against him, knowing he'd feel the softness of her breasts.

"What is it, Wes?" she asked softly, afraid that something out of his political past now threatened him. She knew more about his past activities than she ever let on.

He said without looking at her, "John Junior is alive."

180

"Oh, my God!"

He faced her, and nodded.

She let go of him. "Are you sure, Wes? This time are you sure?"

He moved back to the couch, and she followed him.

"You've been disappointed in the past," she said.

"Not too long ago I received a letter from a young man named Richard Gault, who spent time with him at a lamasery somewhere north of Katmandu. I had Gault checked out, and he was where he says he was."

He continued to tell her everything he knew about Gault, including that he'd hired Gault to help Marylee with the cataloguing.

Isabel listened without interrupting him, and when he was finished, she offered him a drink. "I know I can use one."

"A spritzer will do fine."

She needed something stronger, and poured better than two fingers of Chivas in a shot glass for herself.

"To John Junior," she toasted.

Anderson stood up.

"To my son," he said passionately.

"Does Wally know?" she asked, already divining Anderson's intentions.

"Neither does Augusta, not yet anyway," he said.

She gestured back to the couch. "Did John Junior ask to see you? I mean, did he ask that you come to him?"

"No. He only said that he loved me, and understood."

She was on her feet, and went as far as the sliding glass door, but did not turn around.

"What's wrong?" he asked.

181

She didn't answer, but she could see his reflection in front of her in the glass. It was as if the entire living room was suspended outside the building.

He set his glass down on the coffee table, and came up behind her.

"You're going to try and convince this Gault person to take you, aren't you?"

"Yes."

"Has it occurred to you that you might be making a mistake?" she asked.

"How could—"

"Wes, if he really wanted to see you, don't you think he would have asked you to come?"

"I think—"

"Wes, he went on the crazy mountain-climbing trip to get away from you, to spite you . . . to hurt you, the way you hurt him."

A sudden chill passed through Anderson, making him shudder. He stepped back.

"I never hurt him," he mumbled.

She turned around, and nodding very slowly, said, "You did, Wes. We did."

He clenched his jaws together, and when he finally unstuck them, he answered, "He said he understood."

"Wes, he found us in bed. You were on top of me, and I was moaning."

Anderson backed away.

"He was there, in the doorway, looking at us."

"We were never sure it was him. Never!"

She nodded. "It was him, Wes. You know it and I know it."

Anderson threw his hands above his head. Then lowering them, he retreated to the couch and sat down again, suddenly overcome by a wave of exhaustion.

"I had almost forgotten about that," he admitted, his voice almost a whisper.

She sat down on the couch too, but this time she was next to him. "I never have. It's one of the few things that make me feel guilty. Not because I was committing adultery, or that you were—I never felt any guilt about that. I knew then and I still know that we were good for each other. What I feel guilty about has to do with what I—we—took away from John Junior without being able to give him something back. You know what that was, don't you?"

"His trust in me," Anderson whispered.

Isabel sighed deeply, and rested her head against Anderson's chest.

He put his arms around her.

"That was why I ended our relationship after he was reported lost, then dead. I couldn't bear the pleasure you gave me and the guilt I felt each time we made love. I knew the guilt would never leave me—"

"So you gave me up."

"Yes."

Anderson held her fiercely to him.

She had come into his life like spring moving across the land, reviving everything in its path. She'd given him back his youth, his dreams of love, but more important than anything else, she'd given him herself, completely, without reservation.

"I just don't want you to be hurt, anymore than you already have been," she said, without moving.

"I have to see him, now more than ever."

"Yes, I know that. When will you go?"

"Soon, I hope," Anderson answered.

"Wes, will you hold me?"

He nuzzled the top of her head.

"Make love to me," Isabel whispered.

He kissed the back of her neck. "I'm not the man I used to be," he told her.

She raised her face to his. "Nor I the woman, but I think we'll be right for each other."

"I think so," he answered, kissing her on the lips, while his hand moved gently over her breasts.

Chapter 16

Isabel smiled at the ceiling. Anderson hadn't spent the entire night with her, but he had spent enough of it for her to still be aware of his presence, and to know that they still loved each other.

"God, it's so very good to be loved!" she declared aloud, and then with her inner voice she added, "It's truly new life." And she laughed out loud.

She was almost tempted to phone him, but as she reached for the telephone, she saw the digital clock. It was only six-thirty.

Much too early to phone him. Though she knew from past experience with him that he was a very early riser, she still doubted that he'd be awake.

"Eight o'clock would be more reasonable," she said. By then she was sure he'd be at his desk.

She puffed up the pillow, and settled down on it with her hands behind her head, hoping to sleep a while longer. But she began to think about Gault.

For a young man, from the way Wes had described him to her, he seemed like an old man, a very wise old man at that.

"Too wise, if you ask me," she said aloud, and leaving the bed, she slipped on a white silk dressing gown, padded into the kitchen, and began to measure out drip-ground coffee into an old-fashioned coffee pot.

"And too damn self-effacing for my tastes."

She put water in a kettle, and put the kettle on the stove, over a high flame. Then she sat down to wait for the water to boil.

"Yuppies are too damn taken with themselves to really be wise, let alone self-effacing, and Gault is certainly in the yuppy age group."

Suddenly Isabel frowned, and shook her head. "Wes can't see the damn forest for the trees," she declared aloud. "More like doesn't want to, when it comes to John Junior."

She left the chair, padded to the door of the apartment, and opened it. Picking up the Monday edition of the *New York Times,* she returned to the chair in the kitchen.

On the bottom of the third page there was an article, datelined Washington, D.C., with the headline: *John Wesley Anderson the Most Likely Choice for CIA Ombudsman.* The article said that rumors emanating from the White House pointed to Anderson as the front-runner. It also gave a brief summary of Anderson's government service, and then stated, "Insiders at the CIA have mixed reactions over the possibility of Anderson's appointment."

The kettle began to whistle.

She folded the paper, went to the stove, shut the gas off, and then poured sufficient water to make four cups of coffee into the top section of the coffee pot. She placed the cover on it and put the pot on a burner, over a very low flame.

She returned to the table, but did not resume reading the *Times*. The story disturbed her on two counts: Wes had never mentioned the possibility to her—if he had, despite her feelings for him, they would not have wound up in bed; and secondly, the moment he had any visible connection with the CIA, he would become a target for the assassination squads sent by governments from the right and the left in Central and South America.

The phone rang.

She answered it with a sharp, "Yes, who is it?" At the same time she looked at the kitchen clock, on the wall opposite the stove. It was seven-fifteen.

"You must have read the story in the *Times*," Anderson said.

"Yes."

He laughed. "And you're angry as hell, right?"

"Absolutely seething."

"You're wasting precious energy," he told her. "I'm not after that job."

"What are you after, Wes?"

"You."

"Be serious."

"I am. I want you, Isabel, but we'll talk about that later. I want to see my son, and then other things will fall into place."

"What other things?" she asked.

"I'll tell you, but not now, not on the phone. Will you have dinner with me tonight?"

"I can't. I have to be at a reception. Tomorrow night?"

"Yes. I'll be by about eight."

"See you then."

"I love you, Isabel."

"I love you too," she answered, and with a smile, she put the phone down.

She would have hugged herself, and twirled around once or twice with joy, if she hadn't thought herself too old for such girlish expressions of happiness.

She poured coffee for herself, and started to drink it, standing up.

Gault still bothered her. She wasn't able to resolve the image of him that Wes had described with what she knew about men and women in his age group.

"Even if he has spent a year in India and, according to him, a couple of months with John Junior in a lamasery, he's too different to be real. And if he's not real, what is he?"

She suddenly became agitated. "Who sent him, and why?"

Isabel put her coffee mug down, went back to the phone, and quickly punched out the seven digits of a phone number.

From her previous connections with various revolutionary groups, she still had sources of information that even the CIA would covet, if they knew of their existence.

It took a half a dozen rings before a man answered, *"Si,* who is it?"

Ignoring the question, Isabel said, speaking in Spanish, "I need your help, Jose."

He immediately recognized her voice, and answered in Spanish. "Now, at this hour in the morning?"

"Can you meet me later, say two o'clock in the afternoon?"

"Yes. Where?"

She thought for a moment, and looking toward the window, she saw the sun was shining. "The Staten Island Ferry terminal. We'll take a ferryboat ride. Two o'clock, at the top of the escalators."

"I'll be there."

"Thank you," Isabel said.

"For you, anything, anytime, anyplace," Jose said.

Isabel waited to hear the click on the other end before she put the phone down.

Jose Yaglias was a Mexican national, employed by the Mexican government to increase tourism between his country and the United States. But clandestinely he also acted as a conduit for information coming from revolutionary groups in Central America.

Anderson was ebullient; he had the door to his office open, and could be heard whistling as he read the morning's mail.

Neither Marylee, Pat, nor Jeff remembered him ever doing that.

"Seems like Mr. Anderson is in very good spirits this morning," Gault said, directing his comment at Marylee, who appeared to be definitely out of sorts.

"Yes, it does," she answered curtly.

Gault said nothing, allowing the silence to build over their desks, like some gigantic summer thunderhead.

Marylee bit her lip.

Even before Anderson had "discarded" her, she had started therapy with Doctor Hasse in an effort to become "a more complete person." But now, the circumstances in which she found herself had incredibly diminished her.

Suddenly, Anderson was at the door. "Richard, I'm for a walk. What about you?"

Marylee's head bobbed up.

Gault smiled at Anderson. "The best offer I had all morning," he said, turning his smile on Marylee, who looked daggers at him.

Anderson said to Marylee, "I have a call into my lawyer, Max Grenville. Tell him that Wednesday will be fine. But it will be all day."

"Certainly."

He looked questioningly at her, then at Gault. Gault shrugged.

"Is anything wrong, Marylee?" Anderson asked.

She managed a small smile. "I'm just very tired," she told him.

"Well, take a few days off. The cataloguing doesn't have to follow a precise time schedule. Take a long weekend, this Friday and the following Monday and Tuesday. I'll talk to you about it later." His face turned toward Gault. "Ready?"

"Ready."

Gault was already on his feet, and moved out from behind the desk.

Pat and Jeff fell in behind them, and in moments the four of them—Jeff in front, Pat bringing up the rear, and Anderson and Gault, together, between them—were on the street, headed toward Fifth Avenue.

"A champagne day!" Anderson exclaimed as they entered the park. "New York is a very special place on a day like this."

"You won't get any disagreement from me on that point," Gault answered.

"The usual way, boss?" Jeff asked. He was a dozen paces in front of them.

"Sure, why not."

Not too far along the path they reached a fork,

and turned onto the arm that connected with a pathway running south, parallel to Fifth Avenue, where the traffic also moved south.

"I consider this my front and rear lawn," Anderson said with a chuckle. "But not on Sunday, when the boom boxes are out. Then I can't be quite so liberal."

"No boomers around today, only mothers and nannies with babies."

"I can remember this park when you could walk through it anytime at night and be perfectly safe."

Gault shook his head. "That was way before I was born."

Anderson agreed, and said, "I don't wallow in nostalgia. Those times were very hard for tens of millions of peoples. But there were certain things— well, you could drink cream off the top of the milk, and the milk came in bottles, not in waxed containers that hold a liquid whose only resemblance to milk is in its color."

Gault wasn't sure what his reaction should be, so he made a few wordless sounds that he hoped Anderson would accept. He didn't give a rat's ass which way milk was packaged, or what it had tasted like years before. He only knew what it tasted like now.

"I'd have to say the pace was less frenetic then, and there's something to say for that."

"I think that's why I love Nepal so much," Gault said, giving his voice a soft tone. "There everything moves not much faster than our pace now. And in the lamasery, movement follows an even slower pace, tuned to the larger rhythms of the universe and the teachings of Buddha."

It was his turn to speak, and Gault made the

191

most of it, giving Anderson some of the basic concepts of Buddhism. "It's not a religion so much as it is a way of life, a philosophy that allows you to come to terms with yourself, and then go outward to the universe."

"Yes, I understand that. But I have to admit that I have little appreciation for its mysticism, or for that matter the mysticism associated with Christianity. But I respect those who do."

Almost without Gault realizing it, they reached the entrance to the Children's Zoo, turned around, and began to retrace their steps.

"Tomorrow night, I will be dining with a very good friend, Richard, and I'd very much like you to join us," Anderson said. "That is, of course, if you're free?"

"I have nothing planned."

"Then you'll come?"

Gault was sure the other person was Anderson's wife, Augusta. "Yes. But I would like to know—"

"Yes, certainly you'd like to know who the other person is," Anderson said. "Mrs. Isabel Aroyo. She's the former wife of the Mexican Ambassador. I'm sure you have seen her name in the newspapers from time to time. She's very active in the arts, and politically."

Anderson spoke about Isabel with pride—no, with obvious love.

"I consider it an honor to join you and Mrs. Aroyo," Gault responded.

Anderson said, "Honor has such a formal ring. I'd rather it be a pleasure."

"A pleasure then."

Anderson smiled, and said, "This time I hope you

won't object too much if we dine in a less off-beat restaurant. If you wish, I can have Marylee phone ahead and tell the chef to prepare your food in any way you choose."

The request would send Marylee into orbit. There were other and better ways of doing that, some of them even enjoyable.

"No. No. That's very considerate, John, but not really necessary. I'm back in Rome, so to speak, and must do as the Romans do. I have already begun to make the adjustment."

"It will be someplace that serves nouvelle cuisine. That is light and can be very tasty."

They were approaching the huge outcropping of rock that rose steeply some distance in from the path and sloped down toward Fifth Avenue.

Anderson slowed, and gesturing toward the dark gray rock, said, "John Junior climbed that when he was a boy of six, maybe seven. I think—"

Gault saw the little girl walk in front of them; her mother, wearing a tight gray jersey, was sitting on the bench. He wasn't the least bit interested where John Junior had climbed.

Had he been alone, he would have sat down next to the woman and tried to get something going between them. He had been successful with young mothers on several different occasions.

His eyes moved from the woman to the rock.

The bluish glint of gun metal registered.

"Get down!" Gault shouted.

Two shots exploded.

Anderson ran forward, and scooping up the child, dropped flat on his stomach, covering her with his body.

The mother was screaming.

"Stay down," Anderson shouted. "For the love of God, stay down!"

Gault spun around.

Two more shots were fired.

Pat staggered, and fell backward.

In a crouch, Jeff moved toward the rock.

Gault crawled to where Pat lay.

"Cover me," Jeff shouted. "Cover me."

Four shots exploded in rapid succession. Two of the bullets ricocheted off the pathway.

Gault pulled Pat's .357 from his hand, rolled over, and from a prone position saw the top of a head just above the rock and fired.

A man leaped up; then toppled over.

Jeff was working his way up the left side.

Suddenly the air was full of screaming sirens. Two blue and whites came toward them from opposite directions, and four mounted cops galloped down the slope on the other side of the path.

"Hold your fire!" a voice shouted from on top of the rocks. "Hold your fire!"

Two uniforms appeared at the top of the outcropping, and waved their arms.

Gault scrambled to his feet, and went back to Pat.

There was blood all over the man's shirt.

He hunkered down beside him, and felt for a pulse.

There wasn't any.

He stood up.

The cops swarmed around Anderson, who handed the child to its hysterical mother.

The child was screaming now.

Jeff scrambled down the rocks, and knelt down

next to his dead partner.

Anderson, with the woman holding her child, and the cops in tow, came to where Gault was.

Jeff moved Pat's eyelids down, and stood up.

"I'm sorry," Anderson said.

"I think it's better if I tell his wife," Jeff said.

"Do whatever you think is best," Anderson said. Then he turned to Gault. "That was quick thinking, Richard."

Gault flushed. He was still holding Pat's .357.

A black car, with a red light flashing on its roof, raced to where they were and came to a screeching halt. Four plainclothesmen got out.

"Better give me that," Jeff said, taking the weapon from Gault.

Anderson knew one of the men — he was the Police Commissioner — and told him that two men had been involved in the shooting.

"One is dead. The other got away."

"You must have nailed one," Jeff said, looking at Gault.

"A lucky shot."

"Didn't look lucky to me. Looked like you knew what you were doing."

Gault shrugged. He was anxious to leave the place. But he had to give his version of what had happened to one of the cops, and then wait until Anderson, Jeff, and the woman, whose name was Marie Tosti, gave their statements — and by that time the TV and newspaper reporters were there.

While the reporters and TV people were attempting to get their stories, Pat's body was placed in an ambulance to be taken to Bellevue for an autopsy.

Marie stood before the TV cameras. Holding her

195

daughter, she said, "Mr. Anderson saved my daughter's life. He's a very brave man to have done what he did." And she explained how Anderson had scooped up the child and then lay flat on the ground, covering her with his body.

Anderson went before the cameras. Visibly shaken, he spoke very slowly. "I owe my life to quick action of Messrs. Jeff Hunter, Richard Gault, and Pat Ryan, who was shot and killed."

"Do you know who sent the assassins?" a reporter asked.

Anderson shook his head. "Like every man who has held sensitive posts, I am sure I have made enemies, but none who would want to kill me."

"Mr. Anderson, will this incident have any effect on your decision to accept or reject the President's offer—"

"I have nothing to say about that matter," Anderson answered. "And now, please excuse me." And he stepped away from the cameras.

The reporters tried to buttonhole Jeff, and he completely ignored them.

Gault fell in alongside Anderson, and refused to either step before the TV cameras or speak to any of the reporters.

The Police Commissioner detailed the driver of a blue and white to take Anderson, Gault, and Jeff back to the town house, and another to drive Marie Tosti and child to where they lived, on East Seventy-eighth Street and Lexington Avenue.

"I'll go straight to Pat's house," Jeff said, once they were in the car.

"Tell his wife not to worry about anything," Anderson said. "Tell her—" He faltered. "Pat was a real talent. I mean a genuine primitive." He stopped again to clear his throat. "Tell her that she doesn't have to worry about money. I'll take care of that."

"Thanks, boss," Jeff responded.

Anderson uttered a ragged sigh, but didn't say anything.

By the time they reached the town house, the TV and newspaper people were there, and Jeff and Gault, with Anderson between them, elbowed their way through, up the steps, and finally into the safety of the house.

Marylee and the entire staff were there to greet them.

"I'm going to my room to rest," Anderson told her. "The only calls I'll take are from Mrs. Aroyo, Augusta, or either of my brothers."

"Boss, I'm going to Pat's family," Jeff said.

Anderson nodded.

"I'll be back as soon as I can."

"Take your time."

"Are you going to be here?" Jeff asked Gault.

"Whatever I have to do can wait until you get back."

"A couple, three hours ought to do it."

Jeff turned, reopened the front door, and left.

"I am tired," Anderson commented as he started up the steps. He called out to Gault, "Richard, why don't you get some rest too. There's no need for you to continue to work this afternoon."

"I'm fine, Mr. Anderson. I'd rather work than do nothing," Gault said.

He was in trouble, and he didn't want or need the time to think about it.

"Suit yourself," Anderson replied, and disappeared

into his room.

"You look beautiful, as always," Yaglias said, speaking in Spanish as he greeted Isabel with a kiss on the cheek. He took hold of her arm possessively.

"And you are as gallant and handsome as you always were," she responded. "I can't believe almost five years have past since we saw one another."

Yaglias, a tall, dignified-looking man with a gray mustache and a dark complexion, guided her deeper into the terminal.

"Would you care for a cup of coffee?" he asked.

She shook her head. "But don't let me stop you from having one."

"I'm hopelessly addicted," he answered.

They stopped at a food concession, and in less than two minutes Yaglias was sipping hot black coffee.

"You said we haven't seen each other for almost five years. That sounds like a long time, and maybe it is. But somehow, meeting you doesn't have the weight of time behind it." He smiled. He'd always been in love with her, from the first moment he had met her, some twenty years before, when he was a young, very young lieutenant in the Mexican army.

"For old friends, for good friends, it is always like that," Isabel answered.

An electric sign came on indicating that the ferry would come in at the slip on the right side of the terminal.

They joined the queue of people waiting for the steel doors to open.

Isabel was surprised by the number of pigeons

198

that seemed to make their home on the various steel beams and ledges, and the many homeless men and women who'd appropriated the benches for themselves. She was about to comment on both when the green light above the door came on, and the door was opened by an attendant.

Instantly, the crowd surged forward, many running to be first to board the boat.

Isabel and Yaglias walked onto the ferry, and along its full length to what would be its bow for the trip to Staten Island. Then they went out of the cabin, and stood at the railing on the left side.

Yaglias finished his coffee, and tossed the plastic container into a nearby trash can. Then he said, "So, John Anderson has come back into your life."

A momentary flush came into her cheeks.

"He never really left it," she admitted.

Yaglias was amazed at how girlish she suddenly looked when she spoke about Anderson.

The ferry's horn sounded three times, its engines reversed, and as the deck shuddered, it moved out of the slip.

"All right, he's back in your life. Now tell me why you need my help."

"Because a man by the name of Richard Gault has convinced him that his son is alive, and living in a lamasery in Nepal."

"I thought Anderson was finished with that, and it was a closed issue."

Isabel shook her head. "This Gault isn't like the others. He has not asked for anything."

"And that's what frightens you?"

She nodded. "It frightens me," Isabel said. "It frightens me very much."

Her hands were on the railing, and Yaglias put his over the one closest to him. "For you, I will find out whatever there is to know about Richard Gault. But there are some things you should know about Anderson before you become . . . become too committed to him."

"There is nothing political about this—"

Yaglias held up his free hand.

"I don't doubt that. But if you hadn't phoned me, I was going to phone you."

She raised her eyebrows.

"I recently received some very interesting information on John Wesley Anderson."

The tone of his voice brought goose bumps to Isabel's back and arms. She trembled, and hugged herself to ward off the inner chill coursing through her body.

"I have had this information for over two weeks, Isabel, before I finally decided to share it with you."

"Is it that serious?"

"Yes. Anderson was CIA. Even when the two of you were lovers."

She nodded. "I knew that."

Yaglias continued. "His code name was Cobra. He personally directed Venom."

"Oh, my God!"

And a moment later, she said, "I'd like to go inside and sit down."

He helped her to an empty bench.

"I am sorry," he told her.

"Is he still involved that way?" She spoke without looking at him.

"Not that we know. Now, those who would kill us are themselves being killed."

She lifted her eyes to him. "I don't understand."

"We don't either. But it's happening. And because it's happening, and because there are rumors that Anderson might run for the Presidency—"

"That's not so!"

Again Yaglias holds up his hand. "My people aren't interested in what he does or does not do politically here. We wanted you to know, because we respect and love you, that if anything happens to Anderson, none of us would be responsible. Though God knows, we have reason enough to kill him."

Isabel squeezed his hand. "Thank you, and thank our mutual friends. You can tell them that Anderson hasn't any political goals. He has other things on his mind."

"I will tell them," Yaglias answered.

When the ferry reached Staten Island, Yaglias left the bench, while Isabel walked to the far end of the boat for the return trip to Manhattan.

Gault wasn't able to leave the town house until six o'clock, and by that time the story of what had happened to Anderson had been on the five o'clock TV news programs, and on the radio hours before.

By the time Gault had left, Anderson's wife and two brothers had called, and so had Isabel Aroyo. There had been at least a hundred other calls, including calls from the heads of various unions, at least two dozen assorted senators and members of Congress, several officials from both the Democratic and Republican Parties, and the President of the United States—all of which Marylee had fielded with amazing coolness.

201

Gault went straight to Fifth Avenue, hailed a cab, and told the driver to take him crosstown to Eighty-fifth and Broadway; then he took a bus down to Columbus Circle, hailed another cab, and gave the driver an address on East Thirty-sixth Street.

The doorman checked him out with an internal security system, and after an elevator ride up to the twenty-eighth floor, he knocked at the door of Apartment 2805.

George Tops, a tall, thin black man, opened it.

Gault stepped across the threshold.

The other man he knew, Don Ricks, was coming out of the bathroom. Grier was standing in the living room.

Without preliminaries, Grier said, "I had to come here because you fucked up."

Tops passed Gault on the way back to the living room, and Ricks, a short, chunkily built man, nodded and went into the kitchen.

Gault moved into the living room.

"You saved his fucking life!" Grier exclaimed.

"I saved my own fucking life," Gault answered, trying to appear unruffled.

"The hit—"

"Was that ours?"

"No. But what the hell difference does it make whose hit it was?"

"It makes a fuck of a lot of difference when you're the one being shot at," Gault answered. He was close to Grier now, within an arm's reach.

"Safe Deposit isn't thrilled with you," Grier said.

"That's his problem, not mine."

"Anderson's resigning his chairmanship of the Foundation, and he is going to donate—"

"Yeah, yeah, I know that. I already told you that I'm doing some of the cataloguing for the appraiser," Gault said, taking several steps to Grier's right and then sitting down on an easy chair. "I have him hooked."

Grier faced him. "He's more of a hero now than ever before. Christ, he shielded that little girl with his own body."

"What the hell did you expect? He's the American Eagle, isn't he?"

Grier sat down on the edge of the couch. "How hooked is he?"

"Waiting for me to tell him that I'll take him to his son."

"Depending on what?"

"My judgment of whether or not he deserves the privilege," Gault said, paused, and added, "You're going to blow your whole fucking plan now. It will happen just the way you planned. I'll take him to Nepal and there, on the way to meet his son, he'll have a tragic accident. Hell, if you think he's a hero now, wait until you see what kind of hero he'll be then." He grinned, and bracketing the air with the fingers of both hands, moved them through the air. "Banner headlines—JOHN ANDERSON KILLED ON THE WAY TO REUNION WITH LOST SON. How does that grab you?"

Grier frowned. "Bushwick is on my back."

"Does he know where I am?"

"He doesn't even know who you are."

"Can you string him along for awhile longer?"

"How much longer?"

"Two, maybe, three weeks. A month at the outside. I have to play this very carefully."

Grier left the couch, and walked to the window. "I can't see a fucking thing."

"Clouds," Gault said. "Sometimes either they're too low, or we're too high."

Grier turned from the window, but didn't say anything. Gault was his creation, and using him to take out Anderson while going to his son was his idea. "I can live with that if nothing else puts Bushwick into orbit," he told Gault.

Gault pressed the palms of his hands together. "There are no guarantees in the cosmos, only the eternal cycle of life and death."

"Cut the shit," Grier snapped. "Save it for Anderson."

"If I had enough time with him, I could turn him into a Buddhist."

"Sure, and all you would need is luck and a couple of millennia."

"I didn't say how much time I'd need," Gault answered. "And as for needing luck — hell, I have all I need. I have you as my boss, and the Company as my god — what else could I possibly need?"

Grier pointed a finger at him. He was going to tell him that someday that mouth of his would get him into more trouble than he could possibly handle. But it would have been wasted breath. He dropped his hand. "Just get Anderson on a mountain road in Nepal," he wound up telling him.

Gault stood up. "No sweat, boss. No sweat." He turned to Tops, who had been standing at the side of the room during his exchange with Grier. "What's for dinner? I'm starved."

"Chinese. Don has gone to get it."

"Are you staying?" Gault asked Grier, not caring

204

very much if he stayed or left.

"I have to go. I told the wife I'd be home before midnight. Tell Don good-bye for me." He started for the door, and when he reached it, he turned and said, "That was good shooting, Richard. Good shooting."

"A lucky shot," Gault answered.

The door was opened and closed before Tops went over to lock it.

"Don has a key. Or if he can't manage to use it, he'll ring the bell."

"Any beer?" Gault asked when Tops came back into the living room.

"In the fridge."

Gault went into the kitchen, took a bottle of dark Mexican beer out of the refrigerator, and began drinking it before he returned to the living room.

"Some kind of excitement today." He uttered a deep sigh, dropped into a club chair, and pressed the cold bottle to the side of his face.

Tops sat down on the other chair. "You should have seen Grier when he first walked in here. Man, he was so fucking excited, I thought he was going to start throwing things."

"He's a lot calmer now."

"That's because you made him believe you can get Anderson. Can you really get him?"

Grier looked toward the window. The cloud was no longer there, and he saw the soft blue of a twilight sky.

"Yeah, I can really get him, but to do it I have to play out my role to its finish." Then he moved his eyes to Tops, who was staring at him.

"Grier isn't worried so much about whether you

can set Anderson up," Tops said. "He knows you can."

"Then what's the problem?" Gault got to his feet, went to the window, and looked out over the East River, at the lights of the Fifty-ninth Street Bridge, and off to the northeast where planes were landing in the yellowish white light of LaGuardia Airport.

"Will you do it—that's the problem," said Tops. "Will you be able to kill Anderson when the time comes for you to do it? You don't know that, and he doesn't know that. You won't know until you do it, and Grier has a lot riding on this one. So that's the problem."

Gault was now looking to the east. Far out over Long Island the dusk seemed to have already gathered into darkness. He took a long swallow of beer, then said, "Yeah, I can understand that being a problem."

"Do you think it's going to become your problem?"

Gault rested one hand against the window frame. "Like you said, man, I won't know until I'm there." He drank again, until he finished the beer.

Chapter 17

Augusta's penthouse was filled with the heavy cloying scent of burning incense, and the living room was decorated with paintings, prints, and statuary reflecting her deep interest in — and probably by now, Anderson thought, her deep knowledge of — the occult.

He sat on the couch, while she occupied a high-back chair, emblazoned with a pentagram done in gold and silver thread. He had come there at her insistence, though he would have much preferred waiting a few days to allow the shock he was feeling, and was sure she was experiencing, to have dulled somewhat.

Neither of them had mentioned the incident yet, though when he had first arrived, she had not only kissed him on both his cheeks — which she always did, whenever they met — but had also hugged him, something she had not done in more years than Anderson could remember.

"We could have some sherry if you'd like," Augusta offered.

"No, thank you. Coffee perhaps, and a sandwich, but later."

She was on her feet. "How foolish of me not to have realized that you haven't had your dinner. I have only one meal a day, and that's at noon. I'll have the cook prepare something for you."

"Later," Anderson said authoritatively.

Her blue eyes opened wide.

Anderson nodded, and in a more moderate tone he asked her to sit down.

She hesitated.

"Please," he said.

She acquiesced, folding her hands and keeping them on her lap. She was tall for a woman, with a graceful neck, a face that might have been comely if it hadn't been for badly occluded teeth, and long gray hair, which she wore as a bun on the back of her head. "I am satisfied that you are alive . . . not hurt. None of the other details interest me."

"I came here for you to see with your own eyes that I am unhurt."

She nodded. "I appreciate that, John."

Anderson stood up and walked to the far side of the room, where there was a very large and very clear quartz crystal. Aware of the power imputed to it, he looked back over his shoulder, and asked, "Have you rubbed it lately?"

"John—"

He moved his hand over its surface, and faced her. "I have three things to tell you."

She started out of the chair; then changed her mind. "I could feel something—"

"Augusta, what I'm about to tell you must not go beyond this room. You must not confide—"

"Yes, yes. I will not tell anyone. What are they, John?"

"I'll begin with the least important. I'm giving up the Foundation."

This time she did stand. "But why?"

"I no longer want the responsibility, and more to

208

the point, whatever time I have left, I want to devote to my own interests."

"The rest of the family—"

"Wally already knows, and is very upset. As far as George goes—well, I really don't give a tinker's damn what he thinks or doesn't think about it."

"Do you care what I think about it?"

The question surprised him.

They had gone their individual ways for so many years that he seldom if ever consulted her about anything, or considered whether or not she approved or disapproved of something he had done or didn't do.

"I think you need a change," she said, not waiting for his answer.

"Thank you, Augusta. That's very kind of you."

She smiled at him. "Now, tell me the second item on your agenda."

"I'm going to donate my art collections to an institution."

"Long overdue, John. It's time to share what you have with others. So far, I approve of everything you intend doing."

Anderson came around to the front of the couch again. "This last one concerns us."

She pursed her lips. "If you're going to ask me for a divorce—"

"Augusta?"

"No, let me finish, John. What we have between us, we have, and I won't give it up."

Tears filled her eyes, and began to run down her cheeks.

Anderson crossed the distance between them, and giving her his handkerchief, gently pressed her head to him.

"Listen very carefully to me," he said in a tender voice. "I have not come to ask you for a divorce."

Drying her tears, she looked up at him. "I'm sorry, John."

She handed his handkerchief back to him. "Now tell me what you want to tell me."

There was no easy way, no circuitous route he could have taken that would spare her the shock.

"John Junior is alive."

He could feel her tremble, even as a low moan escaped from her lips.

"Oh, John!" she whimpered. "Is he really alive?"

He nodded. "He's living in a lamasery."

She gathered herself together.

Anderson took several steps back.

"Can we go to him? I want to see him. Oh, John, I must see him."

She was on her feet once more, pacing and wringing her hands.

"For the time being, we must settle for the knowledge that he is alive," he said gently.

"But—"

"Augusta, the lamasery is deep in the mountains of Nepal. It is very difficult to get to."

"Are you sure he is alive?"

"Yes. The person who brought me the information is very reliable, and has asked nothing."

"My God," she exclaimed, "I almost feel young again!"

"I know the feeling."

"John, you will go to him, won't you?"

"Yes. Yes, that is my intention . . . sometime in the very near future."

"Why not now, John?"

He could not tell her that their son had said

nothing to Gault about wanting to see either of them. Nor could he expect her to understand the relationship he had formed with Gault, much less who he was.

"The time is not propitious for me to undertake the journey, or to meet John."

He hoped her mystical inclination would make the most out of the word propitious. "Yes, yes. Everything must be propitious."

"I will tell you when I'm going," he said, almost breathing a sigh of relief.

She took hold of his hands, and pressed them to her breasts. "I never believed he was dead. If he had been on the other side, he would have made contact with me."

Anderson nodded, knowing that would please her.

Gault was surprised to see Marylee still working when he returned to the town house.

"Here late, aren't you?" He stepped inside the office.

She looked up. "I didn't expect the hero of the day to be back so early. I thought you'd be out celebrating."

"I killed a man," he said with feigned humility.

"Somehow, I wouldn't have expected that to bother you."

There was something about his connection with death that excited her. There also was, she had to admit, something physically attractive about him — cobraesque, and if her intuition was right, deadly.

Gault was feeling too mellow to let her snide remark bother him. He, Tops, and Ricks had had a good dinner, and had spent a couple of hours shooting the bull.

"Anything I can do to help?" he asked, moving closer to her.

He had not been unaware of her physicality, but had chosen to ignore it. But now the tea-rose scent of her perfume was in his nostrils, and he was looking down into the valley between her breasts.

"How can you help me, when you can't do what you're supposed to do?" The edge in her tone matched the edge of her words.

Gault's hands went up, palms out, and backing away, he said, "I'm out of here."

"I wish to hell you had never come!"

Fire came into her green eyes. She stood up. "You don't know a damn thing about . . . about all of this. Nothing."

The good feeling he had was gone now. He was being challenged. "Tell Mr. Anderson," he answered.

"You think you're something wonderful."

He pointed his finger at her. "You have the problem, not me."

"Problem? Problem? What problem?"

"Lady, you're just jealous because—"

"Who are you?" she shouted, coming out from behind the desk.

"Richard Gault," he answered.

She shook her head. "No. No. That's not who you are. That's just a name. Why are you here? Why? You don't know anything about art."

"Because Anderson needs me," he shot back.

She was stunned. "Needs you? John Wesley Anderson needs you?"

"That's right. He needs me more than you can ever imagine." This time, his voice was absolutely flat.

"Needs you," she repeated.

Gault just looked at her.

Her lips quivered, then twisted back, baring her teeth. "Needs you," she hissed out.

She flung herself at Gault, beating on his chest with her fists.

The attack staggered him. Then he grabbed hold of both her wrists and forced her hands down.

Breathing hard, she glared at him. "Let go of me."

Her body was against his.

Suddenly, he bent her arms up behind her and brought his lips down hard on hers.

She twisted her face away, and tried to break his hold on her hands.

This couldn't be happening. It couldn't be.

Gault tightened his hold, and again bruised her lips with his.

"Bastard!" she gasped, pulling her head back as far as she could.

Gault too was breathing hard.

"Let go of me," she rasped.

He shook his head. "That's not what you really want me to do."

Her face colored more deeply than it had been moments before.

"And that's not what I want to do," Gault said, his voice almost a growl.

Marylee's eyes locked with his. She could feel his cock against her, and the sudden wetness in her crotch. "I hate you."

Gault smiled thinly. "Maybe that's why it will be the best fuck either of us ever had."

She said, "It won't change anything."

Gault didn't bother to answer, and scooped her up in his arms. She was lighter than he'd thought.

213

"Where?" she managed to ask.

Any moment she half expected him to throw her over his shoulder and carry her that way.

He started for the couch on the opposite side of the room.

"Not here. Your room."

"My room," Gault answered.

She was surprised he could take the steps two at a time.

"Reach over and turn the knob," he told her.

The door opened, and the next moment they were in his room.

He kicked the door shut with his right foot, set her down, and switched on the lights.

"I want to see you naked," he said, fixing his eyes on her.

She started to open her blouse.

She had been told that by other men, but hearing it from Gault gave her a peculiar feeling of satisfaction, almost of power.

"No," he said.

She stopped. Her blouse was half open. "All right, you do it." And she thrust her breasts out to him.

"Suck my cock," he said, unzipping and freeing his penis.

Marylee looked down at his organ, then at him.

She had done it that way for Anderson several times, but it was always because she wanted to. But now she was being ordered.

"Games," he said.

She repeated the word.

"Do it!"

She knelt down, put her lips against his prick, and then began to use her tongue.

Gault closed his eyes, and brought his hands down

on her head, forcing his cock deeper into her mouth.

"Games," he muttered. "Just fucking games!"

Marylee heard him, but didn't understand.

Then suddenly he pulled away, opened the remaining buttons of her blouse, then undid her bra and fondled her breasts.

She was still on her knees. His cock was still in front of her, and she began to stroke it.

"Yeah. Yeah, that feels good."

His hands on her breasts felt good too, but she wasn't going to give him the satisfaction of telling him. Her nipples were erect, and teasing them with the balls of his fingers shot tendrils of heat through her.

Suddenly, he lifted her to her feet.

"Now, strip," he said harshly.

She reached around to the back of her skirt, unbuttoned, then unzipped it.

By the time she was naked, Gault was too. He ran his hand over her pubic mound.

"A real blond," he commented. "Not too many around."

With a sudden flash of anger, she said, "That's some fucking compliment, especially coming from you."

"Believe it!" he shot back.

The anger was still there. "What the hell am I doing here?"

"I'll show you."

He had her on the bed, and was on top of her before she could answer him.

Her anger vanished, just as quickly as it had come.

His hands were all over her body. His fingers entered it, probing, teasing . . . making her gasp

215

when he stroked her clit.

He was stringing her out, as far as he could.

"Do it," she moaned. "Do it . . . fuck me . . . fuck me."

He drove his cock into her, and she met his thrust. He pounded into her, his sweat dripping on her breasts.

Writhing, she raked his back with her nails.

She found herself where she'd never been before with a man.

Gault slowed purposely to string her out even further.

Hoping to regain the frantic pace that moved her closer and closer to the final burst of orgasmic release, Marylee thrust her naked hips against him.

He pinned her motionless beneath him.

She rolled her head from side to side.

"Why . . . why are you doing this?"

He began to move, slowly, in long strokes, penetrating her the full length of his prick.

"Faster," she demanded, her voice, a throaty whisper. "Faster."

The exquisite sensation of heat swirled through his groin.

Gault had no feeling for the woman beneath him, other than the pleasure that came from knowing that he controlled her, that he could have her any time and anywhere. The physical pleasure she was giving him he could have gotten from any other woman. There was nothing special about her, nothing.

Suddenly, the need to move faster gripped him.

"Oh . . . oh!" Marylee moaned, her body taut. "Oh . . ." the tension stretched out, teased out, becoming something like a white-hot strand stretched out in the back of her brain, stretched out deep inside of her. Then it snapped. Her body heaved up.

She could hear herself scream, muted shrieks mixed with body-shaking spasms that some how seemed connected to the whirl of red, yellow, and orange in the center of her brain, and then the words—

"Fuck me . . . fuck me . . . oh, God . . . God . . . I hate you, Gault . . . I hate you . . . hate you."

Gault half heard her.

He had heard the same words from women whose names he couldn't remember, and from women whose names he never knew.

Then his own pleasure tore through him, bringing a satisfied grunt, and an immediate grin.

"You look like the fucking Cheshire cat," Marylee said.

He rolled off her, and stretched out.

She lifted herself up, and resting on one elbow, she looked down at him.

"I'm going to sleep. You can spend the night here or leave."

"And that's it?" she asked, on the ragged edge between anger and humiliation.

"We fucked. That was it. Your words, remember? 'It won't change anything.' Well, it hasn't."

He turned his back to her and could hear her muted sobs. Sometime before he fell asleep, Gault was vaguely aware that he was alone. Marylee had left the bed.

Chapter 18

When Grier entered Bushwick's office at eight-thirty the following morning, he found Bushwick in his usual stance, smoking a large foul-smelling cigar at the window.

"Something went wrong," Bushwick said, trying to control his anger. As he spoke, large puffs of smoke burst from the tip of the cigar.

Grier crossed the room, and had gotten as far as the desk when Bushwick took the cigar out of his mouth and pointed it at him.

"Why isn't Anderson dead? And just who the hell is Richard Gault?"

"That wasn't one of our hits," Grier answered.

Bushwick looked puzzled.

"Remember the two guys the police—"

Bushwick nodded vigorously; then he said, "Who is Gault? The fucker sure knows how to shoot." He smiled. "We could use him on our side."

Grier waited a moment, and to keep from laughing, he even advanced several steps closer to the desk.

In a low voice, Grier told him, "He is on our side."

Bushwick squinted at him. "But he's on Anderson's staff."

"Yes, that's true."

"But . . ." Bushwick returned to his desk, and

faced Grier across it. "Then he's our hit man?"

"He's our man."

Bushwick's face splintered into a grin. "You're one hell of a devious individual!" he exclaimed, dropping down into his swivel chair, and then gesturing to Grier to the chair alongside the desk.

"Thank you," Grier said.

"Now tell me, how did you manage to get a man, our man, inside the Anderson house?" Bushwick said.

Grier leaned back.

There wasn't much point to him being coy about, he decided. Sooner or later, Bushwick would have to know everything.

"As soon as I began to suspect Anderson's involvement with the deaths of our people, I recruited Gault. I needed an actor, and that's what he was, Off-Broadway anyway. But good enough for my purposes. Then he went through our training program for six months, including the small arms course, and just by happenstance he turned out to be a crack shot. After he completed our training program, I sent him to our special Asian School, where he learned Hindi and some other things that would be valuable to him when he went to Nepal."

"Nepal?"

"Anderson's son was killed in a mountain-climbing accident there some four years ago."

"So Gault pretends to have found Anderson's son," Bushwick said, now puffing vigorously on the cigar.

Grier momentarily pointed a finger at him. "Right on target."

"All right, that gets him inside. When does he make the hit?"

"He doesn't, not in the usual way, and not here in

the States. Anderson will go to Nepal, where he'll have an accident. The American Eagle will fly off a mountain road. He'll be a hero, and our skirts will be absolutely spotless."

Bushwick took the cigar out of his mouth. "I like it," he said, nodding. "But I have two questions. Are you sure Anderson will go to Nepal?"

"I'm sure."

"How can you be?"

"He has already spent several millions of dollars trying to find his son, and along comes Gault, who wants nothing. He doesn't even want to take him to John Junior."

"Wait a minute, you just lost me. I thought—"

Grier interrupted him. "Anderson is going to convince Gault to take him."

"How?" Bushwick put the cigar back in his mouth, and rolled it to the right side. Grier was a lot smarter than he gave him credit for being, and therefore, probably a lot more dangerous.

"By making Anderson prove himself worthy."

"You mean making him follow the scent?"

Grier nodded. "That's the idea."

"How long will it take to get Anderson to Nepal?"

"Two, three weeks from now. At the outside, a month."

Bushwick tapped the ash off the front of his cigar, but didn't immediately put it back in his mouth. "And after the American Eagle is down, what happens to Gault?"

"If he chooses to continue with us—"

Bushwick shook his head. "No fucking way. He's dead." His voice was steely, and his eyes slits.

"What?" Grier asked, startled by the General's answer.

"Can't be any other way."

Grier's brain was suddenly filled with crashing waves, and he was desperately trying to calm them.

Bushwick started puffing on his cigar again. He'd obviously jumped far ahead of Grier on this one, and was pleased with himself for having done it. "You make sure your plan works, and I'll take care of Gault."

Grier cleared his throat, and was about to speak, but Bushwick began first. "Believe me, it's repugnant to have one of my own taken out. But in this situation, it's our insurance policy." Then in a more intimate voice, he said, "I'm headed for the Vice Presidency, and you have my word that you'll occupy the chair I'm now sitting on. Neither of us wants to jeopardize our chances."

"Yes, I understand," Grier said, but the words came hard.

"Good!" Bushwick exclaimed, then with a smile, he asked, "Is there anything I should know?"

"I'm going to keep Anderson as much off balance as possible before he leaves for Nepal."

"How?"

"Threatening phone calls, when the appropriate time comes, made by men having Hispanic accents."

"Oh, why Hispanic?"

"I received a call from the NYPD late last night. The man who Gault took out was ID'd as Frank Velez, a Nicaraguan linked to the Sandinistas' special police."

Bushwick raised his eyebrows. "The attempted hit should have come from the other side, shouldn't it?"

"Yes, but it didn't. Not if my report is right," Grier answered.

Bushwick removed the cigar, now a stub, from his

mouth, and squashed it into the ashtray. "Maybe he's got both sides after him. Maybe the Commies are turning on each other." Bushwick was on his feet, and planted his palms on the desk. "My God, just imagine if Anderson is a Soviet agent. I mean, with him as our watchdog our whole structure could be compromised. And if he makes a bid for the Presidency, and wins it . . ." He stopped, and pulled away from the desk.

Grier had heard something like this about Anderson from Bushwick before. "I doubt if his direct affiliations extend to the Kremlin."

"They must, if he supports the leftist groups in South and Central America. My God, do you realize that we are probably the only two people in this country who know just how dangerous Anderson is? And this time . . . this time the two who realize the danger are in a position to do something about it." Excitement came into his voice. "By God, we are!"

Grier thought Bushwick had finished, but he was wrong.

Bushwick pointed a finger at him, and said, "Tell Gault not to interfere."

In an instant, Grier was on his feet.

With his finger still extended toward Grier, Bushwick said, "This is an order. Pass it on to Gault. He's not to stop another attempt on Anderson's life. He's to let it happen."

"But —"

"Your idea, yes. I'll go with it. But if Providence intervenes on our side, who are we to obstruct that intervention. Let it happen, I say." Bushwick finally lowered his head.

"I'll pass the word to Gault," Grier said.

"Good. Good. We have the situation under control.

Let's keep it that way."

Grier stood up.

"Keep me informed of any changes," Bushwick told him.

"Yes, certainly," Grier answered, and managed a smile.

Despite the emotional upheaval resulting from the attempt on his life, Anderson slept soundly, and awoke refreshed.

By nine o'clock, he was at his desk in the downstairs office, waiting for his lawyer, Max Grenville, who was scheduled to arrive at ten.

Marylee had prepared a list of the people who had phoned the previous day, and as Anderson scanned it, he put neat, red lines under the names of the various officials of the Democratic party, the President, and several members of the House and Senate.

Done with that, he was about to ask Marylee to contact the appraiser, David Lee, and confirm the day he would start when his private number began to ring.

Only a few people had that number. Among them was Isabel, and he hoped it was her.

"Anderson here," he said.

Augusta was on the other end.

"John Junior is not alive," she said, sobbing. "He's not alive."

"Augusta, Augusta," Anderson called out in an attempt to stop her.

"John, he came to me last night."

Anderson uttered a deep sigh. He should not have told her anything about John Junior until he had seen him. That would have been indisputable proof, and free from mystical interpretations.

"All right, Augusta, stop crying, and tell me what happened," he said.

"I was overjoyed when you left, John. Not only because of the news you gave me about John Junior, but also because we seemed to have touched one another on a spiritual plane that I never thought would exist for us."

Anderson didn't want to hear this long preamble; he wanted to get to the heart of whatever it was that caused the problem.

"By the time I got into bed, I was totally at peace with myself, and then as I began to drift into sleep, I felt a disturbing influence. I began to feel very cold, very cold. I started to reach down to the foot of the bed for a light blanket, when suddenly I saw John Junior. I—"

"Augusta, your imagination was working overtime," Anderson said gently.

"John, he was on the floor, trapped in millions of tons of snow and ice. Frozen for—oh, John, our son is dead. It doesn't matter what someone has told you. He's dead."

For several moments, Anderson was unable to speak.

He himself was suddenly so chilled that goose bumps skittered down his back and arms. Then he broke out into a cold sweat.

"John, are you still there?" Augusta asked, her voice quavering with emotion.

Anderson forced himself to respond. "Yes, yes." Then in an even harsher tone, he said, "Where would I be, Augusta? Certainly not with your damn spirits."

"You're angry."

"No, I'm pleased that you called me with another one of your cockamamie stories about your visions."

He didn't want to be sarcastic; he didn't want to hurt her. But there was a limit. He needed his dreams, as much as she needed hers.

"Oh John, John. I know what you think of me, and my—"

"I don't have time for this discussion," he said. "Besides, we have had it more times than I care to remember."

"My vision—"

"Your vision, Augusta, is the result of an overactive imagination. I don't want to discuss it now, or any time in the near future. I will prove to you our son is alive."

"He's dead, John."

"The hell he is!" Anderson exploded. "Now, goodbye."

Before she could answer, he slammed the phone down into its cradle and stared moodily at the opposite wall, where there was a large painting of the sea crashing against black rocks.

"This is your life," he mumbled, using the title of a 1960's TV show that presented the biographies of famous and not-so-famous people. "Or at least a portion of it."

Anderson shook his head.

Suddenly his anger vanished, and with it any self-pity he felt. He picked up the phone and punched out Augusta's number.

She answered after four rings.

"Listen," he said, "I'm sorry I became angry."

"Thank you for calling, John."

"Are you all right?"

"Yes, John. But I'm so very worried about you."

"Worried about me?" he asked, astonished.

"I saw you dead next to our son," she told him.

"Augusta?"

"We don't have a marriage, the way other people do. But we do have a deep affection for each other—"

"Augusta, nothing is going to happen to me." He was almost embarrassed by her frankness.

"Let me finish, John. I count that affection as my chief asset in this world, and if, for any reason, I should lose it, I would not want to continue living."

"Nothing is going to happen to me." Then, with a forced laugh, he said, "I'm not good enough for heaven, though I just might squeak into hell."

"Don't make fun of me, John."

"I'm not. I just don't want you to worry. I'll be around for a long time yet."

"John, don't go to Nepal. Please, John, don't go."

More in control of himself than before, he answered, "We'll discuss it, Augusta. I promise, I won't go without first telling you."

"If we discuss it, you'll convince me that you're right, and I'm wrong. You do it all the time, John."

"Augusta . . . Augusta . . ." He was at a loss for a response.

Then, with an audible sigh, she said, "I know in the end you will do what you want to do."

"I promise you, nothing will happen to me. Nothing. If I have some time later in the day, I'll call you. Good-bye, Augusta."

"Good-bye, John."

In a better mood than he'd been a few minutes before, Anderson put the phone down.

His feelings for Augusta were the same as hers for him, and so very different from the passion he felt for Isabel. But only part of Augusta, her body, existed in this world, and even that was denied full physical existence by a "higher power," as she referred to it. Years ago, even before John Junior had vanished, sex to her had become less a meaningful expression of need, love, or even fantasy, and more an obligation that she found more and more difficult to fulfill. But while her need had waned until it had almost vanished completely, he had felt more and more sexually starved. Then he'd met Isabel.

Marylee came on the intercom, and announced the arrival of Mr. Grenville.

"Send him right in," Anderson told her as he stood to greet his visitor.

The door opened, and a tall, thin man, wearing a small, blue velvet yarmulke and carrying a brown leather attaché case, strode into the office.

Anderson came out from behind the desk.

"Welcome, Max," he said, offering his hand.

"I'm glad to see you, especially after yesterday's incident," Max responded, vigorously shaking Anderson's hand. "I was sorry to hear about Pat, though."

"I want to make provisions for his family," Anderson said.

"You're a good man, John."

Anderson shrugged, and returned to the chair behind the desk, while Max sat down in the one alongside it.

"Your lovely secretary told my lovely secretary that you wanted to see me this morning," Max said.

Anderson smiled.

Max's "lovely secretary" was a middle-aged woman with a voice that sounded like a tuba.

"All of what we discuss here today is highly confidential."

Max rubbed his long hands. "Tomorrow I take out

a full page ad in the *Yazoo Free Press*. John, the *Yazoo Free Press* is read by everyone who has a particular interest in what John Wesley Anderson is doing and intends to do."

"I just happen to own that newspaper."

"All the more reason for me to do a little payback."

Anderson said, "I'm leaving the Foundation."

"That is serious," Max commented.

"There's more."

Max opened his attaché case, removed a yellow legal pad, and readied a gold Cross ball point.

"I'm also going to donate my art collections."

"And you want the tax benefits?"

Anderson nodded. "I want to take them over a period of years. My best guess is that the collections are worth between forty and sixty million on today's market."

"I'll have to check with the IRS. But how does ten years sit with you?"

"I'd prefer longer. Not so much for me, but for Augusta. I will probably predecease —" Suddenly remembering what Augusta had said, he felt oddly disconcerted.

"Yes, how is she?" Max said.

"Well. She's well."

Max knew about Augusta's involvement with the "spiritual world," and a great deal more.

Anderson trusted him with more than just his financial and legal affairs. He had met Max just after the Tet Offensive in Viet Nam, Max had been a lieutenant in the Navy, a SEAL who had racked up a great deal of highly specialized combat experience of the kind Anderson needed for his operations in Central and South America. But Max hadn't been interested. He'd wanted to return to the States and become a lawyer and a rabbi. He'd become both, and was successful at each.

"That's good. Augusta is one of the most gracious women I know."

"She is that," Anderson responded. "And speaking about wives and family, forgive me for not inquiring about yours, Max."

"Shulamith is fine, and my son Nathan will soon get his doctorate in English, and Benjamin's latest novel, *Full Alert,* is already out."

"I haven't decided which institution, or institutions, I will donate the collections to, but whichever one it will be, it will have to guarantee to house the collection in its own halls."

"Any time limit?" Max asked.

"Five years?"

"If the institution fails to provide the—"

"The collection will be offered to a second institution. There will be no second chances."

"There are some institutions that will immediately object to the five-year limitation."

Anderson waved Max's comment aside. "Starting tomorrow, say fifteen minutes before the market closes, I want you to sell off a ten-thousand-share block of my holdings in Anderson Oil."

Max tried to take the request in stride, but couldn't, and shifted his position in the chair. "At yesterday's closing market price, you're talking about fifteen million dollars."

"Do the same every day until my entire interest in the company no longer exists. Then you can start on my other holdings. I want everything I own liquidated within a period of five business days."

Max could feel himself blanch. "That kind of sale, John, will not go unnoticed . . . and certainly will have repercussions."

"My brothers will no doubt buy up the Anderson Oil stock, and as for my other holdings — well, they might even buy those too."

"The tax on those sales will be in the millions."

Anderson shrugged. "I really don't care, Max. I'll still have more money than I could use in a thousand lifetimes. And eventually, I intend to give most of it away. And that reminds me: I want you to create a trust fund for Mrs. Ryan and her children so that they will never have the usual financial concerns. She is to continue to draw Pat's salary, with yearly increments that match the cost-of-living index, for the rest of her life. And establish a trust fund of a quarter of a million dollars for each of the children to provide for their education."

"That's very generous, John."

"No matter what I do, it will be a poor substitute for Pat," Anderson said.

Max silently nodded, then said, "You already told me that you are going to give most of your fortune away. Now would you tell me why?"

"Ah, yes. Why." Anderson settled back in his chair. "Do you remember Wordsworth's poem that begins with, 'The world is too much with us, little we see in nature that is ours/ getting and spending we lay waste our powers'?"

"Yes, I remember it." He was surprised that Anderson did.

"Well, that's exactly where I think the 'world' is. And to quote from a more contemporary source, 'Stop the world, I want to get off.'"

Max raised his eyebrows.

"No, no, you've taken my comments too literally. It's just that I don't want to be part of the Foundation for one, and the various corporations whose boards of directors I'm either chairman of or I control because I hold a majority of the company's stock. Max, I want my own life."

"I thought everything you just mentioned *was* your life."

"Until very recently, I thought so too," Anderson said. "But unlike the leopard, who cannot change his spots, I can, and will." He smiled. "I want to make the most of what time I have left."

"I certainly understand that."

"In addition to the fund I have put aside for Augusta, put an additional five million in it," Anderson said.

"To whom and in what amounts do you intend to distribute the remainder of your capital?"

"Several millions to existing medical research facilities . . . to universities, where I will establish special grants for young artists . . . to the United Nations child health care programs . . . to groups throughout the world that struggle for a free society . . . and there are many more."

"You will certainly have to be more specific, John."

"Over the next three, or four days — I imagine it will take that long to put all of this into some order — you'll have the specifics that you need."

"Those last bequests will cause you some problems," Max said.

Anderson shrugged.

"I'm going to ask a question, John, that I know is out of line, but nonetheless, I will ask it."

"You want to know what my motivation is for the changes I intend to make, don't you?"

"Yes. These changes are not just the ordinary changes a man would make. Because you are who

232

you are, the changes will have repercussions here and abroad."

Anderson leaned forward, resting his elbows on the desk. "Two very diverse causes. The first, and the most important, is that John Junior has been found—"

Max started out of his chair.

Anderson smiled. "That really grabbed you, didn't it?"

"Believe it!"

"He's living in a lamasery north of Katmandu."

"Proof?"

Anderson shook his finger at him.

"Even Moses asked for proof that God was God."

"I will be going to him soon, Max," Anderson said.

"And John Junior has been positively identified?"

"Positively," Anderson responded with a vigorous nod.

"Then congratulations," Max said, offering his hand.

Anderson shook it.

"When will you be leaving?"

"Very soon, if everything goes smoothly."

Max settled back in his chair. "You said there were two causes."

"There are. I'm going to run for the Presidency."

Max emitted a low whistle.

"Now you understand why I made specific mention of the confidentiality that must surround our discussions here."

"Yes."

"You're one of a very small circle of people who know about John Junior, and an even smaller circle who have any knowledge of my political plans."

"I appreciate your trust."

"Now you tell me the kinds of information you will need from me, and we can get started. Oh, by the way, on Friday, after the market closes, I will hold a press conference during which I will only announce my coming departure from the Foundation."

"That certainly will be front-page news," Max answered.

"The chair or the couch, Marylee?" Dr. Hasse asked, from his chair behind the desk, after they had exchanged greetings.

Marylee's eyes went from the chair, alongside the desk, where she usually sat, to the couch against the wall, at the far side of the room, under a framed reproduction of the *New Yorker* magazine cover showing Manhattan big and bold, and everything else west of the Hudson River to the Pacific Ocean squeezed into a narrow band.

All of her other sessions had taken place with her sitting on the chair, but this wasn't her scheduled time. She'd called Hasse late the previous night, after her third sexual encounter with Gault, during which she'd allowed him to bind her, spread-eagle her, and then do things to her that drove her into a sexual frenzy which left her quivering and sobbing.

"The couch."

Hasse came out from behind his desk. He was a tall, round-shouldered man, with a shiny, bald pate and a nose that seemed to be too large for his face.

"Please," he said, gesturing toward the couch, while he moved a chair next to it and sat down.

He was well aware of his patient's connections. She'd started therapy shortly after she became John Wesley Anderson's mistress, and now that Anderson had turned her away, and she had come face to face with a predator like Gault, she was, as some Nam vets would say, "in deep shit."

Marylee stretched rigidly out on the brown leather couch, and stared at the ceiling, where there was a round globe of frosted glass protecting the light bulbs.

"I understood from what you said on the phone that the reason for this session is your deepening sexual relationship with Richard." Hasse didn't speak directly to her, but rather let his words float above her, or so it seemed.

She closed her eyes. Her bowels churned, making her feel as if she was going to pass wind any moment.

"Marylee?"

Her name came right at her.

She opened her eyes, and immediately began to sob. "I let him do things to me. He tied me up. I knew what he was doing, but I enjoyed it. He worked on my clit with a feather, and—I begged him not to stop."

Hasse handed her a tissue.

She wiped her eyes, and then blew her nose.

"I don't know why I went to bed with him again. This was the third time, and it was the most degrading. I hate him. I've never hated anyone in my life, but I hate Richard Gault."

"Despite your negative feelings, you're sexually attracted to him, aren't you?"

"He—he somehow manages to get a hold over people."

"The way he does with Mr. Anderson, and with you?"

"He doesn't have a hold over me, not anymore. I

235

see him for what he is."

"And what is he, Marylee?"

"He's evil. Yes, he's evil."

Hasse asked, "Did he force you to go to bed with him?"

"No. But he expected me to."

"Did you allow yourself to be tied up, or did he—"

"He suggested it!" she said angrily.

"Did you tell him that you didn't want him to stimulate you with a feather?"

"No, but—"

"But what, Marylee?"

She squinched her eyes shut, and rolled her head from side to side.

"Weren't you the slightest bit excited by being tied up and the prospect of having a new sexual experience?"

Again, she had the feeling that Hasse's words were floating above her, and even after she couldn't hear them anymore, they seemed to be there.

"You don't understand," she said. "He makes me do things, the way he does with other people. He's not like other men."

"Admittedly, some of his sexual activities are unique, but he certainly enjoys being with a woman."

"Richard doesn't enjoy anyone, or anything. He does what he does to do it, nothing more or less, and that's why I don't trust him. That's why I think he's trying to put something over on John."

For several moments Hasse considered what Marylee said, then he asked, "Have you any idea what that something might be?"

"I wish to God I knew," she answered vehemently.

"And what would you do if you did know?"

"Expose him."

"Ah yes, and by exposing him, eliminate him from Mr. Anderson's life and regain your place. Isn't that right, Marylee?"

She bolted into a sitting position. "That's not true!"

"You'll admit that it's a possibility, then?"

She dropped back on her elbows. "If that's true, then why have I let Richard do the things he has done to me?"

"You can answer that better than I can. You think about it, and maybe by the next time you come here, you'll be able to tell me."

She stretched out on the couch again and closed her eyes. "Gault isn't like any other man I have ever known. All he has to do is look at me, and my . . . pussy becomes wet . . . He doesn't ask. He just says, 'I want to fuck you.' And I go with him. But there's nothing there. He's not even with me when he's inside of me. He's somewhere else."

"Will you go with him again?" Hasse asked.

Marylee uttered a deep sigh, and sat up. "I really don't know. I'm very much the moth, and he's even more the flame."

237

Chapter 19

Isabel met Yaglias at the south end of the Brooklyn Heights Esplanade that overlooked both Lower Manhattan, across the East River, and the very wide reaches of the upper portion of New York Harbor.

He was already there, leaning on the iron railing with his forearms, staring into the distance, in profile looking very much the Aztec he was. Yaglias could trace his family line back to the time of Montezuma, and before. He was truly "a stranger in a strange land."

Yaglias turned when she was still several paces behind him.

"Your friend was very lucky," he said, without preliminaries. "Have you seen him yet?"

They started to walk. "Tonight. I am dining with him and Richard Gault."

Yaglias nodded. "That Mr. Gault is a very good shot."

"Has he any other unique attributes?"

"No. His credentials are very ordinary."

"I know he has visited India."

"Yes, that is true. He appears to be a photojournalist."

"And what about his family?" Isabel asked.

"Local people, here in Brooklyn. His father is a

239

retired cop, who now works as a guard in a neighborhood bank. He has one sister, who is married. He himself was involved in the theater, mainly Off-Broadway productions."

"Thank you," Isabel said, touching his arm.

Neither of them spoke for several moments, then Yaglias asked, "Are you satisfied, Isabel?"

She moved toward an empty bench in front of the railing, and said, "Let's sit for awhile. It's such a beautiful day, and such a spectacular view."

After they were seated, she answered his question. "Part of me is satisfied, but . . ."

"Yes, but what?"

"The other part of me will reserve judgment until after I meet and have the opportunity to speak with him."

Yaglias smiled, and shaking his finger at her, said, "No wonder why you were so effective in the movement."

She blushed. "It's my nature to be suspicious," she said, "especially when everything is so neat."

"Neat?"

"Fits together so perfectly."

Yaglias looked at the graceful curve of the Brooklyn Bridge for a moment before he said, "There is one piece that doesn't fit all of the others."

"Yes, I know."

"A man who is able to shoot that way would have to have been trained."

"Well trained," Isabel answered.

"The way you were."

"Yes, the way I was by you," she said, putting her hand over his.

Several more moments of silence passed.

"That has to be seen for what it is by others," Yaglias commented. "Anderson must be aware of it."

"You know people see what they want to see, and most often question, if they question at all, those things that give them the answers they want, and not the answers that might lead to more questions."

He turned toward her. He had in the course of his life had many women — even, for several years, a wife — but Isabel was the only woman he had ever loved, and he had never touched her. "What will you do?"

"Wait for Gault to do something."

"By then it might be too late to save Anderson."

"It will also be too late to save Gault," Isabel answered, suddenly tightening her hold on Yaglias's hand.

Jesus Ortega made it back to the funeral parlor by the early evening of the next day.

Immediately after Frank had been shot, he had driven the car straight from Fifth Avenue and Sixty-eighth Street to Newark, New Jersey, and left it on a street, with its doors unlocked, not far from the PATH train station; then, from the window of a nearby luncheonette, he'd watched four black teenagers strip it in a matter of minutes. He'd waited a few minutes before he left the luncheonette and hailed a cab that took him to Newark Airport. There he'd rented another car. From the airport, he'd driven to the Ramada Inn, near Middlesex College in Edison, New Jersey, and spent the night there. In the morning, he'd taken the car to the parking lot adjacent to the Staten Island ferry, left it there, and boarded the ferry for Manhattan, where he'd spent a few hours before going by subway to the Eastern Parkway station in Brooklyn.

All of his movements had been previously planned by Sanchez. But had the hit been successful, he and Frank would have been back in Bogota by now.

People were at the funeral parlor for a wake, and he had no difficulty mingling with them until he could slip behind a curtain and open the door leading directly to the preparation room.

Under a bright light, Sanchez was working on a body that was on a metal table.

"This one is old. Maybe ninety, or older," he said, without looking up, speaking in Spanish.

Ortega could see that it was a black man.

"Scars on his arms and chest. Probably from knife fights. Still has a good-sized cock for a man his age." Sanchez laughed. "I wonder when the hell he used it last. Yeah, you can bet not too recently."

Ortega didn't give a damn if the old man had died screwing some bitch.

"You're booked for a flight tomorrow night for Madrid, and two days later from there to Bogota," Sanchez said.

Ortega lit a cigarette, and asked, "What happens to Frank's body?"

"It's in a refrigerator now, or soon will be after the coroner is finished with it. Then, if no one claims it after a certain amount of time, it will be handed over to a medical school, and when they're finished with it, it will be buried in a place called Potter's

242

Field."

"Can't you claim it and give it a decent burial?"

The question made Sanchez look up. "I do that, and I'm finished here. What happens to Frank's body isn't important. Killing Anderson still is."

Ortega didn't answer. He took a deep drag on the cigarette and held the smoke in his lungs for several seconds before releasing it. Sanchez didn't understand. Frank was like a brother to him.

"We'll choose another time, and maybe another way to get Anderson," Sanchez said.

"Frank killed one of Anderson's watchdogs."

"Did the other get him?"

Ortega shook his head. "There was a third man there. He took the dead man's gun, and got Frank with one shot."

"Lucky."

"Shit lucky. The man was a professional. He knew what he was doing. I'd like to blow that cocksucker away."

"You're going home, that's the only thing you're going to do," Sanchez told him, and pushing his glasses up on his nose, began to work on the corpse again.

Ortega didn't move.

Sanchez slowly looked up from his work. "Go upstairs. There's half a roast chicken in the refrigerator, beer, and a number by the telephone if you want a woman."

Ortega shook his head. "I don't want Frank's body to be sliced up. He was a good man, and should get a decent burial. He'd want the same thing for—"

Even as Ortega was speaking, Sanchez eased open

243

the table drawer, wrapped his right hand around the butt of a .38 already fitted with a silencer, and pointed it at him.

"It has to be this way," Sanchez said, squeezing the trigger twice.

The shots sounded like the corks popping from champagne bottles.

Ortega didn't even have time to look surprised.

They were having after-dinner drinks.

This was Gault's first time in the Four Seasons, which was decorated for spring with hundreds of different-colored tulips and hyacinths, daffodils, and paper-white crocuses.

He'd dressed for the occasion, and wore a white linen jacket, a light blue shirt, a red and blue diagonally striped tie, dark blue slacks, blue socks, and white shoes.

Throughout dinner, Isabel had more or less dominated the conversation, or more precisely, had directed it.

She had purposefully kept from mentioning anything about John Junior, and had instead chatted about various people she and Anderson knew, about world events, and now, even about the erratic weather conditions.

"When we have rain, it's more like a tropical downpour than anything else," she said.

Anderson, still warming his brandy with his hands, commented, "I understand that for the fourth year in a row there are severe drought conditions in the Midwest."

"What about the snow in Nepal?" Isabel asked, smiling at Gault.

For an instant, he didn't respond. The weather conditions around the world didn't interest him at all, but Isabel's breasts did. They were clearly visible under the green silk off-the-shoulder cocktail dress she was wearing . . . especially the left one, where the dress came down almost to the nipple.

"I'm sorry," he finally said, "but I was thinking of something else." His eyes locked with hers.

Her smile became a chuckle. "Yes, apparently you were."

The bitch had caught him ogling her.

"I asked whether there was more or less snow than usual—"

"Ah yes, in Nepal. Well, from what I was told, it was normal. The mountains are snow-covered all year."

She smiled at him again, but purposely didn't say anything.

Then Anderson said, "Didn't you lose your way in a snowstorm and wind up in the lamasery where you found John Junior?"

Gault nodded.

"Wes says that you produced a book of photographs of your trip to Nepal," Isabel noted.

Gault nodded, his mind racing ahead to deal with what he was certain was coming next.

"I've always been interested in photography," she commented.

"She's done some spectacular work of her own," Anderson said.

Isabel placed her hand over Anderson's. "He's naturally prejudiced."

Then to Gault's complete surprise, she changed the subject. "Yesterday, that was a very brave thing you did."

Gault flushed. She was referring to the shootout.

"If you hadn't acted so quickly — well — that really was spectacular shooting, especially for someone totally unfamiliar with firearms. You *are* totally unfamiliar with them, aren't you?"

Gault took a sip of brandy. She was playing head games.

He smiled, almost childishly, he hoped. "Well, not totally. My father took me hunting with him now and then."

"Then yesterday was the first time you used a revolver?"

"I did some plinking with a Ruger twenty-two," Gault answered.

"Do you hunt now?" Isabel asked.

He could stop her cold now. "Only with a camera," he answered, smiling at her.

"Well, I'm certainly glad of that," she came back at him, "because if it was with a gun, I would be a very nervous lady indeed."

"Only with a camera," Gault said.

She sipped her brandy, waiting for the conversation to begin again, and when it was apparent that neither Wes nor Richard was going to start it going, she decided to ask the critical question.

"When do you expect to return to Nepal with Wes?"

That made both of them straighten up.

"Isabel —" Anderson began.

"Isn't that a fair question, Richard?"

"It's certainly a direct one," he answered.

"Can you give a direct answer?"

Gault set his snifter down on the table, and looking straight at her, said, "With all due respect, Isabel, that's—"

"I know what you're about to say, and you're absolutely right. It's none of my business. But I was thinking that I'd like very much to go along with the two of you."

"Isabel, you never said a word about that!" Anderson exclaimed.

"Oh, unless a woman has some surprises . . ."

"What do you think, Richard?" Anderson asked.

She had him pinned, as if he were a bug on a drying board. "The lamasery is almost sixty miles north of Katmandu, and—"

"I'll go to Katmandu with the two of you and wait there until you return. Think about it, Richard."

Gault smiled. "Yes, I certainly will think about it." Then he lifted his glass, and as he sipped the brandy, looked at her breasts again.

"Thank you, Richard," Isabel said, aware of how much he wanted to fuck her, but intuitively knowing that his reason for being there, to use the vernacular, was to fuck Anderson.

But exactly how Gault would do it—other than that it somehow involved convincing Wes that John Junior was alive, which he had already done—she could not even begin to imagine.

"That was a wonderful idea," Anderson commented. "I really hoped you would get on well with one another."

247

"We have, haven't we, Isabel?" Gault asked.

"Absolutely," she answered, realizing that Anderson, for whatever reasons, preferred to ignore the less than friendly interaction between herself and Gault.

She didn't trust Gault, and from what she could divine, he felt the same way about her.

"Friends," Gault said.

"Friends," Isabel echoed.

Anderson kissed Isabel gently on the lips, and separating from her, caressed her face.

"If it were possible for the two of us to escape —"

"Oh, Wes, there is never any way to escape," she answered, running the tips of her fingers over his bare chest.

That this man could have headed Venom was inconceivable, as inconceivable as his obvious blindness to Gault's true nature.

"But if there were," he pressed on before he kissed each of her nipples.

"Someplace by the sea, someplace where we could enjoy its many moods."

"God, I love you!" he exclaimed, suddenly taking her in his arms. "I don't know how I managed to be without you for so long."

She laughed. "Come, come, Wes, you weren't exactly alone. Even now, there's Marylee."

"That's over. I swear, Isabel, that's over."

She put her finger across his lips. "Yes, I know that. I was only teasing you."

"Marylee is upset about Gault —"

248

"I shouldn't wonder."

"Why do you say that? I thought you and he—"

"Oh, Wes, you just didn't want to see what was really happening between us."

Anderson relaxed his embrace. "Suppose you tell me."

"The only way he'd like me is for me to have my thighs wide open and for him to be between them."

"Isabel, you're old enough to be his mother."

"A cunt is a cunt is a cunt," she said harshly.

He'd seldom heard her resort to that kind of language, except when she was close to having orgasm, and then those words, whether she used them or he did, seemed to bring her to a higher pitch of excitement.

"Wes, he wants something from you," she said.

Anderson shook his head. "He hasn't asked for anything."

"That doesn't matter. He will, and when he does . . ."

Anderson let go of her, and pushed himself up on his elbows.

"Doesn't it at least seem odd to you that he hasn't asked for something?"

"At first, yes. But then I realized that he was one of those individuals—"

"Don't tell me he's selfless," she challenged.

"I am telling you that he wants nothing from me, Isabel," Anderson responded forcefully; then almost immediately afterwards, he said, "No, that's not exactly true either."

"Ah, then he did ask for something!" she exclaimed with satisfaction.

"No, he never asked anything for himself or anyone else."

"You're confusing me."

"Without asking, he asked that I change, that I give evidence that I'm worthy of being reunited with my son." His voice had drifted lower and lower, until it was a barely audible whisper when he finished.

"Is that why you're resigning—"

"No. No, I had made that decision awhile ago. And as for the art collections, well—I had also decided that those collections should be available to the people."

"Are you telling me that Richard Gault will be your judge?" she asked in disbelief.

Anderson's ire rose. "That's not it at all. It's not a matter of him judging me."

"Then you tell me what it is," she shot back.

Anderson dropped down on the bed again. "You would not understand," he said, placing his hands behind his head.

"Oh, Wes, Wes . . ."

"I need to see my son. I need to know he's alive, and . . ."

He felt as if his voice would break, and he swallowed to stop it from happening.

"And ask his forgiveness," he finally whispered.

Isabel didn't answer.

She thought she knew everything there was to know about Wes, but this was a side she would have never dreamed existed. There was almost a religiosity about it which made it all the more frightening.

"Isabel, I don't mean to hurt you with what I'm about to say," he whispered, "but if you had a child of your own, you'd understand what I'm talking about."

She stiffened. "That was a cheap shot."

"I'm sorry," he said, putting his hand on her bare shoulder.

The afterglow of their lovemaking was rapidly fading . . . or had already faded.

Isabel turned her face toward him. Her heart raced.

"You're wrong, Wes," she said softly. "I did have a child." She let that hang in the air between them. "Your child, Wes."

He bolted up.

"What?" he shouted.

"That's why I divorced Carlos. I knew I was pregnant —"

"My God, why didn't you tell me? Where is — was it a boy or a girl? My God, Isabel . . . all these years . . ."

He didn't know whether to be angry, or pleased, or both at the same time.

He draped himself over Isabel's body. "Is that all you're going to tell me?" he asked.

"I never intended to tell even that much," she said.

"Is it a boy or girl? For God sakes, Isabel, that child is an Anderson, and —"

"That child is a young woman of fifteen who lacks for nothing and who —"

"Where is she? I want to see her."

Isabel gently touched the side of his face. "She lives with her parents in Mexico City."

"Parents? What parents? You mean you gave her up for adoption?"

"Yes," she whispered. "There was nothing else I could do. I was in no position to raise a child."

He moved away from her. "You should have come to me. You should have told me."

"I didn't want her to be John Wesley Anderson's bastard," Isabel said softly. "I wanted her to have her own identity, and she has. Her name is Carmen Valdez. Her father is a professor of archaeology, and her mother is a professor of English."

"Do you see her?" Anderson asked.

"Yes, several times a year. We are great friends."

"Who does she think you are?"

"A very good friend of the family."

Anderson said, "I want to see her."

"You will."

"When?"

"Just suppose I was to play the same game as Gault, and tell you something like, when you prove yourself to be a better man."

"Isabel—"

"Just think of how much power you've given to that young man."

"Isabel, I want to see my daughter."

"She's spending the summer with me. She'll be here from mid-June to late September."

"I'll have to make certain financial—"

"Please, Wes, nothing while you're alive. Please?"

"Are you sure she has—"

"Yes, she has everything she needs, and she has the love of her parents."

After a few moments, Anderson said, "If she looks like you, she must be beautiful."

"She has your eyes and chin."

252

He kissed Isabel gently on her lips.

"You're not angry with me?"

"I am, but I also love you very, very much."

"Enough to make love to me again?" she asked, embracing him and splaying her bare thighs.

For some reason, at that moment, she loved him more than she ever had, and needed to feel a oneness with him.

"Enough for an almost old man to try," he answered.

Chapter 20

Anderson was pleased with his newfound fatherhood, though he knew, of course, that he was reacting foolishly. Nonetheless, he indulged himself, and through the indulgence experienced an almost childish happiness.

For the next several days he worked with Max, getting the necessary legal documents in order that would be required by the Foundation when he resigned, and those that would be needed by the Internal Revenue Service when he finally donated his art collections. The financial statement would not be available until the appraiser finished his work.

Each evening and each night, he spent with Isabel. Twice she prepared dinner for him—the first time, she made a veal dish, and the second time, she broiled swordfish steaks.

Anderson was enchanted with her domesticity, and he was totally enchanted with her.

The night they went out for dinner, Isabel suggested a small local eatery that was, in her opinion, the best Mexican restaurant in the city.

Both knew they were rediscovering each other, and more important for Anderson than for her, she seemed to provide him with a voice for his conscience, social and ethical.

It was in the Mexican restaurant, after they had finished eating the most delicious flan he could remember having, that she took his hand. He'd realized that Isabel was well known to the two waiters and everyone else connected with the restaurant, including the chef, who'd come out from the kitchen while they were eating to ask if they were enjoying the food. Now, in a very low voice, she asked him if the name of the chef meant anything to him.

"Not that I recall." And he repeated the chef's name. "Miguel Santos." He shook his head. "Should it?"

"Think, Wes."

He started to shake his head, stopped, and stared at her. "There was a Santos, a Major Santos—"

She nodded. "That's him."

Anderson's brows knitted together.

She knew about Venom.

"That was a long time ago," he said in a whisper. "When I first met you. It's not the same now."

"The past is the past," she answered.

He was going to be totally honest with her. He had to be, more than she would ever know. He needed to be, especially about Venom.

"There is a fraternity among its former members. Now and then we meet, but there is nothing else. I swear to you, Isabel. There is nothing else."

She stroked his hand. "I believe you."

"Thank you," he said, then he asked if Miguel knew who he was. "He has reason to kill me. I had him tortured for eight consecutive days, and then—"

"You ordered him castrated," she whispered.

Anderson nodded.

She could see the pain in Anderson's face evoked by the memories.

"Isabel, I carry a huge, huge sack of guilt on my back, and I hope I have the opportunity to not so much reduce its weight—because the truth is, I deserve to carry it for the rest of my life—but possibly to make sure that the outrages I committed can never again take place."

Tears came into his eyes as he spoke, and when he finished, Isabel handed him a tissue.

"I can never make it right with that man," Anderson said, looking to the door on the other side of the room that led to the kitchen. "Money won't give him back his manhood."

"He never stopped being a man, Wes. A stiff cock is only a stiff cock, and is not an ensign of manhood, by any stretch of the imagination."

With a silent nod, Anderson agreed; then he spent a few moments looking around.

The restaurant consisted of one small room. The place was really a storefront operation, with ten tables, all with red tablecloths, and green painted walls decorated with framed travel posters from the Mexican tourist bureau.

"I think I know what you're thinking," Isabel said.

Anderson faced her and smiled. "You would be his silent partner."

"That I didn't expect," she admitted.

"He would become a restaurateur."

Again Anderson looked around, and started to ask about the other people who worked in the restaurant.

"They hold green cards," she told him.

"I'll have Max take care of the legal and financial details. You'll have whatever monies it requires to open and operate a larger and more elegant restaurant."

"Even if it operates at a loss?"

Anderson patted her hand. "Oh, I will make sure that doesn't happen. But that is between the two of us." And he smiled.

"I have a sudden vision of you as a little boy," she said, "who has just been caught with his hand in the cookie jar, or is guilty of some other bit of mischievousness, and is smiling as you do now."

"You see the wrong boy. Smiling was for other children, not for the Andersons. The world was a serious place, and they learned that lesson early. My brother Wally hardly ever smiles, and George wouldn't know how to."

"Thank God that you do," she said, and lifting his hand, she kissed the tips of his fingers.

Late the following afternoon, Anderson and Max were at the computer waiting to see the effect Anderson's stock offering would have on the market.

Three minutes after it was on the ticker tape, Wally phoned. "That's your stock, isn't it?" he practically shouted.

"Yes."

After a few moments of silence, Wally said, "You're making a mistake, John, a very big mistake." And he hung up.

Not more than a minute elapsed before Anderson's older brother, George, was on the line.

"Yes, that's my stock, and there's more to come," Anderson said before George could ask if the stock was his.

"I take a dim view of this," George said in a high-pitched voice. "You're making it possible for outsiders to have more of a say in the operation of Anderson Oil."

"And that's long overdue," Anderson answered.

"John, you were always a fool," George said, and hung up.

Anderson put the phone down. "My brothers are upset," he told Max.

"Wouldn't you be if you were either of them?"

Anderson shrugged. "That's something I can't imagine." Then he said, "Shut the computer off. There's something else that I want you to do for me."

Max exited the program, switched off the computer, and sat down in the chair alongside Anderson's desk.

"Last night . . ." Anderson began and stopped, then began again. "You know that I have over the years been linked to Isabel Aroyo."

Max nodded. "That's what I have read in the newspapers."

"Last night she told me I'd fathered a child, a girl, some fifteen years ago. That would be about a year after we met. I had no idea that she even had a child at that time, and we ended the relationship. She divorced her husband, and dropped out of sight for almost two years. Then we met again, and—well, our relationship has been off again, on again." He chuckled. "Of course, that has a double meaning, and either way you take it, it's true."

"John, the question pops into my mind, and I must ask it. Are you sure it's your child?"

"Isabel gains nothing by having told me. Nothing, that is, materially. But certainly, this binds us even closer together than we have been before.

"This daughter of mine—by the way, her name is Ann-Sophie-Pascale Giroux—lives in Mexico City with her parents."

"Adoptive parents," Max said.

259

"She believes them to be her real parents, and there is no real reason to upset that belief. But I want you to set up a trust fund for her from an anonymous donor for two million. Set it up so that she will receive fifty thousand a year from her eighteenth year until her fortieth, at which time she will be able to draw on the principal if she wants to."

"Do you want her parents to know the source?"

"Absolutely not."

"John, will you ever see your daughter?" Max asked.

"She'll be visiting with Isabel this summer," Anderson answered with a grin.

"And who does she think Isabel is?"

"A very good friend of the family," Anderson said.

"You're being extremely generous, and very trusting," Max commented.

Anderson didn't like the tone of Max's voice, and told him so.

"Sorry," Max said. "But—"

"You object to what I want to do?"

"I object to the way you're leaving yourself open for difficulties in the future by being so generous in the present. Let me explain, John. Should your daughter in the future discover who her real father is, and that he had already acknowledged her to be his daughter by providing a substantial trust fund for her—and there are ways she would be able to prove that—then, depending upon whether or not she was avaricious, she could lay claim to additional monies from your estate, if you are dead, or from you directly, if you are still alive. Either way, it could mean a nasty court fight."

Anderson stood up, went behind the desk chair, and leaned on it. "You, then, must make sure that she can never trace the source of her trust, even if it means using monies I have abroad."

"John, there's always a way, especially if someone is determined to do it."

"I have to believe that she will not cause difficulties."

Max stood up. "Is there any rush on this?"

"Not really. As long as I have the papers to sign before . . ." Anderson stopped himself. "Say, in two, or three weeks. A month at most."

"You'll have them," Max answered.

"You know, I find the idea of having a daughter very appealing," Anderson said. "And when Pascale visits with Isabel, I'm hoping that we become great friends."

"You will. That Anderson charm will make it happen."

Anderson laughed. "Yes, I'm counting on it to make me something special in her life."

Since dining with Anderson and Isabel, Gault hadn't seen much of Anderson, who spent the days with Grenville and his nights with Isabel.

The first part of that didn't sit well with him at all. He had no idea what Anderson was doing, and that made him feel as if he was losing his hold on the man. But the second part gave him free reign to play his sexual games with Marylee.

These thoughts were going through his mind when the phone on his desk rang, startling him. He almost never received calls, unless all the lines were being used and an incoming call was automatically switched to his phone.

"Gault here," he answered.

"Call your red number," the man on the other end said.

That was Grier's code phrase.

Gault put the phone down.

"Who was it?" Marylee asked without looking up from her work.

"Wrong number," Gault answered, and immediately became interested in a small stack of file cards on which various items of the Mezo-American collection were listed.

He was concerned. Grier had never before phoned him. And now he had to come up with an excuse that would enable him to call Grier back from an outside phone—not just any outside phone, but a specially designated one, because it was put there for only his use. Anyone else who used it always got a dial tone, but nothing more.

Suddenly, Marylee stood up.

He looked at her. No doubt she was off to see her shrink, to tell him of the previous night's "fun and games." When he'd begun fucking her, he'd done it to intimidate and control her. Now he had the feeling that, even though he had accomplished his goal, something else was beginning to operate . . . something that made him want her.

She smiled at him. "When you look at me that way—well, I like it."

"It's only because . . ." He wasn't going to let her get any hint of his shift in feeling toward her. "Because I want you to suck my cock. Now!"

Her cheeks flamed. "What?"

His voice harsher, he demanded, "Now."

She looked toward the door.

"Close it," Gault ordered.

"Richard, be reasonable."

He shook his head.

"I can't. I have things to do. I can't. If I do it, I'll be strung out for the rest of the day. I really do have things to do."

"What's more important than you suck my cock?"

"I'll do it after—"

"What's more important?" He stood up. "Come here and unzip my fly."

"I have to make the final arrangements for John's news conference," she said.

News conference—the two words screamed in his brain, and in an instant he was in front of her. Though he wanted to smash her in the face, he grabbed hold of her arm.

She tried to twist away. "What are you doing? You're hurting me. I said I would do it later, after work."

"It's okay," he said, letting go of her, and throwing up his hands. "I'm cool."

He knew he'd overreacted. She wasn't responsible for Anderson's actions.

Marylee rubbed her bruised arm.

"Tell me about the news conference. I didn't know anything about it." He was already thinking about how he was going to explain this new twist to Grier. "Do you know why he's holding it?"

She shook her head, and offered, "Maybe it has something to do with what he and Max have been doing these past few days."

"When is it going to take place?" Gault asked.

"Tomorrow, at five."

"Here?" he asked, looking around. There didn't seem to be enough room.

"In the Anderson building's auditorium."

Gault rubbed his chin. "Not even a glimmer about

what he intends to say?"

"He never gives any indication about what he's going to say," she explained. "He likes to surprise media people."

Gault looked down at her bare arm. The red imprint of his fingers was still there. He wanted to say that he was sorry, but instead he said, "Later, you suck my cock."

She smiled. "But only if you do me at the same time."

"Yeah, I'll do you."

"Don't sound so enthusiastic. I mean, I know one or two other men who'd appreciate the invitation."

He slapped her hard across her ass. "Do what you're supposed to do," he told her.

She glared at him, picked up her bag, and walked out of the office, purposely exaggerating the movement of her hips and buttocks.

Gault returned to his chair.

That Anderson was going to hold a news conference was close to the worst scenario he could imagine. The worst would be his true role being revealed to Anderson. The next in order would be Anderson telling the world that his son was alive, and that he would be reunited with him. And that was exactly what Gault was afraid was about to happen, or something very close to it.

"Shit!" he exclaimed out loud, getting up, going to the window, and looking out at the street.

Grier could damn well order him to take Anderson out.

Gault moved the curtain aside.

He wasn't prepared to do that . . . not yet.

He heard the door to Anderson's office open, and turning around, saw Anderson and Max step into the

264

foyer.

They shook hands, and Max said, "I know the way out."

Max vanished from Gault's sight, but Anderson stood in the foyer, looking after his friend and legal adviser, no doubt waiting until the front door closed.

Gault made his decision, and used the few moments that Anderson remained in the foyer to go to the door.

"John, could you spare me a few minutes?" he asked, stepping out into the foyer.

"Certainly, Richard. Come into my office."

Anderson led the way, and Gault closed the door behind him.

"These last few days have been hard," Anderson commented, sitting down behind his desk.

Gault occupied the chair alongside the desk.

"I'm listening," Anderson said, leaning back in his swivel chair.

"Marylee mentioned that you will be holding a news conference."

"That's right."

Gault made a head-on approach. "I hope that nothing will be said about John Junior." He looked straight at Anderson. "Something like that would be extremely disruptive. I don't think I could continue to remain here." Then in a much softer voice, he said, "You understand that, don't you?"

Moment by passing moment the silence between them deepened.

Gault was aware of Anderson's labored breathing, and the furrows that came into his brow, but most of all of the muddy look that washed into his blue eyes.

Anderson cleared his throat, then said, "I will announce my forthcoming resignation from the

Foundation."

Gault uttered a controlled sigh of relief.

"I'm sorry you thought so little of my sense of discretion that you felt it necessary to have this conversation." Anderson was visibly upset. He did not appreciate being reminded that he was a "probationer," even if, by putting himself in that role, it would eventually reunite him with John Junior.

"I needed to be sure," Gault explained. "I didn't want our special arrangement to be disrupted by becoming a media event. I have too much respect for you, and for your son."

"I would not jeopardize our 'special arrangement.'"

Gault realized that he might have suddenly put his own position in jeopardy. "I am sorry, but when I heard that you were going to hold a news conference, I became very nervous. My first responsibility is to protect the sanctity of the way of life John Junior has chosen for himself."

"I agree with that, certainly."

"Then the matter is closed," Gault said, and began to stand.

Anderson motioned him back in the chair. "I need to know more about your plans," he said.

"They are exactly the same as they were when I came here."

"Then I will proceed with my plans accordingly," Anderson answered.

Gault looked at him quizzically.

With an amiable smile, Anderson said, "Everyone Richard, is entitled to their own plans, *n'est-ce pas?*"

The answer jarred Gault, and it must have shown in his face, because Anderson added, "But I assure you I haven't changed any of my plans that involve you."

"Nor have I changed those that involve you," Gault responded.

Anderson said, "I'm pleased to hear that, Richard, very pleased. Now if you will excuse me, I have, as you can see by the profusion of papers on my desk, still some work to do before I call it a day."

Gault stood up.

"I'm glad we talked," Anderson commented.

"Yes, so am I," Gault responded, but he wasn't.

Anderson picked up one of the papers from the desk, and gave his attention to it, while Gault quietly left the office. Moments later, he was on his way to call Grier.

Among the various things that bothered him about the conversation was Anderson's veiled threat — not in the words themselves, but in the tone he had used to say them. That was where the threat was.

As Gault walked to Lexington Avenue, he remembered the rumors he had heard about how dangerous a man Anderson was. And of course, Grier had warned him more times than he cared to remember not to be deceived by Anderson's charm, that the man was "instinctively a killer" who'd "go for the jugular every time." But when he'd finally met Anderson, he'd found him very different from the kind of man he had been conditioned to expect. The conversation was the first evidence that Anderson could be dangerous, that so far Gault had been only exposed to the gentle and generous Anderson persona, and that there was — as he had been warned there would be — another, more venomous persona capable of killing.

Gault turned south on Lexington, walked two blocks, and crossed over to the southeast corner, where the safe phone was located.

Moments after he dialed Grier's number, the disembodied voice of a computer said, "This is the hotel. Please give the room number you want."

Gault answered with his own ID number.

Grier came on the line immediately. "What the hell took you so long?" he barked.

Gault ignored the question, and Grier didn't press him for an answer. Instead, he said, "Tell me what the fuck is going on up there."

"Nothing," Gault said. He wasn't going to say anything about his conversation with Anderson until he had more time to think about it.

"Listen, you're there, and you don't know that Anderson sold off a block of ten thousand shares of Anderson Oil just before the market closed. Just what the fuck are you doing there?"

Gault started to sweat.

"We want to know what the hell is happening," Grier shouted.

"I'm not his financial adviser," Gault answered.

"Just find out—"

"He's holding a news conference."

"Holy Christ, when?"

"Tomorrow."

"Why?"

"I don't know. I just found out about it myself. He's going to announce his resignation from the Foundation."

"Yes, Safe Deposit has already told us that was about to happen."

"Maybe he knows something about the sale of the stock?" Gault suggested.

"It caught him with his pants down."

Gault had a fleeting image of Safe Deposit with his pants down. It was sufficiently ridiculous to make him laugh.

"I think the fucking joke is on you," Grier said. "I'll tell you what I think, I think Anderson is jerking you around. This news conference—did he tell you what it was going to be about, or did you get it from that bitch Marylee?"

"He told me," Gault said, angered by the way Grier spoke about Marylee.

"Bushwick is going to go through the roof when I tell him about the news conference."

"He's your problem, not mine."

"He's both our problem. More yours than mine if he suddenly gets a bug up his ass and decides to have Anderson terminated now, instead of letting us play out our game to its end."

"He's stupid, but he's not that stupid."

"He wants the Vice Presidency. That's all that matters to him. And he also wants to protect the Company, because if Anderson becomes its watch-dog, the only thing that will happen to General Bushwick is that he will fade away, if he's lucky, and if he's not—well, I don't want to think about that possibility, because I might wind up behind bars too, and there's a good chance you and several others will be with us."

"Tell him—Christ, tell him to be patient."

"By the end of the month, Richard. Either you take him to Nepal by the end of the month, or you take him out wherever the hell he is. It's your ball game to play."

The line went dead.

"Son of a bitch!" Gault swore, slamming the phone down. "Fucking son of a bitch!" Without waiting for the light to change to green, he stalked across Lexington Avenue, forcing one car to swerve around him.

Grier had just backed him into a corner, and there wasn't anything he could do about it. The end of the month was two weeks away.

When Gault reached Madison Avenue and Sixty-seventh Street, he saw Marylee. She was just ahead of him, and he quickened his pace, catching up to her.

"Everything set for the news conference?" he asked.

"Yes."

Gault reached down and took hold of her hand. She gave him a questioning look.

"I—hell, there's nothing wrong with my holding your hand, is there?"

"Nothing." Then she added, "It's different. We don't usually hold hands."

Gault let go of her.

"I didn't say I didn't like it," Marylee said.

"We're almost at the house," he answered.

"Are we going to be together later?" Marylee asked. She sensed he had changed from the way he had been earlier.

"Yeah, maybe we'll take in a flick, and then have dinner out."

They were at the house, and started to walk up the steps.

"I'd like that." She was certain that something had happened.

At the door, Gault ran his hand over her buttocks. She smiled.

"I like doing that," he said.

"I like when you do it," she answered, and unlocking the door, opened it.

As soon as they entered the foyer, Anderson came out of his office. He was grinning broadly. "If I don't tell someone right now," he said, "I'm going to explode. The President just offered me a job."

"What job?" Marylee asked excitedly.

"It doesn't matter—"

"Yes, it does," Marylee insisted.

Gault went numb. Things were happening too fast.

"I sell a block of stock, and—"

"What did he offer you, John?" Marylee asked.

"To watchdog the CIA," he answered triumphantly. "Imagine that. Me, the ombudsman of the CIA. That's certainly going to rattle some bones, I can tell you that." He was enjoying himself.

"I tried calling Wally," Anderson said. "But he's sore at me, and wouldn't take my call. But when he finds out about the offer, he'll call me, and so will my brother George."

"Oh, John, I'm so happy for you!" Then turning to Gault, she asked, "Isn't this just marvelous?"

"That's for Mr. Anderson to decide."

"But just think of the honor—"

Anderson held up his hand, and said, "Too fast, Marylee, too fast. I told the President that I would think about it."

Gault's heart skipped a beat, then raced.

"I want to keep my options open," Anderson explained; then looking directly at Gault, he said, "I told the President I needed a few days to think it over."

"But you are considering it, aren't you?" Marylee asked.

"No," Anderson said. "But out of politeness to the President, I couldn't reject the offer out of hand. I have some plans of my own, and if returning to government service was among them, it certainly would not be as the ombudsman of the CIA, especially not when I could be more effective elsewhere."

Gault suddenly felt ill. Was he playing Anderson, or was Anderson now playing him? Either way Anderson had to be the loser.

Chapter 21

Bushwick and Grier stood at the TV in Bushwick's office watching Anderson.

Bushwick chomped on his cigar, but didn't light it, while Grier, with his hands clasped behind his back, remained outwardly calm, though his stomach was twisted into a very large knot. It had been that way since the previous evening, when he'd had the distinct impression while speaking to Gault that Gault was losing sight—or worse, had already lost sight—of the mission's goal.

Anderson, behind a podium, holding his glasses in his left hand by one side of their frames, looked confident and cheerful, and even bantered with some of the reporters in front of the cameras before making his formal statement.

Precisely at five P.M., the camera zoomed in on Anderson, and the announcer said, "NBC News live coverage brings you Mr. John Wesley Anderson. Mr. Anderson."

"Ladies and gentlemen, and members of the TV audience, I called this news conference for several different reasons. The first of which is to announce my resignation, effective immediately, from the Anderson Foundation, which I have had the pleasure of guiding for the past twenty years. There are compelling reasons for my having made this decision. I have reached the stage in my life where I need to . . ."

Anderson picked up his notes, smiled the famous Anderson smile, and said, "I knew these weren't worth a damn when I wrote them."

His audience roared with laughter.

Bushwick rolled his unlit cigar from one side of his mouth to the other, and Grier suddenly felt the burning sensation of heartburn.

"I'll speak off the cuff. Please don't quote me," Anderson said.

Another burst of laughter followed.

"Son of a bitch is smooth," Bushwick growled, momentarily shifting his eyes from the screen to Grier.

Grier remained stone-faced. Anderson wasn't just smooth, he was a consummate actor.

"Ladies and gentlemen, at sixty it suddenly dawns on a dimwit like myself that I have lived most of my life, and the time that lies ahead of me should be put to better use than making more money, collecting more art. The time should be used to . . . to do those things that I have always wanted to do, but never had the time to. I'm sure everyone here today, or watching today, has had something that he or she has wanted to do, but for either the lack of time or money—often the lack of both—has not done.

"Well, I have more money than I could spend in twenty lifetimes, and as for time, I have by resigning from the Anderson Foundation given myself the time."

He smiled at them, and they responded by clapping; then Anderson held up his hands for silence.

"Ladies and gentlemen, I am going to put, to use the vernacular, my money—and I have lots of it—

where my mouth is. I'm going to donate my various art collections to several different institutions in the United States, and thereby allow the public access to the great art that was created by the Pre-Columbian inhabitants of Mexico and Central and South America."

A third burst of applause followed this announcement, and when it finally died down, Anderson said, "I'm sure that a great many of you are anxious to know what I intend to do with a fortune that I can't obviously take with me when I finally make the trip over to the other side—and even if I could it would be useless, where I'm going. I'll leave you to speculate whether it will be up or down."

The audience laughed.

"Hell—that's where you'll go to!" Bushwick exclaimed.

Anderson laughed along with the audience, then he continued. "For those who want to know what I intend to do with my money, I ask them to rest easy. I will give most of it away for research on AIDS, cancer, and several other diseases—"

The audience rose to its feet and applauded.

Anderson held up his hands again, only this time he appealed to them to let him finish.

"Thank you," he said, when the auditorium was quiet again. "Other monies will go to various art schools to establish art scholarships for young men and women who have the talent but not the funds to attend a college or university.

"And before you begin to show your approval and appreciation for the way I intend to get rid of my money, I must also tell you that I intend to endow certain institutions whose purpose is to save our environment, promote world peace and the better-

275

ment of all mankind. That, ladies and gentlemen, is what I will do."

The members of the press were on their feet again, clapping and shouting, "Anderson . . . Anderson . . . Anderson . . ."

And he responded by coming out from behind the podium and opening his arms to embrace all of them.

Bushwick switched off the TV.

"The fucker never mentioned the President's offer. You would have thought he'd say something."

Grier finally popped two antacid tablets into his mouth.

The red phone on Bushwick's desk rang. He answered it.

The President was on the other end. He said, "Anderson is going for the brass ring."

"Is that the way you read it?"

"Yes."

Bushwick cleared his throat. "I don't think you have anything to worry about, Mr. President. My people here assure me that within a relatively short period he will—"

Grier was holding up two fingers and mouthing the word "weeks."

Bushwick nodded. "In two weeks, Mr. President, it will be a very different situation."

"Are you certain of that?"

"Absolutely."

"That's very reassuring, especially coming from you," the President said.

Bushwick thanked him.

"I'll be in touch," the President said, and hung up.

Bushwick put the phone down, looked up at Grier, and said, "Get Anderson out of the fucking country."

"Two weeks," Grier said, taking two more antacid tablets. "I'll go up to New York and let Gault know exactly where it's at."

"Do that," Bushwick said. "If you want to sit in this fucking chair, do it, and make sure Gault will do it when the time comes to do it."

Despite the tightening of the knot in Grier's stomach, he managed to nod and mumble, "I'll take care of it."

Isabel waited on the steps outside B. Altman's. She preferred to do her shopping there, rather than in Bloomingdale's, which, though more trendy, was also more crowded and more frenetic. But this time she was there to meet Marylee Terrall.

She had called Marylee the day after Wes's news conference, which made the front page of every morning newspaper in the city, and probably the front page of every newspaper in the country.

Isabel had considered meeting Marylee after she'd met Gault, but had delayed making the call partly out of inertia, and partly because she had no real wish to meet Wes's other woman. But the fallout from Wes's news conference had made it absolutely imperative. She didn't trust Gault, and Wes had looked very much like a political candidate on TV. The combination of her distrust and Wes's TV appearance had forced her to phone Marylee.

They were to meet at eleven-thirty in the morning. But Isabel had arrived a few minutes earlier, and just as she was about to look at her watch, a cab pulled up to the curb, the door opened, and Marylee emerged.

She was even more beautiful than she had appeared to be in the various photographs of her that Isabel had seen in newspapers and magazines.

Without the slightest bit of hesitation Marylee came directly toward her.

She had no idea why Isabel had asked to meet her, but she was determined to act with as much aplomb as she could possibly muster, despite the constant fluttering of her stomach.

"Thank you so very much for coming," Isabel said, taking Marylee's hand and gently shaking it.

"To tell the truth, your invitation surprised me."

"And you were just a little bit curious about why I called?" Isabel said. "In your place, I would have been curious too."

Marylee found herself looking at a forty-five-year-old woman whose exotic attractiveness was even more striking than if she had just been beautiful, which she was. There was a Parisian chic about her that enabled her to wear, as she was, a simple green neckerchief folded into a narrow band and tied, Indian style, around her head of red hair. It made her startlingly lovely.

"What I have to say to you would be better said while we walk," Isabel told her.

"That serious?" Marylee asked, wondering what it could be. Certainly, it could not be about her relationship with John, since that no longer existed.

"Yes, it is very serious." Then Isabel asked if Marylee preferred to walk uptown or downtown.

"Uptown," Marylee said.

Isabel waited until they were across Thirty-fifth Street before she asked, "What can you tell me about Richard Gault?"

Marylee immediately began to cough.

Isabel waited until Marylee's coughing subsided

before she said, "You're sleeping with him, aren't you?"

Another fit of coughing erupted, this time so severe they were forced to move off to the side until Marylee brought it under control. Then she started to say, "What I do, or don't do—"

Isabel cut her short. "You're absolutely right. I'm only interested in his connection to Wes. I don't care a pin for Richard Gault, but I care very much for Wes, and I know you."

They started to walk again.

"Wes chose you," Marylee said. "Isn't that enough for you?"

"Marylee," Isabel said, using her given name, as if she were a friend, "I asked you to meet me because I need your help."

"My help to do what? To keep John?"

"To protect him," Isabel answered.

They stopped for a red light, waiting in silence until it turned green.

"Gault is my concern," Isabel said, as soon as they began walking again.

"Why? John knows him. They worked together on a dig."

Isabel didn't give an immediate answer. That Wes had had previous dealings with Gault was obviously his cover story, and she couldn't reveal Gault's real purpose for being there without betraying Wes's confidence.

"The truth is he doesn't know a damn thing about archaeology, much less Mezo-American art," Marylee blurted out. "I have to redo almost everything he does."

Had Isabel believed in God, she would have at that moment thanked Him, but she was a confirmed atheist, and the most she could do was to nod and say, "That should tell you something."

"Only that John wants him there."

"Yes, but . . ." Isabel stopped herself from saying "but why," and took off in another direction. "Gault is certainly an expert shot," she said.

"Lucky, he claims."

"Don't you believe it. I know something about that, and that shot was made by an expert."

Marylee glanced at the woman. And suddenly remembered that Isabel Aroyo, for all her chic, had been, and possibly still was, a member of a revolutionary movement. "Are you trying to tell me that Gault is some sort of a revolutionary?"

"I am not trying to tell you. I *am* telling you that Gault is dangerous."

They paused for another red light, and stopped their conversation.

When they were on the other side of Fortieth Street, Marylee asked, "If he's a danger to John, why did he save his life?"

"I can't answer that," Isabel said. "Or maybe I can, and I just don't want to accept it. Gault could have acted reflexively, that's a possibility. But he also could have done it to prove his loyalty—for want of a better word—to Wes."

Even as she spoke, Isabel felt the goose bumps on her back and arms. Gault had done just that, and Wes would not only believe his story about John Junior, he would insist that he be taken to John Junior. But Wes would never return.

Her stride suddenly faltered, and she almost fell.

Marylee grabbed hold of her. "Are you all right?"

Isabel nodded, forced a smile, and assured her that nothing was wrong.

"I really don't know what you want me to do," Marylee said.

"Help me protect Wes."

"From Gault?"

"Yes, from him or anyone else."

Marylee wondered what Hasse's reaction would be to all of this.

"Do you love Gault?" Isabel asked.

"I would if he'd let me," Marylee said in a low voice.

Isabel suddenly wondered if she had made the wrong move by meeting Marylee. "If you tell Gault about our conversation, you might very well be putting your life, as well as mine, in danger. And I'm not telling you this to frighten you. I'm telling it to you because I sincerely believe it. Gault is a very dangerous man."

They stopped at Forty-fifth Street for the light.

"He can be very persuasive, especially in bed," Marylee said, as soon as they stepped off again.

Isabel guessed as much.

"I'm sorry. I wish I could promise you that I won't tell him, but I can't. I'm not a very good actress, and he has a much stronger will than I have."

"Thank you for being honest."

"But I will help you protect John, at least as much as I can."

"Just call me, Marylee. Call me if Gault or anyone else does something unusual," Isabel said. "It doesn't matter what time of the day or the night."

"Yes, I should be able to do that."

"Good, very good!" Isabel answered.

Marylee laughed, and said, "That's what John usually says when he's pleased with something."

"Yes, he does, doesn't he!" Isabel responded.

But she was far from pleased. She was even more frightened for Wes than she had been before, and now she was also frightened for herself and for Marylee.

"I thought you came here to congratulate me on my news conference," Anderson said, smiling at Wally, who was standing stiffly in front of him.

"I did not come here to congratulate you or discuss that . . . that performance," Wally responded.

Anderson gestured to where a small couch and two easy chairs were positioned around an elliptical glass-topped coffee table. "Whatever you came here for can certainly be discussed from a seated position as well as a standing one, and I much prefer to be seated."

Anderson took the lead, and sat down in one of the easy chairs.

Wally settled on the couch.

"All right, now tell me the real reason for your visit," Anderson said, expecting his brother to launch into a tirade.

"I need you to come with me to Paris," Wally said.

Anderson smiled broadly. "Ah, so the deal with the Saudis has finally been made. Then I must congratulate you. You worked hard enough to bring it off."

"Three years hard," Wally said.

"I think this calls for something of a celebration." Anderson started to stand.

"No need . . . no need to . . ."

"Of course there is," Anderson insisted, finally getting to his feet. "Now, tell me what you would like to drink."

Wally shook his head. "You should know I never drink before five."

Anderson snapped his fingers. "Damn it if that very important fact didn't escape me," he answered, and sat down again.

"The Saudis want your signature on the deal," Wally said, looking absolutely pained as he spoke.

"My signature!"

"The initial deal was set up with you as one of the principals."

"What did you finally get from them, Wally?" Anderson asked.

"Let me put it to you this way. The fleet of Anderson Oil tankers will over the next ten years transport a full sixty percent of all the oil the Saudis produce, and have the right to buy and process up to a hundred percent of that crude at the lowest market price."

"And what did you give them in return?"

Wally's face almost fractured into a smile. "Nothing that Anderson Oil has to pay for."

"Arms?"

"I gave them what they wanted, and I got what I wanted. Now, all we need to do is fly to Paris and sign the official documents. I have already taken the liberty of booking us on tomorrow's Air France Concorde flight out of Kennedy. Overnight in Paris, and we'll be back here for a full business day by the following morning."

Anderson stood up, walked as far as the desk, turned around, and said, "I'll sign, because I was one of the principals, but I want you to know now, so that it doesn't come as a shock to you later, I will resign from my position in Anderson Oil within the next few weeks."

Wally leaped to his feet. "Are you completely mad?" he shouted. "You do that, and it will eventually lead to breaking the family tradition."

"You mean breaking the family's hold on the company, don't you?"

"Yes . . . yes."

"It needs breaking, if it trades oil for arms, arms that it doesn't own."

Wally's face colored. He couldn't believe what he was hearing. "I have nothing more to say to you, John. I'll see you at the airport. I hope you have the good sense not to mention your future plans to the Saudis."

Anderson went to his desk; he wasn't going to honor his brother's comment with an answer.

Grier was waiting for Gault in a black limousine parked across the street from the apartment house where Tops and Ricks had their safe apartment.

There were just the two of them in the rear of the car, and the bullet-proof plastic partition between the front and the rear positions was up.

"Have trouble getting away?" Grier asked as the limo eased out into the middle of the street.

"None. Anderson wasn't around, and I'll see Marylee later."

"She any good?"

"Yeah, she's good. I'm kind of sorry that I come on to her the way I do."

"Once this matter is settled, you can apologize," Grier said.

Gault didn't answer. He'd probably never see Marylee again, and that didn't sit well with him. Besides, if he did, how was he going to tell her what he'd done to her was an act—and for what? An act for whom?

"It's a quarter to twelve, Richard, and Anderson has fifteen minutes to live," Grier said.

Startled, Gault looked at him.

"Those fifteen minutes can be stretched into two weeks, or become, should the situation require it, a matter of hours."

Gault let his mind absorb that. Then he uttered a deep sigh, but didn't say anything.

"I'm going to spell the whole thing out for you," Grier said. "Maybe I should have done this at the very beginning."

"Yeah, maybe you should have," Gault answered, looking out of the dark tinted window, and realizing they were on the East River Drive heading north, toward the Triborough Bridge.

Grier said, "Years ago, before you reached the age of puberty, Anderson worked for the Company."

"I knew that, or rather I heard about it."

"He ran a very particular operation, a group of hit men who were totally loyal to him."

"His own hit team?" Gault asked incredulously.

"Believe it. And just to make it more interesting, he was the only one who knew the identity of each member."

Gault uttered a low whistle.

"The group's code name was Venom."

"Yeah, I certainly heard of it, but I had no idea Anderson ran it."

"Only a select few in the Company know that." Grier paused, then he said, "And now you're one of them."

Gault accepted the honor with a nod.

"So now you know that Anderson's hands are stained red with blood, a great deal of blood, Richard. And that brings me to my next point. Recently,

285

we've lost a half a dozen good men over the past several months. All of them had some connection with our operations in Central and South America."

"That doesn't tie Anderson to the killings," Gault said.

"It does if you're Anderson," Grier shot back.

"I don't see it."

"Suppose you're Anderson and for whatever reasons you have had a change of heart, of politics. His speech last night is a good indication of where he's going."

"Where do you and General Bushwick think he's going?"

"Well, you know the President has offered him the job of watchdogging the Agency."

"He's not going to take it," Gault said. "I thought you guys would be smart enough to read between the lines." He would have expected Grier to be sharp enough to understand what Anderson was doing in front of the TV cameras. "For Christ sakes, Grier, I have Anderson hooked. He's going to go with me. He's giving his worldly goods away to prove to me that he's worthy of breathing the same air as his son."

Grier positioned himself catty-corner on his side of the rear seat. He wanted very much to believe what he'd just heard. In a very low voice, he said, "We don't want Anderson anywhere near the Agency, either as its watchdog or worse, as the President. It's not only Bushwick who feels this way about Anderson. I do too, and there are others, including Safe Deposit. With our present leader, and Bushwick in the number-two spot, we will be able to bring power to bear either here or abroad where it will do the most good for the people who hold it. The stakes are very high, Richard, very high. And Anderson — well,

286

he can make the difference." By the time Grier finished, his voice was racked by an emotional tremolo.

"Anderson will be history," Gault responded. He too was caught up in the emotions generated by the whole idea of a government within a government. "He'll go to Katmandu."

Grier nodded. "That's very reassuring to hear, Richard, very reassuring."

It was in the Mexican restaurant, after they had
finished eating the most delicious flan he could ...

Chapter 22

"This trip to Paris . . ." Isabel began. Then realizing that Anderson was out on the terrace and couldn't hear her, she stopped.

But even if he could hear her, he wouldn't listen. He'd still go.

She came up behind him, and put her hands on his shoulders, pressing herself against him.

"I love you," she said.

He covered her left hand with his right. "And I adore you."

His voice had just enough of a melancholy tone for her to respond, "The words are right, but the enthusiasm seems less than burning."

Anderson gently squeezed her hand. "I've had several disturbing phone calls," he said. "Prank calls in the middle of the night."

He turned, and put his arms around her. "Nothing to worry about."

But he couldn't quite make himself sound convincing. The calls had been from dead men, from some of the men Venom had killed on his orders.

She shook her head. "For something that I shouldn't worry about, you seem awfully worried."

Anderson separated himself from her and walked back into the living room. He couldn't tell her anymore about the phone calls. As it was, he'd probably told her too much. Enough to make her question him. Though she knew about his involvement with Venom, he still wanted to keep her knowledge at a minimum, for fear she might not be able to live with his past, and turn away from him.

"Some people have a sick sense of humor," he said. "Eventually the calls will stop."

"I hope you don't say anything. That's the worst thing you can do."

"No, I just listen, and that's enough."

"They're obscene, aren't they?" she questioned.

He nodded, and was going to say, "if you interpret the word 'obscene' in its broadest sense," but she spoke first.

"I had phone calls like that, about two years ago. Mine came complete with filthy language, and lots of heavy breathing."

"Mine are the same," Anderson lied.

Isabel sat down on the sofa and patted the cushion next to her. "Come sit down, Wes."

He joined her, and said, "I imagine that I'll be going to see John Junior soon, but before I go I'm going to hold another news conference, and—"

"Your last one still has some people twirling," she commented.

"The next one will send those same people ricocheting off the wall. I'm going to declare myself a Presidential candidate."

Isabel jumped up.

"You're not, are you?"

Anderson grinned.

"My God, Wes, you never gave me any hint that you were even thinking about it."

"It's been in the wind for awhile."

"With the Democrats?"

"Well, they want me to be their standard-bearer, and I said I would, but I've been doing some hard thinking about that, and the way I see it, I don't want to be aligned with either the Democrats or the Republicans. I want something fresh and exciting to offer the people, something that they could really believe in. I'm going to run as an independent. I don't want to be obligated to anyone. I want to be my own man, all the way. I want to be able to make a difference to the people here, and the people abroad."

She dropped down with her knees on the sofa, and put her arms around him. "I know you can make a difference, Wes. I know you can." And she kissed him passionately on his lips.

He held her tightly to him.

Suddenly she pulled herself away. "What will happen to us?"

"Nothing. Nothing will happen to us."

"Even you wouldn't be able to stop, or cope with, the slander. Wes, having a mistress—"

"You won't be my mistress." He stood up. "I want you to be my wife. I have nothing with Augusta."

"Wes—"

"I want you at my side. Even if I wasn't going to run for the Presidency, I was going to ask you to marry me. I don't want to live my remaining years the way I have lived most of my life in the past. I have loved you from the first moment I saw—no, that's not exactly true. I have loved you from that time we were together in Acapulco, and stopped at a place that overlooked the ocean."

291

She smiled. "I didn't think you remembered."

"We were fondling each other. We hadn't made love yet. Then without a word you—"

"Wes, I wanted you as much as you wanted me."

"Yes, I knew it then, and that's when I really fell in love with you."

Isabel flushed. "I needed to have you inside me," she said in a low but intense voice. "And when you finally were, I felt complete."

"And when I finally was, I suddenly knew what I had never before known, that I was in love—not just making love, but actually in love. I still am wildly, totally in love with you, Isabel."

This time he kissed her. "I want you with me for the rest of my life," he told her.

She caressed the side of his face.

"I will discuss the divorce with Augusta when I return from Nepal. I do not think she will oppose it."

"Wes, are you sure—"

"I'm more certain about this—us—than I am about anything else," he answered. "And I'll tell you something else. Once I finish my terms—"

"Terms?"

"Yes, I'll need two terms in office to accomplish everything I want to do. Listen to me. Once I'm done with the White House, I'm finally going to do what I have always wanted to."

"Paint?"

Anderson grinned. "Yes, paint."

Gault and Marylee walked hand in hand up Second Avenue. They'd had dinner at the Ukrainian, a restaurant near the Second Avenue Theater. He'd once had a walk-on part there in *Mahogany,* an opera by Kurt Weill. But he didn't mention that to her, or for that matter, much else, despite the fact that he enjoyed being with her. His meeting with Grier had left him in a pensive mood.

The stakes that Bushwick, Grier, and whoever else was with them were fighting for were no less than the secret control of the government itself. What was just as unbelievable was his own role as the linchpin for the entire operation.

Reflexively, he squeezed Marylee's hand.

She returned the pressure and smiled at him. "I was beginning to think that you forgot I was here."

"Just preoccupied. Sometimes, I get that way."

She suddenly angled toward a women's boutique, taking him with her, and exclaimed, "Isn't that a stunning cape, the light tan one!"

Gault saw the garment, but he also saw a gold ring shaped and worked into a small knot in a jewelry case.

"Would you mind if I went in and asked the price of the cape?" Marylee asked.

"No, I'll go with you."

As soon as they entered the shop a bell tinkled, and a Chinese woman, wearing a long silk green dress decorated with an embroidered red rose over her right breast, came out from behind a curtain in the rear.

Marylee immediately pointed to the cape in the window and asked how much it was, while Gault moved over to the small glass-topped case where various pieces of jewelry were kept under lock and key. Some were made of gold, others of silver, a few of green jade, and one opal was mounted in a simple gold setting. Even in the case, the opal was full of fire.

"The cape is two hundred dollars," Marylee announced, going toward him.

Gault looked up. He was going to point out the ring to her, and then tell her that he'd buy it for her, if she wanted it. But in that same instant the shop bell tinkled and two men walked in.

Gault found himself looking at the same two punks he'd beaten up a couple of weeks before.

Marylee raised her eyebrows, and realizing he was looking at the people who just entered the shop, started to turn.

"Don't move!"

The taller of the two closed the door.

"Just give us what you have in the register, and we'll go," he said, pointing a .38 at the shopkeeper.

The shorter one moved deeper into the store, stopped, and called out, "Brownie, we got our old friend back."

Brownie moved off to the side. "Yeah, the one the cops didn't want to talk about."

"And he's with his lady friend. Now that's real interesting."

"Nice-lookin' piece of ass," the shorter one said. "Okay, cunt, move away from your boyfriend."

Marylee trembled.

"You and me—well, lover boy, I'm goin' to have some fun with your doll here."

Gault said nothing.

"Brownie—"

"Yeah, yeah, fuck the bitch, then I'll do the same," Brownie said.

"Don't move," Gault said under his breath. "Don't

294

move."

"Bitch, get your fucking ass in the back."

Marylee squinched her eyes shut. Her blood pounded in her ears. She expected to feel the ripping pain of a bullet any moment.

"I'm talking to you, cunt," the shorter one shouted, and the next instant he went for her arm.

Gault's hand shot out and grabbed hold of the man's hand, twisting him around, bringing his arm behind his back.

"The mother-fucker got me!"

Gault pushed Marylee aside, and started moving toward Brownie. "You shoot and you're going to kill your friend."

Confusion spread over Brownie's face.

"Put the fuckin' gun down," the man shouted.

"Your play, Brownie," Gault said, pulling the man's arm up higher.

"Christ, you're going to rip my arm out!" the man screamed, trying to twist free.

"Yeah, that's what I'm going to do," Gault answered in a flat voice.

Brownie backed toward the door.

"Where you goin'?" the man shouted. "Where you goin'?"

Brownie stuck the .38 in his belt, flung open the door, and ran.

Gault pulled the man's arm higher up behind his back until he heard it snap.

The man screamed.

Gault let go of his hand.

The man's arm dangled loosely from his shoulder.

"Better have that taken care of," Gault said, pushing him out of the open door.

"I'll get you, mother-fucker, I'll get you," the man shouted, holding his broken arm. "I'll get you." Then he ran.

Gault turned and went to Marylee. She was very pale.

"You okay?"

She nodded.

He looked at the shopkeeper.

"You're a very brave man," the woman said.

Gault flushed.

The shopkeeper said, "I'll give you the cape at cost. One hundred and seventy-five dollars."

Still frightened, Marylee clung to Gault. "Should I—"

"We'll take it," Gault said. "Wrap it up."

"Oh Richard, I . . ." Tears came into her eyes. "I was never so frightened in my life. I thought he'd—they—"

"It's all right," he said, putting his arms around her. "I was frightened too."

"But you didn't show it. You knew exactly what you were doing, like . . ."

She suddenly remembered that he'd known exactly what to do when the two men had tried to kill Anderson.

Smiling, the shopkeeper handed the wrapped cape to Gault, and shook his hand.

"Anytime you come here you can buy at cost," she said.

Gault thanked her.

"You have a brave man," the woman said, shaking Marylee's hand.

"I know," Marylee answered with a smile.

Finally, they left the shop, and started to walk

296

uptown again.

Gault said, "There's no need to mention what happened to anyone. I mean, it's just going to make me uncomfortable." He wasn't sure how much Marylee could put together from what had just taken place and what had happened in the park a few days before.

"But who were those creeps?"

Making a snorting sound, he said, "Just creeps, ordinary street creeps."

"How did they know you?"

Gault suddenly stopped. "I don't want to talk about it. You, me, and that Chinese woman are safe, and that's all that really matters. No more questions, all right?"

Marylee smiled at him. "How could I say no to you?" she said.

"Good. Then let's find a cab, go back to your place, and fuck our brains out."

"If that's what you want to do."

"That's exactly what I want to do," he answered, though it wasn't.

What he wanted was to take her in his arms and tell her that he loved her. But that would have to wait until he finished with Anderson. He bit his lower lip.

"You look pained," Marylee said.

"No, just an odd thought popped into my head."

"Share it?"

"Later. Now we have to find us a cab," he said, leading her to the curb.

The whole idea of finishing Anderson suddenly possessed a definitiveness it had never before had, and for the first time he began to realize the other player in the deadly game hadn't the slightest inkling that he *was* a player. And that he'd end up being the loser.

Anderson stood on the terrace looking out across the darkened Hudson, sprinkled here and there with the red and green navigation lights of tugs moving on its black surface.

"Couldn't sleep," he said, hearing Isabel come up behind him. "Strange dreams."

She put her hand on his arm.

"Down there," he said, pointing to the area along the river south from where they were. "That's where my father used to take me walking. We'd walk and the limousine would slowly follow us. We'd walk and he'd point to the ocean liners that docked there. The *Normandie*, the *Queen Mary*, the *Rex*, the *Bremen*.

"I was on all of them before I was ten. Then later, of course, I sailed on them. You can't believe how luxurious those ships were."

"Is that what you were dreaming about?" she asked. She knew, of course, that it wasn't, that it had to be something sinister to have awakened him and taken him from her side.

"No. Sometimes my father would start walking from South Ferry all the way to where those ocean liners were berthed." He turned to her. "And you know, I don't think we exchanged a dozen words, and if we did, he used most of them."

That was a totally new experience for Isabel. He'd never, ever spoken about his father, mother, or brothers. "That would have been hard for any little boy."

Anderson shrugged. "Whenever I dream about my father, I know something bad is going to happen."

"And you dreamt about him tonight?"

"No." He faced the river again. "When I was in the hospital—I actually had the heart attack while I was there—I had the strangest feeling that my mother and my Aunt Gail were in the room with me. I wasn't hallucinating."

He looked at Isabel. "I felt their presence. My Aunt Gail, my father's sister, was the free spirit in the family. She was the only one who ever asked me about my painting. She died a few years ago, alone and abandoned by everyone, except . . ."

"You."

"Yes, I owed her that much. She and my mother were both dead. Yet they were there in the room with me. My mother sat in the chair and Gail stood alongside her. Neither of them spoke. They were just there, and because they were, I knew that I would survive."

Isabel linked her arm with his. "Sometimes things like that happen, and they don't have a rational explanation."

"I never tried to come up with one," Anderson said. "I never tried to explain it rationally, or any other way."

"There's more, isn't there?"

He nodded but said nothing.

She wasn't going to press him. Whatever it was had set strong emotional forces in motion, and there really wasn't any way for her to calm them.

"My father will come for me when my time comes," Anderson suddenly said. "He'll be there instead of my mother and my Aunt Gail."

His words chilled her, and she was forced to let go of his arm in order to gather her silk dressing gown more tightly around her.

He turned fully toward her. "Isn't it strange that I know that?"

She relinked his arm with hers, and pressed it against her breast. "Yes, strange. Did you dream—"

"No, no. But something else happened, Isabel. Something very important. I've decided not to go to Paris. I can't do it. Isabel, I fought in one war, and became involved in several others. A few years ago, I walked through a Nicaraguan village after the Contras had taken it using arms that I had gotten them. That deal that Wally's set up is just a way for the Saudis to get arms for oil. I can't do that. I can't put my name to any document that makes that kind of an exchange possible."

"What will your brothers—"

"I don't care what they do," Anderson said sharply. "I don't want to be part of that kind of a deal. The truth is, I don't want to be part of any deal."

She lifted her face up and kissed him on his cheek.

"What's that for?"

"For being John Wesley Anderson, the man I love."

He put his arms around her. "There's one more thing," he said.

"Your tone warns me that it's going to be another important thing."

Anderson held her in front of him. "If anything happens to me—say, an accident—"

"Wes, stop it! Nothing is going to happen to you!"

"Listen to me, Isabel. I want you to follow my instructions."

"What are you talking about? What instructions?"

"Just promise."

"But—"

300

Anderson put his finger across her lips. "I must have your word that you will follow my instructions."

She eased his finger away from her lips. "I will follow them. But you make it seem so, so—"

"Dangerous?"

"Yes."

He gathered her to him. "Not for you my love, not for you."

Chapter 23

"I thought this whole matter was settled," Wally stormed over the phone.

Anderson swiveled around in his black leather chair, and looked out through the french doors at his rear lawn, filled with a multitude of flowers. "It was," he said.

He'd arrived back in his office early in the morning after spending the night with Isabel, and had called Wally at his home.

"What's gotten into you?" Wally asked.

"Nothing has gotten into me, as you put it, nothing that hasn't been there all these years."

"It's that Aroyo woman, isn't it?" Wally said in a harsh voice. He never could understand how his brother always managed to bring beautiful younger women to his bed.

Anderson clamped his jaws shut.

"She's nothing but a damn revolutionary whore."

"And you're nothing but a damn stupid man," Anderson growled.

"Listen, John, the family was willing to put up with your extramarital escapades because you looked after family matters, but now you're going haywire."

"That was damn good of the family," Anderson roared. "Damn good. I married a woman I didn't

303

love because of the family, and—and so did you and our brother George."

"We're not talking about that. Now, we're talking about the Saudi deal."

"You don't need me, and more to the point, I'm not in the least bit interested in deal."

"The family will lose ten to fifteen million—"

"How much does the family have? Ten to twenty times that. We don't need it, and we can't give away what we don't own."

"What the hell are you talking about?"

"Arms, that's what I'm talking about."

"It's perfectly legal."

"I'm sure it is. But the Saudis do not need those arms."

"And you're the judge of that?"

"Someone has to be."

"If they don't get them from us, they'll get them from the Soviets, or from the Chinese."

Anderson shrugged and said, "You're probably right, but I would not have been a part of the deal."

He could hear his brother's hard breathing over the phone. His own was equally as noisy.

"My God, John, you've been involved in worse things!"

"What did you say?" Anderson's heart skipped a beat, and began to race. No one in the family had ever known of his involvement with the CIA. They'd never known that Venom existed.

Anderson repeated the question. Suddenly, he was more frightened than angry.

"I'm trying to tell you something and you won't listen," Wally answered.

"I'm listening."

"You were part of deals."

Anderson was on his feet, and stormed out from behind the desk to the full length of the telephone cord. "No, that doesn't cut it. I want to know what you meant when you said I was 'involved in worse things?' " He paced back and forth in front of his desk.

"Deals, John. Deals. Nothing more."

Anderson took a deep breath and slowly exhaled. "Count me out of this one, Wally. Count me out of all future deals that have the stink of death about them, and this one does. From now on, brother, I'll cut my deals."

"And those are your final words on the matter?" Wally asked, his confusion of a few moments before now obliterated by his previous anger.

"Absolutely."

"You're making a big mistake."

"Call me when you return from Paris," Anderson said, returning the phone to its cradle Then he stood motionless until he was finally able to tell himself aloud, "Wally couldn't know. He couldn't."

But even that denial didn't help much. Still disconcerted, he sat down behind the desk, wondering how much his brother knew, or if he knew. And even more important, how did he get to know? Who was he tied to and why?

Anderson leaned forward, and rested his face in his hands.

Wally was suddenly as much of a stranger to Anderson as, no doubt, he was to him; and just as suddenly, perhaps, very dangerous.

As if to rid himself of that horrendous possibility, Anderson raised his head and shook it.

But having learned from experience that, more often than not, even the impossible was possible when it involved human beings, he uttered a deep sigh, almost a moan.

Marylee entered Doctor Hasse's office, and without waiting to be asked whether she'd prefer the couch or the chair, she chose the chair.

Hasse was instantly aware of a change in her and said, "What do we have here, a new Marylee?"

She crossed her legs. "So many things have happened. It's as if I suddenly entered a new world. Yesterday, I met with Isabel Aroyo."

"Oh?"

Hasse was immediately interested. The present mistress of a man like Anderson and the rejected one — that had to be of significance to both women.

"She called me," Marylee said, and she went on to explain the reason why Isabel had phoned her.

"And how did you answer her?"

"She guessed I was sleeping with Richard," Marylee said.

"Did that bother you?"

"Yes, at first. But then it didn't seem to matter. She doesn't trust Richard."

"Do you?" Hasse asked.

Marylee uncrossed her legs, stood up, took a few steps, and stopped, facing Hasse.

"Last night he was as tender and as considerate a lover as any woman could wish for."

"Oh?"

Marylee smiled. "I was as surprised as you are, and I was in bed with him. But he was full of

306

surprises last night."

"He asked you to marry him?"

She laughed, and said, "Almost, almost, Doctor."

Marylee sat down. "He bought me a cape."

Hasse nodded. "So now you envision a different kind of a relationship, Marylee?"

She dropped her eyes to her lap.

"Just suppose," Hasse suggested, "Richard was treating you the way he did for—for whatever reason, reasons—but it was not the real Richard."

Marylee looked up, and her hands tightened around the red strap of her shoulder bag. "Who is the real Richard Gault?" she asked in a low voice.

"You should be able to answer that far better than I can." Her question disturbed Hasse. He had hoped she would prefer a normal sexual relationship with Gault to the sado-masochism she had already experienced.

"Just because I've been fucking him that doesn't mean I know him." She looked straight at Hasse. "Fucking and knowing someone are entirely two different things. Each can happen, and often does happen, without the other."

There was something more behind her words, and he asked, "Who do you think Richard is?"

Again she looked straight at him. "He's the man who saved John Anderson's life with a lucky shot, he claims."

"It could very well have been that."

"Isabel doesn't believe that it was."

"Do you?"

"I would have . . . I wanted to. But last night something happened that made it impossible for me to believe him."

307

She related the sequence of events that took place inside the boutique. "Those men knew him from some previous encounter. The one that wanted to take me into the back and rape me said that the cops wouldn't talk about Richard, that he was something special."

"Afterwards, did you speak to Richard about it?"

"No, I didn't want to risk changing what was happening between us."

"Understandable," Hasse commented; then he said, "And you're sure he snapped the man's arm?"

"Yes. He did it without any hesitation. And if the one named Brownie had started shooting, I am sure he would have used the other one as a shield."

"All right, what conclusion do you draw from all of this?" Hasse asked.

Marylee shook her head. "He knows how to shoot, and he knows the martial arts. And damn few archaeological students know either."

"Then you don't believe he is who he says he is?"

Marylee bit her lower lip, then said, "I want to believe him. I can, and probably have already fallen in love with him."

"And after last night, you think he might be in love with you?"

"I —"

"Have you told him about your meeting with Isabel?"

"No."

"Why not?"

She hesitated.

He pressed her for an answer.

She tightened her hold on her bag's red leather strap again.

308

"I don't trust him," she blurted out. "I don't believe him. God, I want to. I really want to."

"Will you tell him about your meeting with Isabel?"

"She warned me against doing it."

"That's not what I asked."

"I'll tell you the same thing I told her. I won't volunteer it, but if he senses something, and starts to probe, I don't know if I'd be able to hold it back from him."

Hasse recognized her honesty, and complimented her for it, then said, "You have some difficult choices to make, Marylee."

"I have a question for you, Doctor."

Before she asked it, he said, "On the basis of what you have told me I would not believe or trust Richard either. But you have to decide what to do about it."

"Isabel thinks that Anderson is in danger from Richard."

"Do you?"

"I don't know, but I will do everything I can to protect Anderson. Everything."

Gault was smoking a cigarette at his desk, reliving his and Marylee's lovemaking.

She gave "head" that made him horny just thinking about it. And as far as he was concerned, there was magic in her cunt, something he had never felt about any other woman.

"Magic," he said aloud, and smiled.

He was surprised at his own reaction to her, once he'd stopped being the "heavy" and had started to actually enjoy being with her. She was clever, sophisticated, charming, very beautiful — especially when she was nude — and sexually vibrant. And —

The phone on his desk started to ring.

"Gault here," he answered, stubbing his cigarette out in an ornate copper ashtray.

"You're on red alert," the voice on the other end said, then clicked off.

"Shit!" Gault exclaimed, and slammed the phone down.

Obviously something was happening, or had already happened that he didn't know about.

He lit another cigarette, and puffed vigorously on it.

He considered calling Safe Deposit to find out what was happening, but he didn't like or trust him, and was sure the reason for the call would get back to Grier. He'd have to go another way.

Gault squashed the cigarette out, left the desk, and crossed the hall to Anderson's office. He knocked on the door, and when Anderson called, "Come," he entered.

Anderson looked less than serene, but he managed a smile, and invited Richard to sit down. "Strange that you should come at this time," he said.

"Oh, why?"

"I was just two moments ago thinking about you," Anderson explained.

"And I about you, John," Gault said. "I think we're approaching that special time."

Raising his hands, Anderson pressed the palms of his hands together. "When?" he asked.

"Soon, very soon. I must be very sure of what I'm doing, very sure. John Junior has found his peace,

310

and if your meeting with him were to disturb that peace . . ."

Gault purposely didn't define the consequences of such a mistake, but he knew Anderson would, though not verbally.

"I was supposed to go to Paris with my brother Wally," Anderson said, after a moment or two of silence, "but I decided not to."

Gault almost smiled. That was the reason for the red alert.

"I'll tell you this, Richard, I don't want to be part of any more deals, no matter how much money is involved. I don't need the money anymore. I have other things to do that are more important than making more money."

Having discovered the reason for the red alert, Gault was anxious to call Grier and calm him.

"Before we go, Richard, I'm going to hold another news conference—"

Richard immediately started to cough, and when Anderson offered him a glass of water, he drank some of it before he croaked out, "I'm sorry. You were saying something about holding another news conference."

"Nothing that will concern our arrangement," Anderson said, sitting down again.

"Some of the newspapers guessed that you had another shoe to drop," Gault commented. This time he wasn't going to be caught with his pants down.

"Oh, it will make a noise," Anderson said, smiling. "Perhaps even an explosion." And almost as an afterthought, he added, "A rather large explosion, I suspect."

Gault's throat tightened. He began to sweat.

311

"But no more of that!" Anderson exclaimed.

Gault stood up.

"You look a bit shaky," Anderson observed. "Are you sure you're all right?"

"I've suddenly developed a terrible headache," Gault lied. "Would you mind if I went out for a bit?"

"Not at all. I'd go with you, but Mr. Lee called earlier and said he had something very important to discuss with me."

Gault said, "Fresh air sometimes helps."

Anderson agreed, and before Gault was out of the office, he was involved with the papers on his desk.

As soon as Gault was in the street, he headed for the park.

He needed to think before he did anything. If Anderson said his news conference would cause an explosion, he believed it would, and an explosion of the magnitude that Anderson had alluded to could only be caused by announcing his candidacy for the White House.

Gault charged across Fifth Avenue without waiting for the light to change, walked north, entered the park at Seventy-second Street, and headed west.

Anderson's cancellation of the Paris trip had caused the red alert, and no doubt neither Grier, Bushwick, nor anyone else involved understood that they were dealing with the "new John Wesley Anderson." Gault was sure he could explain that to Grier, and get him to buy it, and buy some more time. But now, with the news conference . . .

"Christ!" he muttered aloud, and sat down on an empty bench.

The question is, he told himself, whether or not I do it when the time comes, or do I tell Anderson

312

who I am, why I'm there, and who sent me?

There shouldn't be any questions, especially at this time. But in the short time he'd been with him, he had come to realize that Anderson could make a difference in the world, partly because he wanted to . . . and because he had to.

Gault lit a cigarette, and started to walk again.

But if he went through with it, he'd be one of the insiders, "one of the boys." And there wasn't any way to beat that. That could bring him power and money.

He dropped the cigarette on the blacktop path and paused to grind it under his heel.

Suddenly he realized that if he didn't kill Anderson, Grier, or his replacement, would eventually send someone else to do it. And someone would also be sent to take Gault out too.

Gault lit another cigarette, and realizing that he had been walking very fast, slowed his pace.

He wasn't prepared to risk his life for Anderson, no matter how much he had come to admire and respect him, no matter what possible difference the man might make in future world events.

He'd do what he was sent to do.

Having made his decision, Gault doubled back the way he'd come, but at a leisurely pace.

It didn't matter what time he phoned Grier, as long as he phoned him.

Chapter 24

Lee arrived at two.

Anderson had only met him once, the day he'd started to work. He was a tall, thin man, with very long arms and a prominent Adam's apple. He spoke in a low voice.

Anderson came out from behind the desk, shook his hand, and invited him to sit down alongside the desk.

"Mister Anderson, I . . ." Lee began. He swallowed hard, and found he couldn't go on.

"I hope you have everything you need," Anderson said, concerned that perhaps he'd delegated too much authority to Marylee and she had in some way insulted the man. His type, Anderson knew, was quick to take umbrage, often at imaginary slights.

Lee held up his hand. "Ms. Terrall has been wonderful to me and my assistant, and so has Mr. Gault, though his knowledge is—how shall I put it, yes—at best rudimentary."

Anderson suppressed a smile, and said, "He is certainly a novice in the field. Now tell me, is there anything else I can do to make your work easier?"

"Nothing."

Wondering if Lee was there to ask for more

money, Anderson decided to bring the subject up himself.

"No. No," answered Lee. "We have an agreement, and it will stand. I came here to—I am sorry, Mister Anderson, to have to tell you that many of the pieces in your collection of Pre-Columbian art are forgeries."

"Forgeries," Anderson repeated, suddenly feeling like an exhausted swimmer struggling to breast the next wave, and at the same time knowing that he will fail.

Lee dug into his jacket pocket and removed a small, black terracotta statue of the Zapotec rain god, Cocijo. "This was the first one I found." He placed the statue on Anderson's desk. "The real one is in the museum in Oaxaca."

The wave overwhelmed Anderson. His vision blurred.

"There are many other pieces."

In an effort to clear his vision, Anderson ran his hand over his eyes. It helped. "How many more pieces?"

"Two dozen, and all from the same source, Raul Coronado."

Anderson sucked in his breath, and slowly exhaled. Isabel had sent Coronado to him.

"Have you a list of the pieces?" Anderson asked.

Lee removed an envelope from his inside breast pocket. "The worth—the sum you paid—is two and a half million dollars."

"And their actual worth?"

Lee shook his head. "They have no value."

Anderson realized he was rocking back and forth, and stopped.

"I'm sorry to have to tell you this, Mr. Anderson,

but this puts the authenticity of anything else you purchased from Mr. Coronado in question, and from what I have determined, that would be about a quarter of your collection."

"Yes," Anderson said, after clearing his throat.

"I am very sorry that I had to be the one to tell you," Lee said.

"With all due respect to your expertise, I must ask if there is the slightest doubt . . ."

Lee flushed. "Mr. Anderson, this piece on the desk could not have been made more than ten years ago, fifteen at the most. Whoever made it was skillful, and it was the degree of skillfulness that alerted me to the possibility that it might be a forgery. But if it would suit your purposes, all the pieces that I have called into question can be Carbon-14 tested, though I have no doubt what those tests will reveal."

"Nor do I," Anderson said wearily.

"I'll leave this with you," Lee said, as he stood up to leave.

Though he lacked the strength, Anderson forced himself to stand. "Thank you for coming."

They shook hands, and when Lee closed the door behind himself, Anderson collapsed into the chair.

He'd spent a fortune on that collection, a lifetime of collecting, and now, toward the end of his life, to be told it was worthless . . .

Filled with rage and disappointment, he blamed Isabel as much as, if not more than, he blamed Coronado.

"She had to know," he said aloud. "She had to know."

Suddenly Marylee came on the intercom.

"You have a call from Mr. Hogan," she announced.

"Tell him I can't speak with him now, and then I

want you and Richard to come into my office."

"Yes," Marylee answered.

Anderson waited until the door opened, and then he stood up. "Mr. Lee was here," he said, "and he informed me that a substantial part of my Pre-Columbian collection consists of forgeries."

Marylee gasped.

"That's one of them," Anderson said, pointing to the terra-cotta statue on his desk.

Gault said, "The name of each seller—"

"Raul Coronado sold most of them to me," Anderson said tightly.

"Oh, John, I'm so sorry!" Marylee exclaimed.

"Didn't you tell me, Marylee, that Mrs. Aroyo knew many of the dealers?" Gault asked.

Before Marylee could answer, Anderson said, "I met Coronado through her."

Gault shrugged. He had known that, but had wanted to hear it from him.

"I thought the two of you should know what the situation is," Anderson said, realizing he'd told them because he had to tell someone, to share the disaster—not that it mattered to them, or anyone else. Then he added, in a much lower voice, "This, of course, will change whatever plans I had for the collection."

He sat down. "I don't have anything more to say."

In a matter of moments, Anderson was alone again. He slumped down in the chair, forcing himself to think, not to feel.

First, he decided to confront Isabel, then changed his mind. Switching on the intercom, he said, "Marylee, find Coronado and tell him I want to see him immediately. Fly him here, if necessary, from wherever the hell he might be, but get him here.

And don't give him any hint why I want to see him. But before you do any of that, get my brother Wally on the line."

"Yes, John," Marylee answered.

"Put my brother through immediately," Anderson told her, and switched off the intercom.

He was angry, and becoming angrier at himself for being duped, at Wally for trying to make him feel guilty, and at Isabel because he loved her.

Anderson looked at the phone, ready to pounce on it the moment it rang.

The intercom came on.

"John, your brother is in conference," Marylee said.

"Is his secretary still on the line?" Anderson asked.

"Yes, she's on five."

"I'll take it from here, Marylee," he said, stabbing at the button marked 5.

He knew all about being in conference.

"This is John Wesley Anderson. You put me through to Walter Anderson now."

"But—"

"I said now!"

Wally answered the phone.

"This is John—"

"I have nothing more to say to you."

"But I have several things to say to you, Wally, and you damn well better listen."

"I'm very busy, John, thanks to your—"

Anderson cut him short. "Ever since I could remember, you were my favorite, the one person who understood me, who was as sad about my aborted artistic career as I was; the person who understood why I collected art, and even why I need to have extramarital affairs. Unlike yourself and our brother

George, I could not put all my energies, including my sex drive, into making money. That kind of sublimation was beyond me, and—"

"Where is all of this leading, John?" Wally was at his desk. He had spent the last two hours on the telephone with high-ranking members of the Saudi government, trying to explain why John Wesley Anderson would not sign his name to the agreement, and finding that he was meeting with what he termed professional stupidity, which meant that their failure to understand would eventually be eliminated by gaining some advantage that they did not have before. And that rankled him even more now that John, the individual who'd caused it, was giving him a line of bull shit.

"Listen!" Anderson shouted.

"I'm listening, but I don't want to hear how much you did or did not love me."

Anderson's heart was pounding. He took several deep breaths, before he said, "John Junior is alive."

Wally said nothing.

"Did you hear me?" Anderson asked, his voice choked with emotion. "I said—"

"Are you sure?"

"Yes. That's one of the reasons I'm not going to Paris with you. I'm going to see John Junior."

A few moments of silence followed, then Anderson said, "Richard will take me to him."

"When?"

"Very soon, within the next few days, I imagine."

"I'm happy for you, John."

"Thank you, Wally."

"Will you go before I return from Paris?"

"I might."

"You said there were other reasons."

"Just one, Wally. I'm going to run for the Presidency as an independent."

Wally closed his eyes. That was the one thing he didn't want to hear.

"I think I can win, and I think I can make a difference in—"

"Good God, I really think you're sick," Wally finally exploded. "Why not run for Pope? Why not for the Presidency of the world, John?" Then he clicked off.

Anderson heard the buzz.

"Thank you, Wally," he said, and put the phone down. "It's always good to know your brother is on your side. But if that's the way it is, that's the way it is."

It was well past seven in the evening when Anderson finally arrived at Isabel's apartment.

She greeted him at the door, threw her arms around him, and said, "I was beginning to worry. Usually you're here by six." And she kissed him.

Inhaling her perfume was almost enough to make him want to forget his anger, and though he returned her kiss, he stiffened his resolve to find out if she knew he was being duped by Coronado.

"It's been a day to remember," Anderson said, ending their embrace, and entering the apartment.

She followed him. "I have had a few of those myself."

"I'd like a drink," he said.

"Fruit juice, or—"

He faced her. "Scotch, neat. Make it a double."

"Wes—"

"Better pour yourself a drink too, Isabel."

She didn't answer, but she wondered if it had anything to do with Gault. Marylee had called, and had told her about what had happened the previous night. Gault, as far as she was concerned, was a very dangerous man, and she hoped to convince Wes that he was.

Isabel poured the drinks, took hers on the rocks, and handing Anderson his glass, said, "Do we toast something or . . ."

He was still standing. "Coronado sold me forgeries," he said, then bolted down half the scotch in the glass.

Isabel's eyes went wide.

"One quarter of my collection is worthless."

He drank again.

"Oh, Wes!"

She started toward him.

He put up his hand, stepped back, and drank a third time, finishing the scotch.

"You think—" she began.

"What I think is that you—"

"Wes!"

Anderson shook his head. "Coronado was your man," he said harshly. "You introduced me to him, and to several other so-called dealers."

She could feel the heat in her cheeks. "I think you better go, Wes."

"Yes, I think I better."

He put the empty glass down on a nearby table, went to the door, and faced her. "I won't be back."

She spit the words out. "You're a fool, John Wesley Anderson, a fool!"

And then she turned her back to him.

Gault ran his hand over Marylee's bare breasts, down her flat stomach, and came to rest on the blond tuft of her love mound.

They had made love, and now while they were still wrapped in the warm afterglow, he decided to speak to Marylee about their future together, which was something he'd given a great deal of thought to since his last meeting with Grier. And the phone conversation he'd had with him earlier in the day made it imperative that he bring the matter up as soon as possible. Time, for all of them, was running out.

"I was thinking," Gault began, "that when we were finished cataloguing we might go away for awhile."

Marylee answered with a sigh. She enjoyed feeling his hand on her body, and did not want to hasten her return to reality. The day had been emotionally difficult. She'd never seen Anderson in such a state, and was sufficiently worried about him to have called Isabel again, but Richard had always been too close by for her to risk it.

"We could go anywhere in the world," Gault said.

Again she sighed, but this time she followed it by asking, "Where's anywhere?"

"Paris, Rome, London, or even Tahiti, if that's where you want to go. It doesn't make any difference. I can take you."

She opened her eyes, and for a few moments stared at him, trying to decide whether he was just asking her to spend a week or two with him, or whether a longer duration was implied.

Then for reasons unknown to her, she became very practical. "How? I mean, where would the money come from, and besides—"

"Besides," he said passionately, "I want to be with you." And he kissed her lips, her neck, and finally each of her nipples. Then he said, "Money isn't a problem."

She raised her eyebrows. "You earn less than I do. You're supposed to be almost impoverished."

Immediately realizing he'd made a mistake, Gault removed his hand from her body. "I've saved most of what I earned."

"That can't have been enough to pay for one round-trip ticket to London, not to mention two."

"I have friends in the travel business," he answered, irritated at her for questioning him, and at himself for providing her with the reason.

Marylee pulled herself up and, embracing her knees, said, "You know I want to go."

"Then what's the problem?"

"The problem is . . ."

She stretched out her legs, and as she crossed them, she continued to look at him.

He was handsome, sexually exciting, and an unknown.

"Well, tell me what the problem is. You want to be with me, and since I asked you to come with me, I want to be with you."

She summoned up her courage. This was the time to place her secret doubts in front of him. "That's not enough, Richard."

Gault nodded. "All right, I understand. I'd like to try living together before we make it permanent. I think it will work between us, but I want each of us to be sure."

He moved closer to Marylee, expecting her to respond in a similar manner. With some tender, loving stroking on her part, he'd be ready for another lovemaking session.

She didn't move, though she very much wanted to.

"I'll go with you, and I'll live with you, but first I want to know who you really are and why you are here."

The question made him pull away.

"Your shrink has really put wild ideas into your head," he said, saying the first thing that came into his mind, though he wasn't sure that the questions came from the shrink.

"Okay, tell me why you went out of your way to make John name Isabel—"

"Oh, so it's Isabel, is it? I didn't know you were on a first-name basis with the woman who took John away from you."

"That's an ugly thing to say."

He knew it, but he was going to force her to the wall, even if it meant bringing her to tears. The one thing he didn't want her to do was ask questions, not until Anderson was history, and then whatever answers he gave wouldn't matter. "Ugly, but true."

Marylee bit her lip, fought back her tears, and said, "Tell me about the two men in the boutique. They knew you. One of them said the cops wouldn't talk about you. Why wouldn't the cops talk—"

He moved so swiftly, she never realized he had moved, until the palm of his hand crashed against the left side of her face, jouncing her head to one side, exploding fire on her cheek, and bringing tears to her eyes.

"No more fucking questions!" he roared. "No more!"

The blow had knocked her to one side, and turning her head to one side, she nodded.

"Just what the fuck is that supposed to mean?" he shouted.

"You figure it out," Marylee answered, reaching

325

over to the box of tissues on the night table. "Now, if you don't mind, I want to be alone."

Gault stood up. "You pushed me too hard."

"Please go," she said. Slipping down on her back and rolling onto her stomach, she buried her face in the pillow.

She couldn't look at him anymore.

Chapter 25

Coronado arrived in Anderson's office at ten o'clock the next morning, and Anderson remained at his desk, letting the man stand just inside the room after Marylee closed the door.

Silently, Anderson watched him.

Seconds ticked by.

Coronado stood very still, almost at attention. He was a short, leathery-looking man, with a large black handlebar mustache, a small gold earring in his left ear, and eyes as black as anthracite.

A full minute passed.

And still neither man moved, or made a sound.

Anderson's anger increased exponentially.

An anger that, like a huge snake, threw its coils around all the fragments of his past, squeezing them lifeless.

From where he stood, Coronado could read past Anderson's expressionless face, and into the man's eyes, where the fire raged.

But as far as he was concerned, it was an impotent rage.

The second minute passed.

Anderson suddenly exploded, "You cheated me. You and Isabel—"

Coronado approached the desk. "I cheated you,

yes. But Isabel had nothing to do with it, and whether you believe that or not depends on whether or not you're a fool. She only knew I was a dealer—"

"You're a thief, a cheat."

Coronado smiled. "A cheat in my dealings with you, yes. A thief, no. Not nearly the 'thief' that you were, when you were willing to buy artifacts for your precious collection that you knew were obtained by dubious means. No, no, John Wesley Anderson, if there is a 'thief' in this room, you have the pleasure of being it."

Anderson's cheeks burned.

"What, no violent protestations of honesty?" Coronado chided.

Anderson stood up. "I paid you two and a half million dollars for—"

"You donated that money to the Nicaraguan people."

"You stole—"

Coronado held up his hand, and shook his head. "No, you and others like you stole a country from its people. Not just one country, but many. The two and a half million is a bargain-basement price for what you got."

Anderson pointed his finger at him. "I want my money back. I don't care how you get it, just get it."

"I'm afraid that even with your finger pointed so dramatically at me, you are, as they say, whistling Dixie. Even if I could raise that sum again, I would not return it to you. As I suggested, consider it a donation, though I doubt if your tax people would allow you to write it off as such."

"I want my money!" Anderson shouted.

Coronado shrugged, and said in a calm voice, "I'm happy that your lovely secretary managed to reach me at my hotel, because I was planning to pay you a visit anyway. After your news conference — in which, I must say, you sounded as if you were a sincere, caring man — I realized that it would only be a matter of time before the forgeries came to light, and there was no better person to bring them to light than myself. But I had several other things, more important things, that demanded my attention. But now I am here, and we can conclude our business."

Anderson couldn't stop his jaw from going slack.

"I see that you didn't realize we had additional business, did you?"

"The only—"

"I'm not interested in anything you have to say. I will tell you what I want, and if you don't comply, I will give the world the other John Wesley Anderson, the one who headed his own death squad."

Anderson's heart raced.

"In cash, two and a half million," Coronado said. "By tomorrow afternoon."

"Never," Anderson rasped, "never!"

Coronado smiled. "In cash, tomorrow."

Then he gave a precise salute, turned, and left the office.

Anderson collapsed in the chair. He was sweating profusely, and to stop his hands from shaking, he clasped them together.

Exposure of his connection to Venom would end his bid for the Presidency even before it began.

He closed his eyes.

That Coronado was able to make the connection between him and Venom was almost in the realm of the — the supernatural, it was so closely guarded by the Company, and by everyone else involved.

"There is no other way," he said aloud. "No other

way." And reaching for the private phone on his desk, he managed to punch out a number, despite the continued trembling of his hand.

After three rings, he put the phone down, waited a moment, then redialed the number.

"Pauli," a man answered.

"This is Cobra."

"Yes."

"I have an emergency leak."

"Four o'clock."

Anderson repeated the time, then put the phone down and looked at his hands. They were steady, everything was under control.

He'd bite the bullet on the two and a half million dollars of forged art, but he'd also finish Coronado, and at the moment that was the only thing he had worth savoring.

Considerably calmed, despite the early hour, Anderson decided he could use a drink—a double bourbon with branch water on the side.

"John, your brother, Wally, called," Marylee said on the intercom. "He's on his way here."

"Try him on the mobile phone," Anderson told her.

"Yes, John."

He picked up on an unfamiliar tone in her voice. "Are you all right?"

"I'm all right. Just a little tired."

Anderson accepted the explanation, and said, "Tell my brother I'm in conference."

"But—"

"He'll understand," Anderson said.

He wasn't in any damn mood to put up with recriminations from his brother, or anyone else.

Leaving his chair, Anderson crossed the room to the bar, poured himself the drink he wanted, and belted most of it down without the benefit of branch water. He'd had a very difficult night, and now with Coronado demanding blackmail money—

Marylee came on the intercom.

"Your brother is not answering," she said. "Do you want me to keep trying?"

"No. No. Thank you, Marylee." Then he asked, "Is Richard there?"

"No," Marylee answered—a bit too harshly, she thought, and to counter the harshness she asked, "Do you want to see him?"

"That's all right. I'll catch up with him later. Send my brother in as soon as he arrives."

Anderson drank the remainder of the bourbon, poured two fingers into the glass, brought it back to the desk with him, and waited for Wally to arrive.

Gault entered the office, carrying a bag with two containers of coffee and two honey-dipped doughnuts.

Marylee didn't look up.

As he put the bag on her desk, he saw that she was wearing dark glasses and her left cheek, just below the frame, was purple.

"I want to talk to you," he said. "Call Anderson and tell him you're going out for awhile."

"You can go to hell," Marylee hissed.

"I'm sorry. I really am."

She said, "I don't have anything to say to you. I want you out of my life. I don't know how I ever let myself get tangled"—she looked at him, and felt as if she were suddenly seeing him for the first time—"in your web."

"What are you talking about? What web?" The

331

conversation wasn't going the way he'd hoped it would. He was sorry about slapping her. That wasn't his style. But he couldn't deal with her questions.

"A giant web spun out by a human spider. A web that—ah, what the hell is the use!"

"I thought you loved me."

"You're right, I did love you. But I don't now."

He reached for her hands, but she pulled them away before he could get hold of them.

"Don't you ever, ever touch me again," she said in a low, dry voice. "I made that mistake too many times to make it again."

Gault was beginning to understand that, at least for the present, he wasn't going to be able to resume any kind of relationship with Marylee, that if he really wanted her as badly as he thought he did, he was going to have to find a way to change her mind about him.

"At least have the coffee and doughnut I bought for you," he said, instantly realizing how ridiculous he sounded.

Marylee ignored him.

He picked up the bag, and put it on his own desk. There wasn't any way he was going to be able to work sitting across from her, knowing what she looked like nude, having tasted her cunt, having fucked her.

He faced her. "I love you!"

Marylee pretended not to hear him.

"We're good together."

She looked up at him. "It won't work, Richard."

"I know you love me."

"I did—and probably still do. But I don't know who you are."

"Don't start that again." He'd almost thought something could take place between them again.

"I don't even think you know who you are."

"For Christ sakes, Marylee, this kind of conversation started the whole thing."

"Ended it," she answered. "It ended it, Richard." And she went back to her work.

Gault uttered a ragged sigh. "You don't give much leeway, do you?"

He waited for an answer.

This was a side of her he wouldn't have guessed she possessed.

When it was obvious that she wasn't going to respond, he said, "I'm going out. I'll be back."

He tossed the bag with the containers of coffee and doughnuts into the wastepaper basket, and left the office.

Moments later Marylee heard the front door being opened, then slammed shut.

Anderson was leaning against the back of the chair and had his eyes closed when Wally entered the office.

"Just resting," he said, to squelch any questions.

"I took a catnap on the way here from my office," Wally responded as he settled in one of the club chairs near the coffee table.

Anderson left his chair, and chose to sit on the sofa, facing his brother.

"I guess neither of us slept too well after our discussion yesterday," Wally commented.

Anderson agreed, then said, "I had additional difficulties after you left."

"Anything I can help with?"

"No, I have it under control."

Wally nodded, and took a few moments to remove a cigar from a leather case, cut the tip of it, and light it. "Last night, I thought a great deal about what you said to me, and, of course you're right. None of the Andersons have ever been their own men, or women, for that matter."

"It's like having a congenital disease," Anderson commented.

Wally smiled. "Something like that. But you could have escaped it. You had the talent."

"But not the necessary backbone to go it alone. I couldn't take all the pressure that was put on me."

Wally blew a huge cloud of blue-white smoke toward the ceiling. Then he said, "It's important to me to know that you're not angry at me, even though if I were you, I would be angry as hell."

Anderson rested his elbows on his knees, and clasped his hands together. It wasn't at all like Wally to eat humble pie. "I'd be lying if I told you I wasn't angry."

"That's why I came here, John," Wally said. "I want to . . . to—well, maybe the whole idea of you being angry at me doesn't sit well. I don't think we've ever been out of joint with one another."

"Neither of us can," Anderson responded.

Wally nodded, and smiled. "Nothing like the relationship each of us has with George."

"To have a relationship with George, you have to be George, and then he'd probably ask himself for credentials."

Laughing, Wally pointed his cigar at Anderson, and said, "In some quarters it's said he gives Mary two weeks' formal notice before he has sex with her."

"Imagine being married to him?"

"Can't. I'm his brother, and I have trouble imagining that, let alone believing it."

The two of them laughed.

"You're looking better already," Wally said, and he added, "I didn't really tell you how happy I am about John Junior. I know Augusta must be thrilled too."

"She doesn't believe it. She—you know her. If it's not in the stars, it's not true." His tone betrayed his annoyance, but he made no effort to conceal it. "She's in her world, and I'm in mine. She'll believe it when she sees him, and then maybe she'll join the rest of us."

Wally blew another cloud of smoke up toward the ceiling. "John, I want to apologize for what I said about Isabel, and I have to admit that I envy you."

Anderson accepted his brother's apology with a nod. He had no intentions of telling him about the rift that had occurred with Isabel. Besides, he was sure that the rift was only temporary. He'd send her flowers sometime during the next few days, and ask her to have dinner with . . .

"Now," said Wally, "I have something to say to you that is more important than anything else I have said this morning, and more important, in my opinion, than anything I have ever said or will, in the future, say to you." Wally stood up, went around to the other side of the chair. "It's important to me that you remain alive, that you don't do anything that will endanger your life."

"If you're referring to that shooting—"

Wally waved the comment aside, even before Anderson had finished making it. "I'm talking about running for the Presidency, John. It's a hard run."

"I know I could win."

"Yes, I know that too. But it would cost you your health."

Anderson stood up. "I've been drinking bourbon this morning. Do you care for anything?"

Wally declined the offer.

"Wait a moment," Anderson said, and he poured himself another drink. "I'm not the drinker I used to be, but this morning hasn't been like other mornings. All right, let's get to it, Wally. I want the Presidency because in that office I can make a difference. Even before you say it, *I* will. Yes, it's egotistical. But it also happens to be true. You know it, and just about everyone in Washington knows it too. I haven't done the things I wanted to do with my life, and now I have a second chance."

He downed all of the bourbon in one gulp.

"I'm going to go for the big gold ring," Anderson said, "and nothing you or anyone else says will change my mind."

"It's a mistake, John."

"Then it will be just another one in a long list that litters my past."

Wally puffed on his cigar for several moments, then said, "I'll be leaving for Paris in the next few days. I had to reschedule the meeting because of your—"

"I'm sorry that I caused you so much trouble," Anderson said, replacing the empty glass on the bar.

"It's all taken care of," Wally said.

Anderson came back to where his brother was standing. "I told you that you didn't need me to do the deal."

"Well, I've said all of the things I want to say," Wally told him.

"Then you have a clear conscience."

"I didn't come here to clear my conscience," Wally snapped.

Anderson shook his finger at him. "Prickly . . . prickly."

Wally put the cigar back in his mouth, and rolled it to the right. "Send my best to Augusta," he said, offering Anderson his hand.

"And mine to Clare," Anderson responded, shaking his brother's hand. "See you when you get back from Paris."

Wally let go of his hand, but didn't answer, except to say that he'd let himself out. Moments later he was in the foyer, where he paused. Feeling the necessity to lean against the wall for support, he was about to do it when he realized Marylee was coming toward him.

Though he'd seen her when he arrived, he somehow hadn't been aware of the dark glasses.

"Mr. Anderson, may I speak to you?" Marylee asked.

Wally nodded. "Here?"

She gestured toward her office.

"Please," he said, letting her precede him.

As soon as they were inside the room, she faced him. "I think John is in great danger."

Wally raised his eyebrows.

"Do you know who Gault is, or where he comes from?"

"Didn't my brother tell you?" Wally asked.

"He said nothing about Gault, other than he'd met him on a dig the previous summer, and that he had recently returned from Nepal."

"Yes. He found John Junior there."

"What?" asked Marylee.

"My brother and Gault will soon leave for Nepal. To meet with John Junior."

Marylee shook her head. "You don't believe he

found John Junior, do you? My God, the man is a fraud, an absolute fraud."

"I'm sorry to hear you say that, Marylee."

"It's true, really it is."

Wally suddenly realized that she'd been sleeping with Gault, and something had gone wrong.

"John has a very high regard for Gault," he told her, "and from my own very brief encounter with the man, I'd have to say that my brother's attitude toward him is not misplaced. Now, if you'll excuse me, I have to . . ."

In desperation, Marylee stepped closer to him and tore her dark glasses off. "That's Gault's work!"

Wally stiffened. "I'm sorry, Marylee."

Then he turned around, and left the office.

Chapter 26

Pauli listened very carefully to Anderson, who alternated between speaking English and Spanish.

"I have five thousand in cash for you now, and another five thousand will be deposited in your account by next Tuesday," Anderson concluded.

Pauli smiled, and said, "It's good to work again."

Anderson opened the desk's middle drawer, took out an envelope, and handed it to Pauli.

"It would be best if it was to seem like an accident, or perhaps a mugging."

"Nothing will be traceable," Pauli answered with assurance.

"Yes, I know that."

"Is there anything else I should know?" Pauli asked, speaking in Spanish this time.

Anderson shook his head. "You have all the information you need to find him."

"I'll phone when it's done."

"Use the special number."

"Yes."

Simultaneously the two men stood up and shook hands. Anderson went as far as the door with him, but Pauli opened it, quickly stepped out into the foyer, and closed the door after him.

Just as he started for the front door, it opened and

Gault entered.

Their eyes locked, and for a fraction of a second neither one moved; then Pauli connected the face with the name, and wondered why Gault was there.

And as they passed, Gault was absolutely certain he had seen the man before . . . somewhere, either at one of the Company's schools or in Central America—possibly Panama?

Pauli left the town house, and Gault went into the office.

"Who was that man who just left?" he asked.

Marylee shrugged, but didn't look up. "I hear tell you're another Stanley," she commented.

"Stanley?" he repeated. The name didn't register. He was still trying to make the man he had just seen.

Marylee finally looked up. "Like Stanley and Livingstone, remember? Only this time it's Gault and John Junior."

He understood, and instantly felt a rising sense of panic.

"You're a con man, Richard, just like all of the others," she said.

As quickly as his sense of panic rose, it subsided. "He tell you, finally?"

"If by he you mean John Wesley Anderson, the answer is no. His brother told me."

"Why should he do that?"

Marylee shrugged. "I told him that I thought you were a dangerous man, too dangerous for John to trust."

By puckering his lips and nodding, Gault suppressed a smile. "Well, now you know why I'm here, and why I'm important, and why it's important for you to cooperate with me."

Again she shook her head.

"What does that mean?"

"It means, Mr. Richard Gault, that until I see John Junior standing in front of me and his father says, 'This is my son,' or similar words, you're still just a con man in my book."

She had no idea where the courage had come from to speak that way to him, but it was there.

Gault realized it too. "That's your attitude?"

"That's exactly my attitude."

"Just don't get in my way."

Though Marylee recognized the implied threat, she would not give him the satisfaction of reacting to it.

"That man who was just here . . ."

"I told you I don't know who he is," she answered.

"He gave you a name, didn't he?"

The phone rang.

Gault grabbed it before Marylee could answer, listened a moment, and recognized Grier's voice. He said into the phone, "No, this is not the Snake House."

"Do it tonight," Grier told him.

"Are you sure you have the right number?" Suddenly he was sweating.

"Safe Deposit confirmed."

"Yes, you have the right number," Gault said, and a moment later he put the phone down.

Marylee was looking at him, trying to decide why he'd suddenly started to sweat.

She almost let herself ask him if he was all right, but she didn't want to show him the slightest bit of solicitude — which he could, and no doubt would, misinterpret.

Gault fished out a cigarette, lit it, and announced that he was going out.

"I really don't care what you do," Marylee answered, shifting her eyes from him back to the papers on the desk.

Anderson was alone in his office. A late evening sun slanted through the windows. Its yellow mote-filled light touched only a small area, leaving the rest of the room in a rapidly deepening darkness.

He was having second thoughts about having Coronado killed.

That would have been his way to deal with the situation years before, but now it almost seemed redundant.

Anderson picked up the phone and dialed Coronado's hotel.

"I am sorry, sir, Mr. Coronado is not in," the switchboard operator said, after letting the phone ring several times. "Do you want to leave a message?"

Anderson was about to say yes when he suddenly realized that if Pauli made the hit, he didn't want his name linked in any way to Corondado's.

He put the phone down, then picked up the one with his private number and tried to reach Pauli.

There no one answered either.

Frustrated, Anderson went to the bar and poured himself a bourbon. He'd been drinking on and off most of the day, but somehow didn't feel any the better or worse for it.

"Dumb!" he exclaimed aloud. "Dumb!"

He brought the glass back to the desk, and sat down before he drank. Then, he tried to reach Coronado again, but wasn't successful. He met with the same result when he phoned Pauli.

The light in the room dissolved into darkness.

Anderson switched on the light, started to call Isabel, changed his mind, and took out a piece of notepaper and an envelope. He dated it, then wrote:

My Dearest Love,

My behavior toward you has been less than admirable, and I humbly apologize. I love you, and I am confident that you feel the same tender emotions toward me.

Isabel, I have put into motion something very foolish, which I am powerless to stop. I am too ashamed and mortified at my own behavior to reveal any more about it.

But should something suddenly happen to me which you deem suspicious, dial 844-1454. A man named Pauli will answer. Arrange to meet him, and he will take care of everything else.

Your Loving Servant

Wes

He addressed the envelope, enclosed the notepaper in it, sealed it, and put a stamp on it. Then leaving the desk, Anderson went into the foyer, where there was a small canvas mail bag with several dozen letters already in it for the following day's collection. He put his somewhere near the bottom of the bag.

For a few moments he remained motionless, trying to make up his mind whether to return to his desk or go upstairs to the library to read while continuing to phone Coronado and Pauli.

Anderson decided to go upstairs, and he started slowly up the steps.

* * *

343

For hours, Gault prowled the city from the northern reach of Central Park to the Battery, at the tip of Manhattan. He walked part of the time, rode the Fifth Avenue bus, even the subway, and now in the gathering darkness was making the return trip to Manhattan on the Staten Island ferry. He had already smoked two packs of cigarettes, and had lost count of the number of times he'd stopped for coffee.

Taking Anderson out was proving to be more difficult to handle than he had imagined it would be. He had developed a liking for the man, and despite the enormous stakes involved, he had feelings of real doubt about doing it. And to complicate the situation, he admitted to himself the bad feelings he'd had about the man he had seen coming out of the town house. Not that there was anything particularly sinister about him. The man was very ordinary looking, and that was why he couldn't get him out of his mind.

As soon as Gault left the ferry, he hailed a cab, and gave the driver the address of the town house. Then he sat back, closed his eyes, and tried to relax.

It was important that he be absolutely calm when the time came for him to kill Anderson.

Marylee and Isabel mingled with the people in huge Lincoln Center Plaza. The water from the illuminated fountain in its center looked like liquid gold.

This time Marylee had asked Isabel to meet her, and together they had decided on the plaza as a safe place.

Marylee told her about Gault's reaction to the man

who'd visited Anderson.

"He wanted his name," Marylee said, "but I pretended that I did not know it. The man had said, 'Tell Mister Anderson Pauli is here.'"

Isabel repeated the name. She remembered having heard it before, but couldn't exactly recall where or in what context. "Can you describe this Pauli?"

Marylee shrugged. "Ordinary looking."

"About how old?"

"Forty, or fifty. Maybe even older."

"Are you sure that they recognized each other?"

"I'm not sure whether Pauli knew Richard, but Richard certainly didn't place him, though he might have thought he had known him."

Isabel was in the same predicament, but she didn't tell Marylee, who had already exhibited more courage than Isabel had thought she possessed.

She smiled at Marylee, and suggested they sit down at an outdoor table. "And treat ourselves to—something cool and refreshing."

"That's a wonderful idea!" Marylee responded.

Anderson was totally at odds with himself. He had continued to try to phone Coronado and Pauli without any success, and the drinking he had done during the day was beginning to give him not only a sour stomach, but palpitations that made him close his eyes and take several deep breaths to calm himself.

Then, with a peculiar feeling that he was waiting for something, he drifted into a sleep light enough for him to still be aware of the hum of the air conditioner.

Suddenly, he was awake. His eyes opened. He

345

looked toward the doorway, where for an instant the figure of a man was silhouetted.

Anderson shook his head.

"I thought you might need something," Gault said, entering the room, where the only light came from the lamp on the desk.

Anderson almost sighed with relief. "I was dozing, and thought you were someone else," he explained, managing a smile.

Gault nodded. He was having trouble keeping calm. "I think we should start making plans for our trip," he said.

Anderson smiled. "Somehow, I just knew that was what you were going to say. Not, of course, the exact words, but the essence. I'm happy, very happy. You know, I could use a nice cup of tea. What about you?"

"I'll make it," Gault said.

"You don't mind?"

"Not in the least. I'll be back in a few minutes." And he left the library. It was going to be so easy, much easier than he had imagined. It was almost as if Anderson was giving him the opportunity to do it, or perhaps the opportunity to back away from doing it.

Gault pushed that thought out of his mind, and hurried down to the kitchen.

A few minutes later, he returned to the library with a small wooden tray, and set it down on the desk.

"I take mine without sugar," Anderson said.

Gault handed him a cup and saucer.

"The really correct way to make tea is the way the English do it," Anderson said, raising the cup to his lips and drinking.

346

Gault drank from his.

"They brew it. English tea—" Anderson's hand suddenly started to shake, sloshing the tea over the rim of the cup.

As he watched him, tears gathered in Gault's eyes, and streamed down his cheeks.

Anderson let go of the cup, tried to stand, and turning his eyes toward the door, nodded to his father.

The next instant he fell across the desk, knocking over the lamp.

Gault picked up the phone, and punched out Wally's number.

"John has had a massive heart attack," he said.

For an instant, Wally remained silent. Then he said, "I'll be there in a half hour or less."

Gault put the phone back in its cradle. Then he sat down opposite the desk.

Wally entered the study, went directly to his brother, looked at him for several moments, and then picked up the phone and dialed.

Grier answered.

"It's done," Wally said.

"You'll take care of the other details?"

"There won't be an autopsy. He'll be cremated."

"Excellent. We are very sorry that such a drastic step had to be taken, but we couldn't run the risk of having him remain alive. Sooner or later it would have had to happen."

"Yes, I know that."

"By the way, arrange to have Gault taken out."

"When?"

"Soon, within the next week or two. We don't want

347

any loose ends around."

"Will you be at John's funeral?"

"I wouldn't miss it. After all, he was our Eagle."

Wally put the receiver down, took out a cigar, and cut and lit it before he said to Gault, "Grier congratulates you on a job well done."

Gault shrugged. "I almost believe he knew it was going to happen, and wanted me to stop it."

Wally didn't answer.

A Bermuda high dominated the weather for days along the Eastern Seaboard. From Cape Hatteras to Cape Cod the air was heavy with moisture and filled with pollutants.

Grier and his wife had been in New York for Anderson's funeral. The Company, using its many contacts with the media, had let it be known that Anderson had suffered a massive heart attack while having intercourse with Marylee Terrall—though to some, to further confuse the issue, they also gave Isabel Aroyo's name, intimating it was a menage à trois.

Grier was feeling particularly pleased with himself. The operation had been his from start to finish. He had tagged Anderson as the brain behind the gun as soon as the second agent had been taken out, and now he was in his own den, savoring the success, and knowing that it was only a matter of time before Bushwick would be the Vice President, and he would be the Director of the Company.

His wife called him to bed.

"Coming," he answered, and was just about to turn out the light when the phone rang.

Sure it was Bushwick, he didn't waste time with

preliminaries, and said, "It was one hell of a day, wasn't it?"

Bushwick probably had something to tell him. He had already begun to take credit for—

"Venom lives," the man on the other end said. Then the phone clicked off.

Grier dropped the phone, and grabbed the table for support. He broke into a cold sweat.

When and where would it happen?

He looked toward the glass patio door, and into the night-enshrouded garden.

The bushes that in the sunlight gave him so much pleasure to look at now were ominous, offering a hiding place to his assassin. From now on, his life would be a living death, a nightmare, orchestrated by John Wesley Anderson from the grave.

MYSTERIES TO KEEP YOU GUESSING
by John Dickson Carr

CASTLE SKULL   (1974, $3.50
The hand may be quicker than the eye, but ghost storie
didn't hoodwink Henri Bencolin. A very real murderer wa
afoot in Castle Skull — a murderer who must be found be
fore he strikes again.

IT WALKS BY NIGHT   (1931, $3.50
The police burst in and found the Duc's severed head star
ing at them from the center of the room. Both the door
had been guarded, yet the murderer had gone in and ou
without having been seen!

THE EIGHT OF SWORDS   (1881, $3.50
The evidence showed that while waiting to kill Mr. Dep
ping, the murderer had calmly eaten his victim's dinner
But before famed crime-solver Dr. Gideon Fell could serv
up the killer to Scotland Yard, there would be anothe
course of murder.

THE MAN WHO COULD NOT SHUDDER (1703, $3.50
Three guests at Martin Clarke's weekend party swore the
saw the pistol lifted from the wall, levelled, and shot. *Ye
no hand held it*. It couldn't have happened — but there wa
a dead body on the floor to prove that it had.